PRAISE FOR LuANN McLANE'S CRICKET CREEK NOVELS

"Sweet romance with small-town Southern charm. . . . McLane weaves together walks in the moonlight, stolen glances, and kisses under the stars with seduction and sizzling sex, populating the carefully crafted story with a cast of affable characters." —Publishers Weekly

"[A] wonderful series." —The Reading Cafe

"[A] lovely, sweetly sexy, terrifically enjoyable read. . . . McLane's Cricket series is similar in style to Susan Wiggs's bestselling Lakeshore Chronicles." —Booklist

"[McLane] nails the charm, quirks, nosiness, friendliness, and sense of community you'd experience in a small Southern town as you walk the streets of Cricket Creek." —That's What I'm Talking About

"[An] excellent series." —Debbie's Book Bag

"Visiting Cricket Creek, Kentucky, feels like coming home once again." —RT Book Reviews

"LuAnn McLane has a rich and unique voice that kept me laughing out loud as I read." —Romance Junkies

"McLane packs secrets, sex, and sparks of gentle humor in an inviting picnic basket of Southern charm." —Ft. Myers & Southwest Florida Magazine

"Charming, romantic . . . This new series should be a real hit!" —Fresh Fiction

"No one does Southern love like LuAnn McLane!" —The Romance Dish

Marry Me on Main Street

A CRICKET CREEK NOVEL

LuAnn McLane

WITHDRAWN

BERKLEY SENSATION
New York

BERKLEY SENSATION
Published by Berkley
An imprint of Penguin Random House LLC
375 Hudson Street, New York, New York 10014

Copyright © 2016 by LuAnn McLane
Excerpt from *Wish Upon a Wedding* by LuAnn McLane
copyright © 2016 by LuAnn McLane
Penguin Random House supports copyright. Copyright fuels creativity, encourages
diverse voices, promotes free speech, and creates a vibrant culture. Thank you for buying
an authorized edition of this book and for complying with copyright laws by not
reproducing, scanning, or distributing any part of it in any form without permission.
You are supporting writers and allowing Penguin Random House to continue to
publish books for every reader.

BERKLEY and BERKLEY SENSATION are registered trademarks and the B colophon is
a trademark of Penguin Random House LLC.

ISBN: 9781101989821

First Edition: December 2016

Printed in the United States of America
1   3   5   7   9   10   8   6   4   2

Cover art by Tom Hallman

This book is dedicated to those who love to rescue and repurpose old items and make them beautiful!

Acknowledgments

I would like to acknowledge artists and crafters for the beauty they bring into the world. Repurposing old items and giving them new life was such a joy to research! I would also like to thank my editor, Danielle Perez, for continuing to make me a better writer. And as always, thanks to my agent, Jenny Bent, for believing in me and making my childhood dream of becoming an author a reality.

1

Flirting with Disaster

INSTANT REGRET WASHED OVER SUSAN WHEN SHE REalized she'd underestimated the weight of the box of mason jars clutched in her arms. The thick glass clanked together as she stepped over the curb and onto the sidewalk. She eyed the front door of her shop, praying she'd make it before dropping her cargo to the ground. Setting the box down wasn't an option because she feared she'd tip forward too fast, break the jars, and face-plant onto the concrete.

"Oh boy . . ." Panting, she took another careful step forward, but her hefty purse slipped down her puffy coat sleeve, sending her off balance and causing her to do a staggering dance sideways. A brisk breeze whipped her long, dark hair across her face, making her progress even more difficult. Slightly disoriented, she tried to right her direction but the box started to slip down her arms. Panic welled up in her throat, halting just behind her gritted teeth. Blinded by her curtain of hair, she backpedaled and came up against a big wall of something solid.

"Whoa there!" said a deep voice next to her ear. Long arms wrapped around her from behind, keeping her from falling and the box from sliding to the sidewalk.

"Oh my goodness! Sorry!"

"It's okay, I've got you," he assured her.

"No . . . really . . . I'm okay now." Well, she hoped so, anyway. Blowing at her hair, Susan tried to look over her shoulder but she was trapped between him and the box. "You can let go."

"Can you hold the box? Sounds like something breakable."

"Yes," she said, although she had serious doubts. "Maybe . . ." She squirmed a little bit and the mason jars clanged together.

"Susan, please stand still and let me help. I'm guessing you're heading into the shop?" he asked. His voice seemed to vibrate through her body.

"That's the plan." She nodded. He knew her name, but so many people knew her from her shop that it didn't help her identify him.

"Let's get you in there." The smooth, Southern drawl sounded familiar but then again, most of the men in Cricket Creek had a bit of an accent, so he could be anyone, although it was most likely someone she knew. She tried to look over her shoulder again. "Who . . ." she began, but the box dipped sideways and she decided right this moment she really needed to make it to the front door without breaking the mason jars she was using for her Christmas cookie mix. Casual conversation could wait. "What should I do?"

"Do you think you can hold the box long enough for me to scoot around in front of you and grab the bottom?"

"Oh . . . I don't know." She winced. "My arms are already protesting." *Note to self: join a gym.*

"Well then, just move forward and I'll keep holding on from behind."

"It's kind of hard because the wind blew my hair in

my face and I can't exactly see where I'm going," she explained.

"You have a lot of hair," her hero said with a low chuckle. "I'd brush it from your face but I'm afraid to let go of the box."

Susan nodded, thinking she should get the unruly curls cut short. "I should head next door to the salon and get it fixed," she grumbled.

"Your boyfriend might not like that," he said, carefully moving her forward.

"I don't have one," she said, then immediately wondered why she'd just divulged that embarrassing information. She wasn't exactly thinking straight at the moment. Just then the wind kicked up again, and she could smell his aftershave; spicy with a hint of outdoorsy pine.

"We're almost there," he said near her ear. "Okay Susan, I'm going to take a lightning quick step to the right and grab the box."

"I'm afraid it will fall!"

"Don't you trust me, Susan Quincy?" he asked, but before she could react he suddenly had the big box in his arms. "See?" he asked.

"Not yet," she said, getting another chuckle from him. It took another moment to realize that her arms were suddenly free.

"You can brush your hair back now, Suzy Q."

Oh no . . . Susan's heart thumped as she suddenly realized she had a pretty good idea who the sexy voice belonged to. She wanted the sidewalk to open up and suck her beneath the concrete like quicksand. Inhaling a deep breath, she brushed the curls from her face and looked into the startling, sky blue eyes of Danny Mayfield, the last person in Cricket Creek she would want to come to her rescue. "Hello, D-Danny." *Oh great, now I'm going to stutter*, she thought and nearly groaned. *Ain't life grand*.

"Hi Susan," Danny said cheerfully, bestowing her

with his killer smile. He nodded down at the box, which he held easily in his strong arms. "What's in here?"

"M-mason. J-jars." Feeling heat in her cheeks, she lowered her gaze and dug inside her purse for her keys. She rarely stuttered anymore. *This is so embarrassing*, she thought with another inner groan. *Where in the hell are my keys?*

"If you open the door I'll bring them, and anything else you want from your SUV, inside for you."

"Oh . . . you don't have to do . . . that." Susan was so happy to have kept the stutter at bay this time that she looked up from her search and actually smiled.

"My mother would have my hide for not doing the gentlemanly thing," Danny said with an easy grin. He lowered the box to the tiled floor of the alcove between two big display windows in front of the front door entrance. "And I value my hide."

Right, just like back in high school, she thought and nearly cringed. "It's okay. I'm used to lugging th-things inside."

"Well, I'd love to see Rhyme and Reason, if you don't mind. My mom's birthday is coming up and she raves about the interesting stuff you have in your shop. You could help me pick something out for her."

"Oh, I'm sorry, D-Danny. I'm not really open right now. I stay closed on Mondays to restock after the weekend." Lowering her gaze to her purse, she frantically pushed past a pack of tissues, a tin of mints, a mini flashlight, and hand sanitizer. "My keys are playing hide and seek," she said. "I don't want to keep you. I can get it from here. Oh, but thank you so m-much." She glanced at him and nearly jumped—she hadn't realized how close they were. At just under six feet tall, Susan was used to towering over women and being eye to eye with men, but she had to look up at Danny. She'd forgotten how tall he was, and it made her feel feminine instead of gangly. "Okay, keys, this isn't funny anymore. Oh hey, there's my phone that I couldn't find."

Danny chuckled. "You're funny."

"I get that a lot. Problem is that I'm not trying to be funny," Susan said, and he laughed again. She lifted a corkscrew from her purse. "You know, just in case I need to uncork a bottle of wine on a moment's notice. S-sorry, you can get going. This could take a while."

Danny shrugged his wide shoulders. "I'm in no hurry. I was just going to grab lunch at the deli next door. I'm obsessed with Damn Good Sandwich," he said calmly while her heart raced.

"Ham Good Sandwich. City council made him change the n-name."

"I know, but I'm a rebel and John Clark does make a damn good sandwich, so I still call it that."

"Oh yes, the food there is amazing. It's hard to resist the aroma of the bread baking. I'll l-let you get back to your lunch," she said in a rush.

"Have you had lunch? I'd be happy to get something for you." Danny smiled. "Or you can join me. He has a few tables inside. My treat."

Lunch with Danny Mayfield? "Oh . . . n-no," Susan said, forgetting for a moment what she was looking for in her mess of a purse.

"You sure?"

Susan nodded firmly. "But thank you for the offer." This was the closest she'd been to Danny since he'd been her prom date back in high school, and her reaction to him was just as instant. She picked up another hint of his aftershave and had an insane urge to reach over and touch the dark stubble shadowing the bottom half of his handsome face. He'd been a cute teenager but he'd matured into a very sexy man. A man that she'd done a very good job of avoiding for the past ten years—not an easy task in a small town.

"Did you find your keys?"

"Keys? Oh . . ." Susan scooped her hand around in her purse. "Here they are!" She lifted her Tinkerbell keychain and jangled it in triumph.

"How could you miss that big thing?" Danny chuckled and then gave her a high five that she promptly missed. He laughed, thinking she'd missed on purpose, and she decided she'd let him believe that.

"Gotcha," Susan said, hoping she didn't sound as nervous as she felt.

"You did," he said as he picked up the box.

Susan opened the heavy door and flicked the lights on, illuminating the main showroom. The calming scent of cinnamon and vanilla filled her lungs and she glanced at Danny to see his reaction to her eclectic array of handmade gifts and repurposed items. She simply loved her store. If she won the lottery tomorrow, she'd keep Rhyme and Reason open just for fun.

"Wow, Susan, this is really cool," Danny said, eyeing a display of old silverware made into wind chimes. He put the box down. "No wonder my mother loves to shop here." He walked over and touched one of the chimes, making the silverware tinkle. "Do you mind if I have a look around? I'm really impressed."

"Thanks." Susan felt a warm rush of pride. "Go ahead."

Danny picked up a colorful rug and looked at it. "Sweet. Mom would love something like this."

"Made from old T-shirts."

"Resourceful idea. Did you make them?"

"Most of them. My mom made a few too. They're easy to do."

Danny nodded and put it back in the stack. "I have plenty of old T-shirts I could donate to the cause. How about socks? I have a million of just one."

Susan grinned. "Socks are repurposing gold. Puppets, holiday snowmen, pin cushions, pet toys . . . I have a display over against the wall called Sock It to Me."

Danny shook his head. "This is really amazing."

Susan felt another rush of pride. "I get such satisfaction out of finding new ways to use old things, especially if they're going to be thrown away." She pointed to a colorful display of candles in various shapes and sizes. "Those were all molded from pieces of broken crayons," she explained with a smile.

"Smart and useful." He seemed duly impressed.

"And see those bowls over there?"

Danny nodded. "Oh wow—they're made from vinyl record albums."

"Yes, but I only use ones that are too scratched to play. I collect vinyl. There's just something soothing about listening to music on a turntable," she said with a sigh.

"Yeah, I agree. My sister Mattie's husband got me interested in records. You should see Garret's collection. It will blow your mind, especially listening on his state-of-the-art sound system."

"I'd like that," she said without thinking. Her heart thumped when he nodded.

"Great, I'll be glad to take you. Oh, and if you'd like to sit in on a recording session at My Way Records, I can arrange that too. Jeff Greenfield is working on a new country album and Garret is one of the studio musicians. He said that Jeff's wife Cat is going to do a couple of duets with him and she wrote several of the songs."

"Oh, everyone in Cricket Creek is so proud of Jeff's success. I just love his old-school country voice. I was at the concert at Sully's when Jeff proposed to Cat."

"I was too. I think the entire town was there. Well then, that settles it. You have to come." Danny gave her another bone-melting smile and then pulled his cell phone out of his pocket. "Give me your number and I'll let you know when we can sit in on a recording session."

"Oh . . . um . . ." Reality smacked Susan in the face at the idea of giving Danny Mayfield her number and she swallowed hard. "My schedule is rather full."

"There will be a lot of sessions to choose from." He looked at her and waited.

"Well . . ." What in the world was she doing getting

cozy with the one person in Cricket Creek she wanted to avoid? How could she forget the embarrassing circumstances behind their one and only date? Feeling warm, she took off the puffy jacket that made her look like the Michelin tire man. She seriously needed to shop for a cute winter jacket. And then she remembered she was wearing a green sweater embellished with Santa's sleigh and all eight reindeer, led by Rudolph, who had an actual blinking red nose. Susan's mother didn't get the whole ugly Christmas sweater concept and bought Susan a new addition to her growing collection at the beginning of each holiday season. Susan always accepted the new sweater with ohs and ahs, along with an inward groan, but she wouldn't hurt her mother's feelings for the world. "I wouldn't want to be an imposition." She put her hand over Rudolph's nose.

"It wouldn't be an imposition," Danny insisted and looked at her expectantly.

Susan would bet there weren't many girls in Cricket Creek who wouldn't readily give their number to Danny Mayfield. But just like in high school, he was way out of her league and she knew he was just being kind. She had sort of initiated the invitation, even though it hadn't been her intention. "Well, I appreciate the nice offer but I'm really b-busy with the Christmas season coming up," she said. "I have a lot of decoration to do before the parade and the Christmas Walk."

"Okay, I understand." Danny slipped the slim phone back inside his jeans pocket and his smile faltered. He pointed at the box of mason jars. "Where do you want the box?"

"Up in my . . ." she began and then stopped herself. "Oh, it's okay right there. You've helped enough."

Danny gave her a level look and then sighed. "Susan, I know you don't want that box sitting here in the middle of your shop. Instead of you having to struggle I can take the box wherever you'd like it to go." He jabbed his thumb over his shoulder. "Or if you'd prefer I can get out of your hair," he said with a slight frown. "I get the feeling I've overstayed my welcome."

Susan knew her cheeks must be as rosy as Rudolph's nose. "I'm sorry, Danny," she said slowly, struggling not to stutter. "I don't mean to sound ungrateful for your help. If you hadn't appeared out of nowhere I w-would have crashed to the ground."

"You don't need to be grateful. I was happy to help." Danny tilted his head to the side as if about to ask her a question, but then seemed to think better of it. He also appeared confused and maybe a little bit hurt. If there was one thing Susan hated to do, it was hurt someone's feelings. He was only being polite and it was silly for her not to accept his assistance.

"If you wouldn't mind, I really need the jars taken up to the kitchen in my apartment above the shop," she said, even though her pulse fluttered at the thought of having him in her home.

"I don't mind at all." Danny gave her a slight smile and nodded. He picked up the heavy box with ease. "Lead the way."

"Okay, follow me," Susan said, even though the knowledge that he was watching her walk ahead of him was quite unnerving. Was her sweater clinging to her butt? Was she wiggling her hips too much? She stood up straighter but then felt awkward and tried her best to walk normally down the narrow hallway that led to the staircase to her apartment.

Once she reached the landing, Susan opened the door and flicked on the overhead track lighting. The wide open space and tall ceilings allowed her to decorate in the eclectic shabby chic style she loved. Like in her shop, Susan used old things for new purposes in her home.

The clump of Danny's work boots sounded manly on the hardwood floor. She rather liked the deep sound. *Danny Mayfield is inside my apartment.* How had this even happened? Oh yeah, she'd fallen into his arms.

And today started out so normal . . . She shook her head. "Geez."

"Something wrong?"

Oh damn, she'd said that out loud. Talking to herself was a product of spending so much time alone. "Oh . . . no." Embarrassed as to where her train of thought was going, she shook her head harder.

"Where to?" Danny asked, following her inside.

"Over there, in the kitchen." Susan pointed over to the far corner of the giant room that was sectioned off by a tall counter and three really beautiful bamboo stools she'd found at an estate sale.

"Okay." He followed her through the main living area, weaving past a wide variety of furniture that changed on a monthly basis. "On the counter?"

"On the floor is fine. I'm going to fill the jars with dry cookie mix, tie festive ribbons around the top, and sell them in the shop."

"A great Christmas gift idea. I'm sure they'll sell fast."

"All you have to do is add eggs and butter and you can make homemade cookies in a flash." She snapped her fingers and gave him a quick smile. "I've already done a few." She picked up a jar from the counter. "For you," she said, extending the jar rather awkwardly. When he accepted the gift his fingers brushed against hers and she sucked in a breath. "I appreciate your h-help."

"Thanks, Susan," he said, not sounding one bit breathless.

She bit her bottom lip between her teeth and nodded, wishing she wasn't wearing the silly blinking sweater.

"Your sweater is cute," Danny said, as if reading her mind.

"Oh!" Susan looked down at Rudolph, suddenly having a change of Christmas sweater heart. "A gift from my mom. She's crazy about Christmas. I have an endless supply of these, along with various earrings, necklaces, and hats."

"My family's big on Christmas too," Danny said, but Susan noticed he didn't specify himself. For some reason she wanted to know why.

"How about you?" The thought of anyone not loving Christmas made her sad. "Please don't tell me you're a Grinch."

Danny looked off into the distance. "I enjoy the family gatherings. Now that Mason and Mattie have kids, they're super into the holidays." He shrugged and turned his attention back to her.

"It's a fun time of the year but can be stressful," Susan said.

"Yeah, I try not to stress too much. Your place is awesome by the way," he said, changing the subject. "I love the hardwood floors and exposed brick." He looked up. "The beamed ceiling is really sweet and I really like how the lighting is recessed between the wood." He turned toward the floor to ceiling windows. "And you have an awesome view of Main Street."

"Along with a very short commute to work."

"With no traffic." Danny chuckled and then continued to walk around. He picked up a ceramic frog and examined it. "The poor guy is missing a foot."

"I tend to buy broken things that no one else wants. I drive my assistant, Betsy, absolutely nuts when I find something she knows won't sell and then buy it."

"You feel sorry for it?"

Susan grinned. "My apartment is like living on the island of misfit toys."

Danny laughed. "It's kind of like being in a museum. I wish everything had little cards so I could read the history."

"If you look closely you'll see that quite a few pieces on display are actually telephones," she said, wondering why her mouth kept moving when she should be sending him on his way. It was like her voice had taken on a life of its own while her brain took a holiday. "Something else I can't resist."

"Really? Show me one."

Susan walked over to a shelf and picked up a red car. "See?" She lifted the top to expose the phone. "I collect odd things. Don't ask me why."

"You collect cool things," Danny corrected. "And it's what you do for a living."

"Some are items that didn't sell in the shop and I just couldn't toss away and some things I buy to sell and then can't part with them. Good thing I have a lot of space." She grinned. "Or then again, maybe that's a bad thing." She put the car back on the shelf.

"Not at all. You just see beauty or value in things that other people miss."

"Thank you," Susan said, even though she suspected he was just being kind. "I suppose part of it comes from growing up on a farm. My mom used everything and wasted nothing." When Danny smiled she realized that she was starting to feel comfortable with him and her stutter, thank goodness, had vanished. "We were green way before it became popular." She chuckled. "Or then again, maybe we were just poor but I somehow didn't know it."

"Hey, when hard times hit, everybody in Cricket Creek struggled. Our marina sure did. There was a time when we thought we would lose it," he said with a sigh. "Trying to keep Mayfield Marina afloat nearly put my father in the grave."

"But you, Mattie, and Mason banded together and saved it, not only for your family but for Cricket Creek. I can't imagine this town without the marina, Danny."

"Thanks." He gave her a warm smile. "Well, we have Noah Falcon to thank for coming home and building the baseball stadium. It was the shot in the arm we needed. His rookie baseball card is one of my prized possessions."

"Oh I know, for a while Main Street was becoming a ghost town, one store closing after another. It's so wonderful to see Cricket Creek thriving again. New shops are springing up all over town. The deli next door is ham good," she said with a grin.

"Are you sure I can't treat you to lunch?"

A big part of Susan wanted to accept his offer but she suspected he was only being polite and had no real interest in her. She wasn't about to repeat the mistake she'd made by going to the prom with Danny. She wanted to ask if his mother had put him up to this visit, just like in high school, but she simply shook her head. "I really do have to get to work."

He hesitated for a fraction of a second, as if he might try to convince her. She sure hoped he didn't, because her resistance to Danny Mayfield was hanging on by a thread. "Okay. Well, I'll come back when you're open to shop for my mother."

"Great," Susan said, even though the thought of seeing Danny again made her heart hammer. He was way too good at putting her at ease when she needed to keep her guard up. "I'll show you out."

Danny nodded and fell into step beside her, continuing to look here and there. Susan was used to people wandering around in her apartment and picking up items to examine them, almost like they were in her shop.

They were almost to the door when Danny stopped in his tracks. "Where did you get this rocking chair?"

"I bought it at an estate sale a few weeks ago, intending to sell it." She slid her hand over the smooth wood of the arm. "But I just couldn't bear to part with it."

Danny inclined his head. "Really? Why?"

"It's just so beautiful, obviously handmade. Rocking in it is so soothing after being on my feet all day long." She sat down in it and sighed. "It's like whoever crafted it made it just for me." She looked up at him. "See, it's proportioned just right. I'm so tall that it's hard to find a chair that feels this comfortable. I change things around in here all the time but the rocking chair is a keeper," she said. Danny had a strange look on his face, which made Susan think she was going on way too long about a chair. "Anyway . . ." Feeling a bit silly she stood up and headed toward the door. He followed her down the steps and through the shop.

"Anything else you need brought out of your car?"

"Nothing I can't manage, but thank you."

Nodding, he put his hand on the door to push it open but then hesitated and turned back to her. "It was good to see you, Susan. Funny that we don't run into each other more often."

"Literally," she said, and he chuckled.

"I hope we do more often, even if it's literally. If you change your mind about sitting in on a Jeff Greenfield session, let me know." He reached into his wallet and handed her a card. "That's the office at Mayfield Marina. Just leave a message and I'll return it."

"Thanks." Susan nodded and wondered if he had any idea how hard she worked to avoid him. He stood there for another heartbeat and she suddenly felt shy again. Not knowing what else to say, she nibbled on the inside of her lip.

"Okay, well, I'll let you get back to work," Danny said and then walked out the door.

Susan stood there while fighting the oddest urge to run after him. Maybe she'd just head over to the deli and tell him that she was hungry after all. As if on cue, her stomach growled. "No!" Fisting her hands at her sides, she inhaled a deep breath. Danny was just being nice, and accepting another pity date, even if it was just lunch, would just be stupid on her part.

"Just get a grip." After locking the door, Susan headed upstairs to start working on layering the cookie mix into the jars. But she was feeling a bit unsettled, so she sat down in the rocking chair and tried to sort out her conflicting feelings about her unexpected meeting with Danny Mayfield. Closing her eyes, she leaned her head against the smooth wood and rocked gently. One thing was for sure: her attraction to Danny was stronger than ever, which meant she needed to avoid him at all costs.

2

Chicken Soup for Susan

DANNY OPENED THE DOOR OF HAM GOOD SANDWICH Deli and inhaled the sweet aroma of freshly baked bread. His stomach rumbled in anticipation of the mile-high Reuben and crispy potato pancake he planned to order. A chalkboard sign advertised chicken noodle as the homemade soup of the day and while waiting in line Danny wondered if Susan would like a hot cup of soup while she made her Christmas cookie jar mixes. Would she consider chicken noodle soup a nice gesture or think he was being pushy? Danny rubbed his fingers over the stubble on his chin. But honestly, why was he even considering bringing her lunch when she'd made it more than clear that she wasn't interested in him?

Danny crossed his hands over his chest, debating what to do, but before he could completely decide it was his turn to order. "Oh, hey!" Danny said, surprised that Stephanie Baker smiled at him from behind the counter. She'd been head cheerleader and prom queen, and one of the prettiest girls at Cricket Creek High. While they hadn't exactly been close friends, they had hung out with the same crowd and she'd spent lots of time at the marina. "How's it going, Steph?"

"Not too bad," Stephanie replied with another perky smile that didn't quite reach her eyes.

"I didn't know you were back in town." Danny glanced over his shoulder, making sure he wasn't holding up the line, but the lunch rush was over.

"Yeah, I got in town a couple of weeks ago."

"I'm surprised I didn't hear you were back."

"I'm still getting settled in." Stephanie shrugged. "I haven't gotten out much."

"So you're not just in for the holidays, then?"

"Nope." Stephanie inhaled a deep breath and leaned in a little bit closer. "I'm just working here until I find something in my field," she added in a lower voice.

"Are you back for good?"

"I think so. Big city life isn't all it's cracked up to be." She gave him a small, rather sad smile. "At least not for me."

"I'm sorry it didn't work out for you. But I'm sure there are plenty of people glad to have you back. Especially your family."

"Yeah . . ." Stephanie nodded slowly. Back in high school all Stephanie could talk about was getting away from small town life. "I'm living with mom and dad until I can find a job in my field. I love my parents but they treat me like I'm ten. Seriously, my dad bought me Captain Crunch cereal because he remembered it was my favorite."

Danny chuckled. "I wouldn't mind some Captain Crunch. But I know where you're coming from. So what's next?"

"Well, I'm still in transition at the moment." She rolled her eyes and then glanced over her shoulder. "Not that I don't like working here," she said, even though it was pretty obvious that she didn't really want to be taking orders for sandwiches.

"What's your field? I know a lot of people from working at the marina."

"Interior design."

"Oh, cool." Danny nodded but he didn't think many people in Cricket Creek would need her services. "I'll pass it along."

"Thanks. I appreciate that." Stephanie gave him another overly bright smile. He remembered she'd gotten married to some rich dude a few years after college. The lack of a wedding ring indicated she must have gotten a divorce. He recalled Mattie mentioning it in passing a while ago.

"So, what can I get for you today?" Stephanie asked.

"Reuben sandwich, potato pancake, and a large sweet tea, no lemon, please."

"Anything else?"

Danny hesitated and then grinned. "Yeah, a large cup of chicken noodle soup, extra crackers."

"To go?"

"Yes, please."

"I'll put your order in." Stephanie smiled again but Danny could sense her sadness and he felt badly for her. She'd always been one of those life-of-the-party kind of girls, the ones who seemed to have it all. She walked over to a window to the kitchen and gave the slip to John Clark, the owner of the deli.

"Hey there, Danny." John grinned at him. "You're becoming a regular."

"That's because you make a damn good sandwich."

John laughed. "You got that right. Going for my soon-to-be-famous Reuben this time?"

"Yep. I've been wanting to give it a try, even though the honey baked ham sandwich is hard to beat."

"Thanks. Good alternate choice, though. I have my corned beef delivered from New York City. It melts in your mouth. You won't be sorry." John kissed his fingertips and turned away to fill the order.

Danny had read an article in the *Cricket Creek*

Courier about John Clark a while ago. The story explained how he decided to open up a deli on Main Street. Originally from Cricket Creek, he'd graduated from Harvard Law School but left his job as a successful, high-powered corporate lawyer up East, wanting to come back to a small town lifestyle. Danny had heard somewhere that John had married a much younger woman and had gone through a messy divorce—a shame since he seemed like such a nice guy. There were more rumors flying around town but Danny tried to tune out gossip.

A couple of minutes later Stephanie appeared with his soup. "Here you go. Your sandwich will be ready in a minute."

"Thanks."

Danny stepped to the side while another customer approached the counter. The woman glanced over and then gave him a big smile. "Well, hello there, Danny Mayfield. Were you going to ignore me?"

"Oh I'm sorry, Miss Brock. I didn't recognize you with . . ." Danny pointed to her auburn hair that had once been brown.

"Makes me feel sassy." She demonstrated with a little head bop. Betsy used to be a driver's education teacher at Cricket Creek High and had been loved by all of the students, though she was retired now. She'd had the discipline of a drill sergeant but had used her sense of humor to keep students calm.

"I think you mean sassier."

Betsy tipped her head back and laughed. "And even more so when I drink one of those craft beers at your brother's Broomstick Brewery. I've got to ride my broom over there sometime soon and try the Christmas stout."

"You'll love it. Guaranteed to bring out your Christmas cheer, Miss Brock," Danny said with a laugh.

"Hey, I know I'm old enough to be your mama, but please call me Betsy. How is your mama, anyway? Enjoying her grandkids?"

Danny grinned. "She sure is. When Lily took her first step a few days ago you would have thought she'd won an Olympic gold medal. And now Mom has Mason's little Oliver to spoil too."

Betsy laughed. "I predict that your parents will be spending much more time in Cricket Creek than in Florida. I wouldn't be surprised if they move back full-time."

"You could be right." Danny nodded but he had his doubts. His father loved the warm climate and year-round fishing. "Well, it was good to see you, Miss . . . Betsy."

"You too. Well, I'd better place my order. I promised Susan I'd help her out today even though it's my day off. But she's such a sweetheart that I can't say no. You know Susan Quincy, right?"

"I do," Danny said and his heart pounded a little bit harder just hearing her name. "In fact, I just ran into her. Or rather she ran into me. Literally."

"Let me guess, she was trying to carry something way too heavy for her?"

"Yep."

"Does that all the time." Betsy tilted her head to the side and gave him a long look. "Lovely girl, that Susan. Quiet as a church mouse but then makes me laugh until my sides hurt. I think there's a much bigger personality lurking inside her ready to jump out and say boo!"

"She could learn from you."

Betsy laughed again. "Yep, I don't really know the meaning of quiet, even in my old age."

"Old age?" Danny knew Betsy was around his mother's age. "You're forever young."

"Charming as ever," Betsy said. "That cute smile of yours got you a B in Driver's Ed when your speeding should have gotten you a C. Always polite too. Your mama raised you well."

"Thank you. By the way, how's your daughter doing?" Danny asked.

"Aubrey's doing well. She's fretting over exams right now but she'll be home for the holidays soon. I sure do miss her but I'm proud that she's doing so well in college." Her smile wobbled a bit around the corners. Betsy was a single mom and Danny knew she must miss her only child something fierce. "I wanted her to stay local but her dream was to go to the University of Kentucky. She worked so hard to get scholarship money, so what could I say?"

"Well, you have the right to be proud."

"Thank you, Danny. Aubrey is my pride and joy."

"Hey, will you do me a favor and give this to Susan?" Danny handed Betsy the bag containing the soup.

"Sure," Betsy said but raised her eyebrows. "Funny, I was asked to bring her chicken soup, extra crackers."

"No way . . ."

"I'm guessing that's what's inside? How did you know chicken noodle was her favorite?"

"I didn't." Danny shrugged.

"Interesting." Betsy looked like she was ready to say more but John Clark came out from the kitchen. "I'll give it to her and—" When she saw John she stopped in mid-sentence.

"Hey Danny, sorry for the wait on the potato pancakes. I had to put a fresh batch in the fryer. I threw in a couple extra for keeping you waiting. Oh, and a hambone for your dog."

"I'd say it was worth the wait then, and Rusty will be over the moon. Thanks, John." Danny took the bags and then nodded to Betsy. "It was great seeing you. Maybe you'll pop in the brewery this Saturday? I'll hook you up with a flight of the winter ales."

"Sounds like an offer I can't refuse," Betsy said but appeared a little bit flustered.

Oh God, Danny sure hoped Betsy didn't think he was hitting on her. But just as he started to feel weird, he noticed that she flushed pink after turning to John

Clark to give him her order. Since Danny was pretty sure Betsy wasn't the blushing type, he had to conclude that it was John causing the extra color in her cheeks. Hiding his grin, Danny hesitated so he could see if his hunch was correct.

"Well, hi there, Betsy." John gave her a warm smile. Since Stephanie failed to reappear, he guessed she must be on break. "It's good to see you on your day off."

Danny raised his eyebrows. John knew what days Betsy worked?

"Hello, John," Betsy said. "I'm helping Susan with a Christmas project today."

"Ah . . . 'tis the season." John handed her a candy cane from a basket on the counter.

"Thank you. It's coming too fast this year."

Danny thought Betsy's voice sounded a little bit breathless. Did Betsy have a thing for John? Curious, Danny made slow work of gathering mustard packets and napkins, while both of them seemed to have forgotten he existed. Danny glanced over in time to see John give Betsy a big smile.

"What can I get for you today?"

"I'm not sure yet . . ." Betsy looked up at the menu above the counter.

"May I suggest some hot soup to warm you up on this blustery day? I make it myself."

"You mean it doesn't come from a can?" The humor in Betsy's tone said she knew better.

"You wound me," John replied.

Danny had to grin as he put the condiments in his bag. He wished he could dally a little longer to watch the exchange but he should get over to the Broomstick Brewery to help Mason unload some equipment, so he pushed the door open and headed over to his truck.

The success of the brewery meant continued expansion, something Danny's brother Mason had originally been opposed to, but falling in love with Grace Gordon had changed his way of thinking. Business was also booming at Mattie's Walking on Sunshine Bistro, and now that she had a liquor license she'd been bugging Danny to build a bar where patrons could gather for craft beer and fine wine. Juggling running the marina, bartending at the brewery, and helping Mattie at the bistro left little time for Danny to pursue anything of his own. But if he suddenly bailed on them all, who would replace him?

When Danny approached the truck, his Irish Setter pressed his nose against the window and gave him a woof of greeting. Danny climbed into the truck and patted Rusty on the head. "Sorry I was so long. I had an unexpected detour." He put his takeout on the floor and Rusty sniffed the corned beef in appreciation. "Yeah, there's a little treat for you in the other bag too."

"Woof!" Rusty wagged his tail, clearly excited at the word *treat*.

"I'll hurry home, old boy," Danny promised as he pulled out onto Main Street. While he enjoyed all of his three jobs, he sometimes felt less successful than his older brother and sister. Shaking his head, he looked over as he passed Rhyme and Reason. Maybe he was also feeling the sting of Susan's rejection.

"What will she think of the soup? And why am I trying so damned hard?" he asked Rusty, who did that dog eyebrow thing that meant he didn't know what the hell Danny was getting at. "You sure knew what to do when you fell in love with Abigail." Rusty perked up at the name of his doggie sweetheart. "You went all out by jumping in the river and swimming after her. Maybe I need a big moment like that. Abigail gave you the cold shoulder at first, so maybe there's hope for me after all."

Wanting to lift his mood, Danny turned on the radio and smiled when the new Jeff Greenfield song came on. Wouldn't you know, the country ballad had to be all about falling in love. While Danny had been

in a couple of semi-serious relationships, he wondered
if he'd ever truly been in love. "How the hell do you
know?" His parents certainly loved each other, having
stayed strong through thick and thin, so Danny valued
the institution of marriage. He supposed seeing Mason
and Mattie so happy lately had him wondering if he'd
ever find someone to settle down with for the long
haul. He gave a low whistle, drawing Rusty's attention
from the window. "Want a little more air?" Danny
pushed the button to open the window more and let
Rusty smell the breeze. He laughed when the Irish Setter pushed his nose out as far as he could. "Ah, the
simple things in life, right?"

But seriously, who would have thought Mason would
fall for Grace Gordon, a world traveling marketing genius? And Mattie? She'd married former bad boy musi-
cian Garret Ruleman, son of a legendary rock star who
had married a local real estate broker and settled down
in Cricket Creek. "Maybe I'm looking for love in all the
wrong places," he mumbled with a chuckle, even though
he really wasn't looking for love at all. Having three different jobs kept him too busy for anything other than
work. "What do you think, Rusty? Is it about time I got
back in the game?" When he stopped for a red light he
leaned over and scratched his trusty companion on the
head.

But on his way to the brewery Danny couldn't stop
thinking about Susan Quincy. Although he'd only asked
shy Susan to the prom at the request of his mother,
Danny had thoroughly enjoyed the evening with her.
She'd been so different than the outgoing girls he'd usually dated in high school and he'd felt an unexpected
connection to her that night. Danny shook his head, remembering how he'd found Susan's stutter cute and her
clever sense of humor had him laughing throughout the
evening. He'd wondered about what it would feel like to
kiss her from the moment he'd picked her up and then
posed for prom pictures with both sets of parents. She'd

looked so pretty in a long, soft blue dress that had been less flashy than what the other girls had been wearing. Instead of a fancy updo, her long dark curls were pulled back in a simple style but he found that he couldn't keep his eyes off her all night long. Danny shook his head at the memory, wondering if he still had the prom pictures stashed away with his high school memorabilia. He hoped that he did.

When he'd finally kissed Susan at the end of the date he'd felt a jolt of desire that he still thought about from time to time, usually when he spotted her somewhere in town.

Danny had wanted to ask her out again but she'd avoided him at school and so he'd eventually given up, thinking the attraction wasn't mutual. While Danny didn't think he had much of an ego, her snub had stung more than he'd cared to admit and her refusal to give him her phone number earlier brought back that feeling of rejection.

Danny tilted his head and sighed as he made a turn toward the marina property, which led to the brewery. Come to think of it, whenever he'd seen her around town, Susan headed in the opposite direction. He'd thought it was just one of those not-wanting-to-share-small-talk kind of situations, like when you saw a neighbor in the grocery store and hurried the other way. But now he had his doubts. Even though she'd finally warmed up to him today, Susan had made it clear she wasn't interested in getting to know him better. For some reason, Susan Quincy didn't like being around him.

"I just don't get it, Rusty." His family was highly thought of in Cricket Creek and Danny knew that in general he was considered to be a nice guy. "No, I *am* a nice guy, right? You like me, doncha boy?"

Rusty turned and gave Danny a doe-eyed dog expression of silent agreement.

"And I'm not bad-looking, right?" While Danny

wasn't a gym rat, he kept fit by doing physical labor at the marina and the bistro. On the weekends when he bartended, women tended to flirt with him, so he knew he wasn't without some physical appeal to the opposite sex.

So what was it about him that turned Susan off?

"What is her deal?" Danny grumbled. Well, if nothing else, she sure liked his rocking chair. The thought brought a small smile to his face. He wasn't really sure why he didn't let her know he'd handcrafted the rocking chair but for now he'd decided to keep the knowledge to himself. Woodworking was something he did on the side, mostly as a way to wind down or to create special pieces for friends and family. He'd made a mother's rocking chair with a side cradle for Mattie when Lily was born and his sister had hugged him tearfully when he'd presented it to her.

Crafting a chair to the specifications of the recipient was the key to making it their favorite piece of furniture in the house. But the fact that Susan's rocker felt as if it was measured for her had him shaking his head in confusion. He'd tried to figure out who the chair had been built for but had come up blank. If he'd asked Susan more questions he probably could have figured it out but for some reason he'd refrained. Maybe his hesitation stemmed from not wanting Susan to think of the chair as having been made for someone else? The image of her rocking gently drifted into his head and he couldn't help but smile.

Danny turned into the brewery parking lot. At one point he had considered using woodworking as his livelihood but when he'd had to help his parents save the marina, his talent had been pushed to the wayside and after a while the notion faded into what he considered a hobby.

Other than the rocking chair for Mattie and the bar he'd built for his brother's brewery, he hadn't done much woodworking lately. But over the years he'd accumulated quite a few pieces that were stored in the large workshop behind his log cabin. Maybe it was seeing Susan's appreciation of his work, but he suddenly felt the urge to start a new project. Perhaps something for Lily? The thought of his cute niece rocking in a chair he'd crafted just for her made him smile again. In truth he couldn't wait to build a doll house for her, or anything else she wanted for that matter. Lily already had her Uncle Danny wrapped around her little finger.

Mattie and Mason had both encouraged Danny to do more with his talent after he'd built the bar in Mason's brewery. But if he decided to make woodworking his main source of income, what would they all do without him? Who would run the marina? While the winter months were slow, business picked up in the early spring and lasted through late fall. Hiring someone would be a solution but no one other than a Mayfield had ever run the marina, so the thought gave Danny pause.

"Ah, Rusty, I just don't know . . ." After killing the engine, Danny opened the door of the truck and then walked around to let Rusty out. "Come on, boy." He picked up his lunch and grabbed the cookie mix, deciding he'd give it to Grace to bake. But as he started walking toward the old boathouse that Mason had converted into the brewery, his mood took another dive. While he was proud and happy for both Mattie and Mason's success, he was starting to feel restless. But unless he bailed on his family his hands were pretty much tied. And if he wanted to be truly honest with himself, the fear of failure tapped at the back of his brain.

And to top it all off, Danny had been suffering from bouts of loneliness lately. His closest friends were either in serious relationships or married, making playing pool at Sully's Tavern or poker nights a rare event these days. Weekly bonfires at the marina had fallen by the wayside. And with his siblings married with children and his parents doting on the grandkids, Danny felt a bit like the odd man out at family and social gatherings.

As if feeling Danny's blue mood, Rusty trotted close to his side. "I need to quit feeling sorry for myself, don't I?" He reached inside the extra bag and pulled out the hambone. "Here you go." Danny grinned at how hard Rusty's tail wagged in response to the treat. He watched Rusty run off with his prize and he had to wonder if he would share it with Abigail. "Even my dog's got a girl," Danny grumbled.

With a long sigh, Danny started walking up to the entrance to the brewery but paused when his phone pinged. He pulled it from his pocket and read the text message: *Hi Danny, it's Susan. Thanks for the soup and for helping me today. I called the marina and the message said to call this number to reach you. Oh, and I hope you enjoy baking your cookies.*☺ Danny grinned at the smiley face at the end of the message. After storing her number in his phone, he typed: *You're welcome. I'm sure I will love the cookies.*

"Well now, that's a start, anyway." He looked at the jar and his grin remained. "I think I'll bake these cookies tonight." His mood lifted another notch when he pictured Susan rocking in the chair he crafted. Eating warm cookies while doing some woodworking would be a relaxing way to spend the evening. He tried to remember if he'd ever baked cookies. Maybe the slice and bake kind.

Danny looked at the jar and noticed Susan had forgotten to add the baking instructions. Well, he'd just have to pay her another visit then, wouldn't he? And now he had her cell phone number. Danny grinned. Susan Quincy might have tried to avoid him but he was suddenly determined to show her what she'd been missing.

3

Truth or Dare

BETSY TWISTED THE LID ONTO THE MASON JAR AND reached for a sprig of holly to tuck into the red raffia bow. "So now, explain to me once more why you turned down Danny Mayfield's invitation to lunch?" She tilted her head to the side and waited. "I'm completely confused. Not that confusion isn't normal for me but this has me really stumped."

"Well . . ." Susan brushed at a dark curl that had escaped the bun she'd piled on top of her head.

"Well what, sweet pea?" Betsy scooped flour into a measuring cup and dumped it into a jar. "I just don't get it."

"He was just being . . . you know, nice."

"Well . . ." Betsy layered a scoop of sugar into the jar and shook her head. "What's wrong with being nice? Handsome? Single! And not to mention has a very nice tush."

"You just mentioned it."

"Haven't you noticed?"

"Did you really check out his butt?"

"Hello . . . I'm old but I'm not dead."

"You're not old."

Betsy aimed her scoop at Susan. "You're avoiding the question."

Susan popped a chocolate chip into her mouth.

"I'm waiting." Betsy sat down on the stool next to the counter and crossed her arms. "I refuse to continue until you answer my simple question."

Susan swept her arm toward dozens of mason jars. "That's not fair!"

"Come on, girl. Danny brought up these jars for you. He asked you to lunch and then sent chicken soup to you, for pity's sake."

Susan lifted her chin. "I thanked him."

Betsy still didn't understand. "Danny Mayfield is one of the most eligible young men in Cricket Creek. What's not to like?"

"I didn't say I didn't like him." She picked up another jar and went to work.

Betsy arched an eyebrow and remained defiant. "So . . . ?"

"I could ask you the same thing about John Clark. He's nice, handsome, and single. Although I can't say that I've checked out his tush."

"I have. It's world-class."

"So . . ." Susan shot back at her. "What's holding *you* back?"

"He hasn't asked me out," Betsy replied, hoping she'd kept her blush in check. The mere mention of John got her pulse going but she didn't want Susan to know it.

"And if he did?"

"He won't. You didn't answer the question."

"And neither did you," Susan countered.

"Since when did you get so feisty?"

"Learning from you, I guess," Susan answered with a grin. "Okay, if I answer your question, you have to answer mine."

"You drive a hard bargain." Betsy inhaled a deep breath of cookie mix–scented air. She really didn't want to divulge her reasons, knowing Susan would give her grief, but she really wanted to know why her sweet friend wouldn't give Danny the time of day. Susan was simply a delightful girl and in her mind would be perfect for a hardworking hometown boy like Danny. A bit on the shy side, Betsy just bet that outgoing Danny would bring out the playful, fun side of Susan that Betsy got glimpses of now and then. "Okay, if you must know . . ." She fidgeted on the stool.

"I must."

"Of course I find John Clark attractive." Betsy had to grin. "He was such a nerdy, quiet guy back in high school. Super smart. He went to Harvard, you know, and became a big-time lawyer up East."

"Oh yeah, I read that in the paper. He wanted to leave the city life behind and get back to his roots. I can understand that."

"He also left an ex-wife behind, after what I heard was a messy divorce."

Susan shrugged. "It happens."

Betsy decided to get straight to the point. "Susan, rumor is that John's ex-wife was a much younger social-ite. I think an actress or model or something. Sure, I find the man attractive, but let's cut to the chase. A man like him wouldn't be interested in a retired high school driver's ed teacher."

"You don't know what he's interested in, and being a driver's ed teacher was a good job. I'm sure you saved a lot of wrecks from happening."

"Sugar, he went to Harvard and I went to the school of hard knocks. I'm not even remotely in his league." Betsy braced herself for Susan to argue the point.

"John gives you extra things with your order most of the time and he even hand delivers lunch sometimes. He gets all flirty with you, Betsy, and you know it."

"That doesn't mean he wants to date me. Some guys are just flirts."

"John doesn't flirt with me." Susan tapped her chest

with her scoop. "And seriously, he doesn't seem like the 'flirt with any woman' type of guy. He likes you."

"I'm a likeable person."

"He's *into* you."

"He's just being nice . . . Oh wait a doggone moment. You led me right into that one. Come on now, is that what you really think about Danny? That he's only being nice and has no real interest?"

Susan nibbled on the inside of her lip and started tying a bow with more concentration than needed. "Yes."

"You've got something more to say. I can tell. Spill, if you want the jars filled."

"You can't be serious," Susan sputtered.

"I'm here on my own time, remember?" Betsy wouldn't leave until she got what she wanted, and Susan knew it, but she lifted her chin. "Come on now. Let's hear it."

Susan sighed. "Okay . . . I went to my senior prom with Danny."

Betsy felt a jolt of surprise. "Really? How come I didn't know this?"

"Well, it isn't something that comes up in casual conversation."

"So were you and Danny dating?"

Susan shook her head. "Nope."

"He must have had the hots for you to ask you to the prom."

"Um, not really." Her cheeks turned pink. "My mom and Danny's mother are friends. I found out that my mother asked Miranda Mayfield to see if Danny would take me to the prom. I had no idea and I was over the moon that he asked me. Shocked, really."

"I don't see why. You're a very pretty girl and sweet as can be."

"Betsy, I was so shy in high school and I had this horrible stutter."

"Oh, I do remember you had a little stutter when I taught you how to drive. A lot of students were brash and thought they knew it all but you were so careful behind the wheel."

"I think you were mistaking careful for scared out of my ever-loving mind."

Betsy felt a flash of sympathy. "Did you get made fun of, sweetie?"

Susan shrugged. "Not too much. I was just embarrassed when it happened. And of course it was way worse when I was nervous about something. It was really bad when I was a child and so I was very quiet. And then I grew like a weed." She shook her head. "I was always so much taller than all of the other girls. I felt like a freak."

"Oh Susan . . ."

"I was so silent that my kindergarten teacher thought I had a hearing problem and insisted that I should get my hearing checked," Susan said with a chuckle. "But she was helpful too and taught me to talk slowly. It was so hard for my mom and dad not to finish what I was trying to say. I had to learn to control the stuttering by talking, not having them speak for me."

"I can see how that would be difficult. Is there a known cause?"

"No, and the bad thing is that although there's evidence that stuttering is genetic, there isn't any real cure or treatment other than speech therapy, which only helps a little bit. My parents were supportive and never critical because they knew it wasn't something I could control. But it was funny—I wouldn't stutter when I sang or read out loud, so I have a huge appreciation for music and reading. That's why I collect so many record albums. Music still calms me down." She pointed to the rocking chair. "I guess I didn't think about it but when my mother read to me it was usually in a rocking chair. Maybe that's why I love that one so much."

Betsy looked over at the rocking chair. "It sure is beautiful." She turned back to Susan. "You're certainly not a freak. You're gorgeous and have your own unique sense of style. I hope you know that." Betsy's voice quivered with emotion.

"Oh, Betsy." Susan gave her a hug.

"Being around you has helped ease the pain of missing Aubrey."

"Well, being around you has helped me come out of my shell a bit more. You're just so full of life."

"That makes me happy to hear you say that. You should be so proud of Rhyme and Reason."

"Oh, having my own thrift shop is a dream come true. My mother hated to throw anything away. I just love it, especially this time of year." Susan reached for another mason jar to fill.

Betsy stood up and scooped up some chocolate chips. "I don't think I've heard you stutter since I started working with you. If you did, I didn't notice."

"I've pretty much overcome it but it pops out when I'm embarrassed or get super nervous. I did struggle with stuttering a bit more when I started high school because I was so shy."

"Oh sweetie . . ."

"So do you see? Danny was only being nice to me back in high school. I had this crazy crush on him and when I found out the truth about why he asked me to the prom I was devastated." She groaned, as if reliving the memory.

"I can imagine. Does Danny know that you know the truth?"

"Probably not." Susan shrugged. "After I overheard my mom talking to Miranda about the whole thing I avoided Danny in the hallways. It wasn't too difficult since we ran in different circles." She chuckled. "Well, I had a few close friends, but I didn't run in any circles. Even today if I see Danny in the grocery store, I duck down the next aisle." She shook her head. "I'd be a fool to put myself through that humiliation again."

"Well, I don't see how it's the same situation. He didn't make any promises to anyone about asking you to lunch."

Susan rolled her eyes. "I literally fell into his arms. It was purely an accident. I'm telling you, he was just being a good guy. He was so popular in high school but he was always friendly to everyone and not stuck up like some of the cool kids. It's the same thing now."

"I don't see it that way at all. But I can imagine how the whole prom thing could have you spooked." Betsy thought about the situation for a moment. "I have to ask you, how was prom night?"

"Magical." Susan's lips curved in a dreamy smile.

"Oh, Susan . . ." Betsy sighed. "Wait, did he kiss you?"

Susan's cheeks flamed but she nodded, biting her bottom lip.

"And?"

"Well, it was bone-melting wonderful."

"Then Danny must have felt something too."

"Oh come on. He was a teenage boy. Kissing is all they had on their mind. I think he was caught up in the moment. Or maybe he didn't want to disappoint me. Who knows?"

"Or maybe he simply wanted to kiss you." Betsy lifted one shoulder. "Danny is a grown man, making his own choices, so I get where you're coming from but I think you should give him a chance."

"So why don't you follow your own advice?"

"Because although John Clark grew up in Cricket Creek, we're still from two different worlds. I was a single mom barely making ends meet and he was a high-powered corporate lawyer."

"And now he's divorced and owns the deli next door. And Aubrey is away at college. You're in a different time in your life and so is he. Maybe you should flirt back and see where it takes you."

"No way. Like I already told you, John couldn't possibly be interested in someone like me. Plus, he obviously goes for younger women. I think we all know that the whole 'age is just a number' thing is a bunch of bull."

"Well, obviously he made a mistake," Susan said with a slight shrug.

"Yeah, but what does that say about him?"

Susan tilted her head. "I don't know. Maybe nothing more than he fell in love with the wrong person. Or that the age difference became wider as he got older?"

"Ah, Susan, you're a very fair-minded person," Betsy said.

"I try to be. I mean, he's obviously trying to simplify his life by coming back to Cricket Creek," Susan said.

"True." Betsy clipped another bit of raffia. "I think we need more of this stuff," she said, trying to divert the conversation.

Susan frowned at the large pile of decorations. "I can pick up more later today."

Betsy nodded absently. Sometimes she craved being in the arms of a man and she couldn't even remember the last time she'd had a long, hot kiss. She'd actually considered getting back into dating lately but the only man she was interested in owned the deli next door.

"So, what would you do if John asked you to go out?" Susan asked.

"He's not going to!"

"You didn't answer the question."

"Susan, I've seen pictures of his ex-wife."

"She's his ex-wife for a reason."

Betsy rolled her eyes. "I didn't know you could be this stubborn."

"I'm just pointing out the facts."

"Humph," Betsy said.

"Okay, let's play truth or dare."

"What's gotten into you? Have you been hitting the eggnog?" Betsy shook her head at her normally low-key young boss.

"No, but I think it's a great idea." Susan headed over to the fridge and pulled out a carton of eggnog. "Nice, almost full."

"Are you adding bourbon?" Betsy asked hopefully. "My house is within walking distance, so I don't need to worry about driving."

Susan pulled two glasses from the cabinet. "It's the middle of the afternoon."

"You started this whole thing. Besides, it's our day off," Betsy said.

"I don't even know if I have bourbon."

"Are you gonna look? If not, if you buy, I'll fly."

"Deal." Susan laughed. To Betsy's delight, Susan opened a door and rooted around. "Well, what do you know?" She turned around with a full bottle clutched in her hand.

"Buffalo Trace. Very nice. Let's crank up the Christmas music and crack that baby open."

A minute later they both had a stiff drink in their hand.

Betsy tapped her glass to Susan's. "Cheers."

"What are we drinking to?" Susan asked.

Betsy nibbled on the inside of her lip. "Christmas?"

"How about to not being scaredy-cats," Susan suggested.

"Did you just say scaredy-cat?"

"Yeah, and I'm fed up with being one."

"I taught driver's ed to teenagers. I'm not a scaredy-cat. And you own your own business. That takes guts."

"You know what I'm referring to. Our love lives. Or lack thereof."

Betsy's heart beat like she'd been running a marathon. She would have declined the challenge but she really thought Danny was the right kind of guy for Susan. So even though she didn't have any intention of pursuing John Clark, she nodded and tapped her glass to Susan's and took a healthy swallow. "Holy moly, did you put any eggnog with that bourbon?"

"A little," Susan replied. "You said you wanted a stiff drink."

"I say a lot of things."

"Well, let's stop saying and start doing. Put your money where your mouth is."

"Wait, so does this mean that if Danny asks you out again, you'll accept?"

Susan looked down at her glass, studying the contents, and then back at Betsy. "Maybe . . ." she replied and then grinned. "Ask me again after I finish this eggnog."

"You mean bourbon with a splash of eggnog."

Susan laughed and although Betsy could see the doubt in her friend's eyes, this was a start. Shy Susan was beginning to blossom, and she was a sight to behold.

4

It's Beginning to Look a Lot Like Christmas

JOHN HUMMED ALONG WITH THE PIPED-IN CHRISTMAS music while he wrapped up the day-old loaves of bread to freeze. On Friday he'd take the package to the Cricket Creek soup kitchen over on Third Street. After delivering the bread he usually hung around and helped serve dinner to those less fortunate. Now that colder weather had arrived and the holidays were upon them, the attendance at the soup kitchen was brisk, and so John started baking more bread than he knew he'd need to make sure there would be a big surplus by the end of the week.

After putting the bread in the walk-in freezer he began that afternoon's daily cleanup. Although the deli remained open seven days a week, he was usually buttoned up by no later than three o'clock since he was only open for lunch. He'd considered taking Mondays off after he'd hired Stephanie, but the control freak in him balked at the idea. In truth, working at his deli felt more like fun than a real job. Flipping the towel from his shoulder, he wiped down the counter and then stepped back to survey the gleaming kitchen. Those who knew him in Boston had given him a month in Cricket Creek before he returned to the city. Now that nearly a year had passed, John knew for certain he'd made the right decision to return to his hometown. Instead of arguing for a living, he chatted and smiled with friendly customers. He fell asleep at night from a healthy kind of exhaustion and he could feel his personality getting softer and opening up at the same time. He used to avoid small talk and now he enjoyed interaction with people.

Picking up a candy cane from the basket that Stephanie had refilled, he ripped off the plastic and took a bite. He rolled the cool peppermint around on his tongue, trying not to feel guilty that he was eating sweets. Growing up, his college professor parents had frowned upon sugary treats and television, preaching healthy eating over junk food and reading over mindless cartoons. As a result, John became serious and quiet, different from the other boisterous boys at school. Although he wasn't really poked fun at, he felt like an outsider, preferring to read at recess rather than play tag or four square.

Popping the rest of the miniature candy cane in his mouth, John stood back and observed the holiday decorations Stephanie had put up before leaving. She'd hummed while she'd put ornaments on the small Christmas tree over in the corner but there was a sadness about her that John understood. The first Christmas after a divorce was tough. He walked over and tacked up a loose loop of silver garland. Over the years, Christmas had become all about buying Rachel and his parents expensive gifts, all of them purchased by his personal assistant. He'd worked all the way up until Christmas Eve and rarely made the trek from Boston to Cricket Creek for the holidays.

Blowing out a peppermint-scented breath, John shook his head. While having Rachel cheat on him with a young lawyer at his own firm had been a blow to his ego, he had to admit that he hadn't given his wife much attention. She was fifteen years his junior and they had little in common, but he'd been arrogant enough to think she married him for love. At the age of forty he'd been a successful attorney, had a huge house, luxury cars, and a gorgeous wife. To the outside world he'd had it all. But arguing for a living had stripped away his gentleness and replaced it with a hard-nosed must-win attitude. Little else in his life had mattered. He'd fought with Rachel over every last detail of the divorce, until one day he woke up in a cold sweat and realized he hated the man he'd become. He'd signed the divorce papers that day, giving in to most of her demands, not caring about possessions or money. His attorney had fumed, telling John that he'd regret his rash decision, but he didn't. Instead he felt as if he'd shed his old skin and had come out of the marriage renewed.

"Snow!" John walked over to the window and watched the flurries dance and twirl in the wind. He suddenly had the childlike urge to walk out and catch a fat snowflake on his tongue. Had he ever been that carefree? Not really. As a lonely only child he remembered asking Santa for a baby brother . . . or he even would have taken a sister if Santa was all out of brothers. When Santa failed to deliver, John had asked for a dog the next year and got a goldfish instead.

John picked up the Santa figurine sitting on the windowsill. "Man, you let me down." Tilting his head, he said, "How about this? Why don't you bring me a lovely lady companion this Christmas? Now that just might make up for the lack of siblings and goldfish that died. Yeah, my mom replaced it, but the lack of a black spot on a goldfish named Spot pretty much clued me in, even though I never let her know."

Hearing laughter, John put Santa Claus down and looked out the window. He had to grin at the sight of Betsy and Susan twirling around in the snow. They weren't even wearing coats and were unsuccessful in capturing snowflakes on their tongues. He walked closer to the window and he could hear what they were saying.

"These snowflakes are wily little things," Betsy said.

"Wait, I got one!" Susan shouted. "I win!"

"Prove it!" Betsy demanded with her hands on her hips.

Susan stuck out her tongue.

"Ha, nothing," Betsy said with a shake of her head. "Thought so!"

"It melted!" Susan protested with a giggle. She zigzagged around, trying to capture another snowflake but nearly running into a streetlamp. "Who put that there?"

John laughed as he watched, longing to join them in their carefree abandon, but he didn't want to intrude upon their moment. Crossing his arms, he watched them delight in the simplicity of falling snow. Their laughter blew puffs of fog into the chilly air. John noticed that both of them had sprigs of holly in their hair and he remembered that Betsy had said she was helping Susan put together a Christmas project. He felt a stab of envy at their easy friendship, wishing he had someone to goof off with.

"When have I ever had that in my life?" John asked the Santa figurine. "Um, that would be never." He blew out a breath that fogged up the window. He looked down at the scripted "Just Believe" painted at the base of the figurine. "Sorry, old chap, I stopped believing in you when I was about six. Told a bunch of kids in my first grade class that you didn't exist and got banished to the hallway to sit all by my lonesome." John shook his head. "Never understood the punishment when all I did was enlighten them with the truth." John frowned, remembering kids crying. He got skipped over by Cindy Cooper, who was passing out star-shaped cookies. She told him he was going to get a lump of coal in his stocking. Then he suffered the humiliation of being sent out of the Christmas party while the teacher tried to calm the class down.

He'd explained to his parents, "I thought I was doing them a favor!" Of course, his parents made a huge stink over the punishment, making matters a hell of a lot worse. Mrs. Sparks insisted the reprimand was for talking out of turn and not for spoiling the magic of Christmas for innocent six-year-olds. For a kid who already had a tough time socially, this early blunder set the stage for his grade school education and he'd been sure to keep his mouth shut about the Easter Bunny and Tooth Fairy.

John had spent twelve long years wishing he could play sports as well as he performed academically. But Clovis and Wendy Clark didn't see the value of chasing a ball around a field when the time outdoors could be better spent hiking and learning about nature.

John looked out the window at Betsy, remembering how pretty and vibrant she'd been in high school. "Still is." He smiled when Betsy finally managed to snag a snowflake. Raising her arms skyward, she cheered, drawing more laughter from Susan.

Susan rubbed her hands up the sleeves of a sweater that looked as if Christmas had thrown up all over it. "I'm getting cold," she said.

"You're saying that because I'm winning."

"We're tied!" Susan shook her head.

"Well then let's break the tie. I could use another eggnog."

John laughed. *Spiked, I bet. That explains a lot.* He was about to turn from the window when Betsy chased a fluffy snowflake right up to the window of the deli.

"I'm after a big one!" Betsy shouted.

Feeling silly for staring, John whipped the towel from his shoulder and started wiping the windowsill, nearly knocking jolly old Santa to the floor.

In spite of his quick reaction, Betsy's gaze fell upon him. Mouthing *hello*, John waved as if surprised to see her. She returned his greeting just as a brisk breeze whipped the snow into a frenzy. With colorful Main Street in the background, Betsy looked as if she were standing inside a snow globe. Her eyes danced with mischief and her cheeks were rosy from the cold. White crystals clung to the auburn layers of her hair and when she smiled John couldn't pull his gaze away. It was one of those time-standing-still moments. Wait, he'd never had a time-standing-still moment . . .

Until now.

John felt a strong pull of longing and nearly put the palm of his hand on the windowpane. A rush of warmth had him breathing harder. He knew he should turn away instead of standing there like a love-struck fool, so he swallowed hard and moved to turn, but Betsy smiled. And it wasn't just a regular old, run-of-the-mill smile, but warm and . . . inviting? Or was he imagining things?

And then Betsy blew him a kiss!

Wait . . . what? Did she just add a wink? But before John could fully react, Betsy's eyes widened and she turned on her heel. She hurried over to Susan, grabbed her arm, and they disappeared inside Rhyme and Reason.

John stood there at the window, dumbfounded. For a moment he wondered if he would wake up from his little winter wonderland display. He looked down at Santa, as if the jolly old soul would give him some answers, but the figurine just stared blankly back, as if reminding John that he was a nonbeliever. Did Betsy really just blow him a kiss . . . and was a wink involved? Maybe he'd gotten it all wrong. But how could he mistake a kiss? And what in the world did it mean? He stood there, twisting the towel, wishing for a replay in slow motion.

"Wow . . ."

John smiled and his heart started beating faster. Being attracted to a woman made him feel energized and alive. Betsy Brock was bringing out a playful side that he didn't know existed. Sure, maybe he'd imagined the kiss, or perhaps it was fueled by spiked eggnog, but he didn't care. He'd felt a strong jolt of awareness at the moment that their eyes met, and he knew she felt it too.

Betsy might rebuff his attempts at flirting, something he was pretty sure he sucked at doing, and she could ignore the extras he put in her lunch order, but there was something simmering beneath the surface between them, and this only served to prove he was right. Of course, he understood her reluctance to give him the time of day. The gossip surrounding his divorce from a younger woman had to be off-putting.

Sighing, John tried to chase away the sudden tug of loneliness. Now that he wasn't consumed with his work he longed for human contact, for friends and laughter. He'd never found his niche back in high school and so he didn't have a circle of friends to return to in Cricket Creek.

Well, if his strict, no-nonsense parents could sell their home to him, pack up just the basics, and head cross country in an RV on a quest to visit every state park, then surely John could muster up the courage to begin a laid-back lifestyle in his old hometown. And some way, somehow, he would convince Betsy Brock to go on a date with him. John looked down at Santa. "You just wait and see."

Fingers of sunshine reaching through the window caused the silver garland to sparkle and send shadows dancing across the walls. Twinkling lights on the tree came to life. John knew it was because of the darkening sky that made the red and green lights noticeable but he had to smile. Maybe he'd finally get a magical, movie-worthy Christmas.

5
Winter Wonderland

"**B**ETSY, WHY DID YOU GRAB ME?" SUSAN SHOOK THE snowflakes from her hair, feeling energized from the cold and activity. "I was ready to catch the tie-breaker." She unlocked the door of the shop. "Whew, now that we're inside, I realize how cold it was out there." She would have said more but Betsy tugged hard at the sleeve of her sweater.

"Oh dear God, I . . ." Betsy paused and looked up at the ceiling. A moment later she doubled over.

"B-Betsy! Oh no! What is it? Should I call 911? Are you in p-pain?" Susan nearly shouted. "Talk to me!" She did shout this time, trying to recall how to do CPR, but her brain was malfunctioning. "Oh God, wh-where is my cell phone? Betsy, lie down. Are you short of br-breath? Going to pass out? Is pain shooting up your arm?" She frantically tried to remember the sure signs of a heart attack.

"No, sweet pea." Betsy shook her head and then moaned. "I'm dying, but it's only of acute embarrassment."

"What? We were just catching snowflakes! Well,

trying to," Susan said, surprised that someone as outgoing as Betsy would feel embarrassment over something so innocent.

"No, Susan, I . . ."

"What?" she asked gently. The stricken look on Betsy's face nearly brought tears to Susan's eyes. "Oh, you can tell me. Did . . . you pee your pants?" she whispered. "I was rather cold. The cold always makes me have to pee all of the sudden."

"No! I wish!"

Susan frowned. "You wish you peed your pants?"

"Yes, rather than blowing a kiss at John Clark."

Raising her eyebrows, Susan took a step back and nearly tripped over a handmade rocking horse. "Say that again?"

"I was going after a snowflake and headed over near Ham Good Sandwich. John was doing something, cleaning the window or whatever, and for some ungodly reason I blew the man a kiss."

Susan kind of wanted to laugh but Betsy looked so horrified that she kept a straight face. "I'm so sorry, Betsy. I shouldn't have cracked open that bourbon."

"Well, it was my idea and damn if I don't need another one right about now. Do you have shot glasses?"

"I don't think so. Wait, maybe somewhere here in the shop."

"That's okay, I'll drink from the damned bottle."

"Oh Betsy." Susan wasn't sure if more bourbon was the smart thing to do but she nodded. "Let's go back upstairs."

"And the day started out so normal." Clearly still shaken, Betsy nodded glumly and led the way to Susan's apartment.

When they reached the kitchen, Susan suggested, "How about some hot coffee instead? Or hot chocolate? I have marshmallows," she added cheerfully.

"Coffee, I guess. Oh no, the caffeine will keep me up tonight." Betsy groaned and sat down on a stool.

"I have green tea."

"I'll just have water."

"You sure?"

"Yeah, a splash with ice and bourbon. Oh, what have I done?" she wailed as if she'd committed some horrific crime.

Susan made a couple of weak drinks, adding a slice of orange and a cherry, and brought the glasses over to the table. She located two bottles of water and brought out slices of Havarti and wheat crackers and then sat down next to Betsy. "It's not the end of the world. I mean, it's not like you flashed him."

Betsy groaned.

"Wait, did you?"

"No!" Betsy picked up a cracker and put a slice of cheese on it. "I don't know what got into me. I mean, we drank a little bourbon but still . . . I can hold my liquor."

"Really? How often do you drink?"

She shrugged. "A little bit now and then. Craft beer at Broomstick Brewery, and that's pretty strong stuff. The wine bar at Wine and Diner, but that's mostly for the half-off happy hour food."

"I rest my case. You got caught up in the moment and we got a little bit tipsy. I did too."

"You didn't blow kisses at anyone!"

"No harm done," Susan insisted, but she understood. If she had blown a kiss to Danny she would feel the same way. Mortified. But she wasn't about to let Betsy know it.

"Oh Susan, what am I gonna do?" She took a gulp of her drink and frowned. "Well, this is weak as all get out."

"You want more bourbon?"

"Kinda."

"Help yourself." Susan took a small sip of her drink and then popped the cherry in her mouth. She chewed slowly, thinking. "I've got it!"

"Oh please enlighten me." She added more bourbon and then reached for another slice of cheese. "This stuff is so good. It's like butter. So what have you got? More of this cheese, I hope."

"You can go over to the deli tomorrow. If John comes out, and you know he will if you're there—"

"Go on."

"You sneeze. Make the sneezing sound but kind of make it look like the blowing kiss thing. He'll think it's just the weird way you sneeze." Susan snapped her fingers. "Easy-peasy."

Betsy perked up. "You really think so?"

"Of course. You just have to make the actual sneeze sound real. Go ahead and practice. Here, no, let me show you. Ah-choo!" Susan flipped her fingers forward like she was blowing a kiss.

"Wow, that actually kind of works. Wait." Betsy slapped the heel of her hand to her forehead. "I might have winked."

"Then blink afterwards." Susan demonstrated. "I think everybody blinks when they sneeze." She grabbed her phone that she'd left on the counter. "I'll look it up." She Googled the question and then nodded. "Yep, blinking is an involuntary response. So then if you winked, he might think you actually blinked." She kept reading. "Listen to this . . . When we sneeze it's about one hundred miles per hour. Hurricane strength. Impressive. Hmmm, we produce four cups of mucus a day, most of which we swallow—"

"Oh yuck! Enough already!" Betsy raised her palms in surrender and then unscrewed the cap on her water bottle. "Do you really think I can pull off a fake sneeze-blink and remember to flip my fingers forward? Come on, I forget where I park my car when I go to the grocery store."

"Totally. Practice in front of the mirror tomorrow and then you can go over to the deli and order lunch."

Betsy blew out a breath. "Well, problem solved. You are a genius."

"Thank you. I get that a lot."

Betsy chuckled and seemed to relax.

"But I have to ask . . ."

Betsy groaned. "Oh, go ahead."

"Why do you think you blew the kiss at him? And I know that you're going to say it was the eggnog, but that was just the liquid courage—I'm not buying that."

"Liquid stupidity, you mean. Have your forgotten we were out on Main Street in the cold without coats, chasing snowflakes with our tongues?"

"And have you forgotten that I'm trying to come out of my shell? And that we toasted to not being scaredy-cats?"

Betsy raised her eyebrows. "So, just what are you getting at, girlie? Does this have something to do with Danny Mayfield?"

Susan pressed her lips together. She remembered the jubilation of having Danny ask her to go to the prom. It was like that Christmas morning feeling when you got just what you wanted beneath the tree. She broke a cracker into pieces while Betsy waited for her to answer. "Because of the stutter I was just always so timid," she said slowly. "And then I grew into such a gangly string bean. I would literally trip over my own two feet." She shook her head. "My parents, bless their hearts, were a bit overprotective. I surrounded myself with music, books, and nature. I preferred being in the woods to hanging out at the mall. Or at least that's what I told myself. And of course I helped out on the farm."

"Your childhood made you into a kind and gentle soul, Susan."

"But socially backward."

Betsy reached across the counter and squeezed Susan's hand. "Well, you certainly moved forward. You're so good with the customers. You're much more confident than you realize."

"Thank you, Betsy. Like I said, you've been a big help."

"We've helped each other." She gave Susan's hand a final pat. "At least give Danny a chance."

"Oh, I think I successfully chased him away. I made it clear I wasn't interested."

"Except you are. Have you forgotten he sent you chicken soup? And don't tell me he was just being nice. The boy is smitten; you mark my words. The rest is up to you."

Susan's heart thudded with the possibility that Danny might actually be interested in her but she was too scared to let the notion sink in. "You've successfully steered the conversation away from you."

"Have you forgotten I was a driver's ed teacher?"

Susan laughed. "Well, don't forget to practice your sneeze tonight."

Betsy sneezed.

"Wow, that was good."

"It was real. Maybe dancing in the snow without coats wasn't such a great idea."

Susan shook her head. "Nope, it was a good idea. Twirling around with the snowflakes felt awesome. If we get the sniffles it will be totally worth it." She dusted the cracker crumbs from her fingers. "Let's get back to work. We have lots of jars to fill."

"I'm ready."

Susan cranked up the Christmas music and tried to concentrate on the job at hand but her mind drifted back to Danny. Would kissing him still make her melt as fast as a snowflake on her tongue? Maybe it was time to find out.

Susan and Betsy sang and scooped until all of the jars were filled and decorated. Betsy stretched her arms above her head. "I'll print out the baking instructions and then we can tie the tags on with ribbon."

"Oh, good idea, thanks," Susan said. She remembered the jar she'd given Danny.

"Why are you frowning?" Betsy yawned. "Tired?"

"Not really. I just remembered that I gave Danny a jar of cookie mix without the instructions to bake the cookies."

"Good."

"Why is that? How will he know what to do?"

"Well, he'll just have to call you, or better yet, show up in person."

"He doesn't have my number." She'd refused to give it to him.

"Oh yes he does. You sent him a text. I'm sure you're saved in his contacts."

"Oh . . . right." Susan felt a jolt of something she couldn't quite comprehend. Anticipation? Excitement? Whatever it was, she liked the feeling and craved more. She nibbled on her bottom lip, trying not to let fear wiggle its way into her brain, but wasn't quite successful. With his act of kindness back in high school, Danny had unwittingly broken her heart. Could she risk letting him do so again?

"What's goin' on in that pretty head of yours?" Betsy asked while wiping down the kitchen counter.

"Just thinking of my to-do list."

"Is Danny Mayfield on it?"

"Betsy!" Susan felt heat creep into her cheeks but Betsy laughed.

"If not, then pencil him in." Betsy dried her hands and came over to give Susan a quick hug. "I'll let myself out and lock the door with my key. See you tomorrow."

"Thanks for all of your help."

"My pleasure. Now you stop working and get some rest. Sometimes you don't know when to take a break."

"I will," Susan promised, thinking a steaming cup of green tea and a good book was on her agenda after she fixed a light supper.

After Betsy left, her apartment seemed so quiet. Susan wondered if she should adopt a cat or dog—that would fill in the silence and keep her company.

And so would a boyfriend.

"Oh, stop it." With a sigh, Susan walked over and sat down in her rocking chair. The gentle movement soothed her sudden blue mood. She looked around at her apartment, the eclectic collection of furniture and accents. Her gaze stopped on her sofa. With the wide cushions and fluffy pillows, the comfy sofa would be the perfect spot to cuddle with her guy. She envisioned a big bowl of popcorn and a scary movie where she would cling to Danny's arm. Inhaling a deep breath, Susan shook her head. "Not Danny, just a guy in general. I need to get out and get back in the game. Well, at least get in the game," she added with a little chuckle, but then her smile faded. Since she was a child, talking to herself had been easier than talking to others, so it didn't feel odd to speak her thoughts out loud. But at the moment her own voice sounded hollow in the big apartment.

With another long sigh, Susan twirled her finger around her hair, a habit of hers that came out when she was tired and went all the way back to her childhood. Yawning, she rocked, thinking that the chair really did put her at ease. She wondered if she could find out who had crafted the chair, because she could surely sell them in her shop, but she'd never give this one up. But what would be the odds that the maker was someone local? Pretty slim.

6

Knock on Wood

DANNY BOPPED HIS HEAD TO THE BEAT OF THE LATEST Jeff Greenfield song playing through his headphones. Unlike Jeff's usual ballads, this country tune had some serious rockabilly kick to it. Danny belted out the verse while he sawed through some maple wood needed for the little rocking chair he'd decided to make for Lily. If he worked diligently, he could have the chair ready for Christmas Day. Danny knew Lily would like cuddling in the chair with her favorite teddy bear.

Mattie complained that Lily had already hit the terrible twos but in Danny's mind Lily could do no wrong. If he ever had a little girl, he'd be toast.

Just as Danny reached for some sandpaper he felt a hand grab his shoulder. Startled, he nearly fell off his workbench. Tugging the earbuds loose, he turned around. "Mason! You damn near made me fall on my ass."

"That would have been hilarious. I shouted your name but you were too busy singing really badly." Mason reached down and scratched Rusty behind the ears.

Danny shifted on the bench. "I've been told I have a good voice."

"Only after a lot of this." Mason held up a growler of beer.

"Please tell me that's some bourbon barrel."

Mason grinned. "It's some bourbon barrel."

"Sweet. What brings you over here?"

"Gracie, Mattie, and Sophia are baking Christmas cookies and drinking wine over at the house. Mom's watching Oliver and Lily. I had to get out of there. Too much laughter over silly girl stuff. Their singing is as bad as yours. About now they're starting to think they sound like Adele." Mason winced. He unbuttoned his Carhartt jacket and looked around. "Wow, I didn't realize you had this many pieces of furniture in here."

"Yeah." Danny shrugged. "I've accumulated a lot over the years."

"What are you working on?" Mason walked over and looked at a table.

"A rocking chair for Lily."

Mason looked up. "Oh man, she'll love that."

"Next comes a dollhouse."

"I think you're gonna get the uncle of the year award."

"I could live with that." Danny grinned. "A rocking horse for Oliver is next on my list."

"You have a list?" Mason gazed around the room and gave a low whistle. "How do I get on that list? I could use a nice bar in my man cave."

"Well, Mattie has been all over me about building a bar at the bistro."

"You gonna do it?"

"Do I ever say no to my sister?"

"Not that I know of. I always had to be the voice of reason when it came to you two rascals. Whenever either of you said *watch this* I knew I would have to come to the rescue or brace for the sight of blood. Being the oldest sucked."

Danny laughed. "I haven't had any stitches lately. Knock on wood." He tapped his knuckles on the bench.

Mason chuckled. "You really are talented. You know we have compliments on the taproom bar all the time."

"Thanks."

"You ever think of selling some of these pieces? You could get a pretty penny."

Looking around, Danny said, "I haven't done much woodworking lately. I'd kind of forgotten how much I had stored in here. This and fishing keeps me sane."

"You think you're sane?" Mason walked closer and gave him a good-natured shove. "I've got news for you, baby brother."

"You've got a point. Hey, wanna go up to the cabin and crack open that growler?" Danny asked.

"I can go up and get a couple of glasses if you want to keep working."

"Nah, I was just puttering around. It's a little cold in here, anyway. Let's go find a college football game or something." Danny whistled. "Come on, boy, grab your bone and let's get outta here."

"Where'd he get that big-ass bone? Did you steal some ham from Mattie, Rusty?"

Rusty gave Mason an injured look.

"I got it from John Clark at Ham Good Deli up on Main. Have you been there?"

"Not lately, but I pop in there once in a while for the clam chowder. Gracie loves it. Wanna get on up to the cabin? I'm thirsty. Got any snacks?"

"I can rustle something up." Danny stood up and walked with Mason. "I'm glad you came over. We don't get to hang out much these days."

Mason nodded. "Between the brewery and fatherhood, I'm swamped. Plus, Gracie keeps coming up with new ideas. My wife wears me out."

"I won't touch that line."

"Are you kidding?" Mason groaned. "Oliver has

cramped my style. We never get any sleep," he said but then pulled out his phone and showed Danny a dozen pictures of his son. "Mom thinks he looks a lot like you."

"Lucky kid."

Mason chuckled. "But, yeah, I'm super busy."

"And now we have the holidays to deal with."

Mason shot him a look. "Deal with? Where's your Christmas spirit? Mom and Dad always made the holidays a big celebration."

"I dunno." Danny turned off the lights and opened the door. "Having a family makes a difference. To be honest, the holidays are kinda a pain in the ass for me." Zipping up his hoodie, he shoved his hands in his jeans pockets, falling in step with Mason. Even though Mason was four years older than Danny, they'd always been close. They'd both been overprotective of Mattie, making local guys reluctant to date their sister. Who would have thought that homegrown, tomboy Mattie would have ended up falling for Garret Ruleman? Danny and Mason had been skeptical of Garret at first but now he was part of the family.

They walked toward the cabin, through the light dusting of snow. The flurries had stopped but more winter weather was in the forecast. "I've got to get you revved up for Christmas," Mason said. "Gracie's planning a big bash at the brewery."

Danny inhaled a deep breath of pine-scented air. "I appreciate the spiritual part of Christmas but the rest is just . . ." He shrugged. "More bother than it's worth."

"That's pretty damned sad," Mason said as they entered the warmth of the cabin. Rusty trotted in behind them.

"I guess . . ." Danny flicked on an overhead light revealing a total lack of Christmas decorations.

"Not even a tree?" Mason shook his head. "You're a total Grinch. Parties, presents, cookies, what's not to like?"

"Fruitcake. Endless diamond jewelry commercials.

Piped-in tinny Christmas music everywhere I go. Shopping with no clue what to buy Mom every year. This list goes on and on . . ."

"You forgot ugly Christmas sweaters."

Danny thought of Susan. "I don't mind those so much."

"Gracie's thinking ugly sweaters will be the theme of the party at the brewery. Come on, don't be such a downer. I thought I was supposed to be the moody one."

Danny unzipped his hoodie. "Don't get me wrong. I don't hate Christmas. I'm just not, you know, into it." Danny wasn't ready to tell his brother that he'd been feeling like the odd man out, nor his insecurities about not being successful like his siblings. They had their lives together while he felt like he was treading water, getting nowhere. His most faithful companion these days was Rusty. He loved his dog, but still . . . waking up to a warm woman rather than a cold nose in his face would be a step up.

"You at least need to get a tree. We can chop one down."

"Nah . . ." Danny shrugged. "I don't have any ornaments or lights. Just give it up. I don't need any of that crap. And whatever you do, don't tell Mom or Mattie. They'll be over here putting Christmas stuff up everywhere. I don't want it, okay?"

"Okay, you've made yourself clear. Enough said." Mason put the growler on the breakfast bar that separated the galley-style kitchen from the great room. He unbuttoned his coat and tossed it over a barstool. "What the hell is this?" He picked up the jar with the cookie mix. "Saw the mason jar and thought you had some moonshine."

"Cookie mix."

"What do you do with it?"

"You bake them in the oven." For some reason Danny felt like grabbing the jar and putting it somewhere safe.

Frowning, Mason raised the jar up higher, inspecting the contents. "Mattie's the expert baker, but don't you need eggs and stuff?"

"Well yeah." Danny opened the growler and poured some of the ale into two glasses.

"But where does it say how much?"

Danny grinned. "I've got to find that out."

"Where did you get it?" Mason put the jar down and picked up his beer.

"Susan Quincy gave it to me," he answered carefully.

"Susan Quincy?" Mason frowned as if trying to place her. Shy Susan must have been lonely in high school. "Did she ever come around the marina?"

"Susan was in my grade at Cricket Creek High. Mom and Susan's mother are friends."

"Oh." Mason took a drink of his beer and seemed to lose interest. "I don't remember her but then again I'd already graduated by the time you were a freshman."

"Susan didn't go boating or come to bonfires." Danny felt another twinge of regret that Susan had missed out on the popular social activities for Cricket Creek teens. The marina was the main hub and between all of their friends, something was always going on.

"So why did she give you the cookie mix?" Mason poured more of the amber-colored ale into both of their glasses.

"A reward for coming to her rescue." He took a swig of his ale, savoring the bourbon-infused flavor.

"Come on, you can't stop there." Mason sat down on a barstool and waited.

Danny told Mason the tale, grinning while he relived the time spent with Susan, including sending her lunch.

"Ah, so she owns Rhyme and Reason?"

Danny nodded. "It's a sweet little shop."

"I haven't been in there but Gracie and Sophia have and they thought it was really cool. So you sent her chicken soup?" Mason shook his head. "Sounds like you have a thing for her."

"I do." There wasn't any reason to deny his attraction.

"And she's single?"

"As far as I know. Sweet girl. Tall and gorgeous. Dark curly hair." He wondered how soft her hair would feel running through his fingers. Damn . . .

"So did you get her number?"

"In a roundabout way." Danny explained how Susan had texted to thank him for the soup.

"You didn't ask her out? You falling off your game?"

"What game?" Danny took a swallow of his beer. "Damn, this stuff is so good," he said, trying to change the subject, but Mason wasn't having it.

"Seems like I remember girls digging you at the parties at the marina, Danny. I'm surprised one of the hometown girls hasn't corralled you yet."

"It's different now. Everybody's got families, full-time jobs."

"You don't lack for attention when you bartend at the brewery."

"Girls out to have a night of fun. Goes with the territory." He pulled some ranch dip out of the fridge and located a bag of baby carrots. "Being an adult sucks sometimes."

"Doesn't have to. Maybe you need to think about getting serious with someone. What about Susan?"

"She made it clear she isn't interested in me." Danny located a bag of potato chips from his pantry, dumped some into a plastic bowl.

"Did she say why? I mean, you might not be as good-looking and charming as me but you're a close second." Mason swiped a carrot through the dip.

Danny laughed but then shrugged. "Susan is super shy." He took a swallow of his ale, wondering if he should tell the whole story.

"Don't do that."

"What?"

"Hold back. Danny, you've always been here for everybody. First Mom and Dad with the marina."

"So were you and Mattie."

"Yeah, we're a close family, and I know we're all busy, but I want it to stay that way."

"There's zero chance of us not staying close." Danny couldn't imagine otherwise.

"No doubt." Grabbing a handful of chips, Mason nodded. "When I was in deep financial trouble with the brewery, you were my voice of reason. You helped me get over my fear of expansion and knocked some sense into me when Gracie was slipping away from me."

"You've always been hardheaded."

"I won't disagree with that. But I want to be here for you." He casually swiped another carrot through the ranch dip. "What do you want out of life?"

"Wow, I didn't expect this to get so deep. At least not until we've had a couple more beers. Then we can solve all of the world's problems and mysteries." He held up a baby carrot. "Like how are these grown with perfectly rounded ends? Are they really baby carrots?"

"Are you really using a carrot to distract me from the question?"

"Yes."

"Baby carrots originated as a way to get ugly carrots to the market rather than just throwing them away. Now a sweeter, smaller version is grown especially for baby carrots. They're not really baby, but peeled and chopped up. The rounded edges happen during the washing process when the carrots rub together."

"Did you just make all of that up?"

"No, I am full of useless knowledge. Just ask Gracie."

Danny laughed. "I'll never look at a baby carrot the same way."

Mason poured more beer into their glasses. "I spend a lot of time reading about ingredients for beer and get sucked into information holes. So back to the original question. What do you want out of life?"

"Geez, Mason, can't we just chill?" Talking about the lack of direction in his life wasn't something Danny wanted to do right now, but judging by the look on Mason's face he wasn't going to get let off the hook that easily. "Seriously?"

"You don't have any problem handing out advice, little bro."

"Who are you calling little? I've got you by two inches."

"In your dreams. I'm the tallest."

"Whatever." At six-foot-two, Mason only had him by an inch. For a long time, it had been Danny's goal in life to outgrow his big brother. He knew part of the feeling stemmed from being the baby of the family. Mason and Mattie always got to do things before him, making Danny feel as if he was playing catch up with them. And with their successful businesses, the feeling was hard to shake.

"All right, at least tell me more about Susan Quincy."

"I actually took her to the senior prom."

"What? Wait, did you date?"

"I wasn't dating anyone at the time and I didn't really care all that much about going. Like I mentioned, Mom is a friend of Susan's mother and I asked Susan to go to the prom as a favor. Like I said, she was painfully shy, with a bit of a stutter, but I thought she was pretty and so I agreed."

"You always win the nice guy award."

"Yeah, well, sometimes it seems like nice guys finish last."

"That's bull but go on. This is interesting. Guess I was away at college when this went down."

"Yeah." Danny took a long pull of his ale. "You know, the funny thing is I had a great time at the prom with her." He smiled at the memory. "Compared to the rest of the girls, Susan was dressed conservatively, but I kinda liked that. She was sweet and quiet but clever.

And I remember a goodnight kiss that knocked my socks off."

"So why didn't you ask her out again?"

Danny raised one hand in the air. "I wanted to but she avoided me. After a while I gave up. I guessed the attraction was only on my end."

Mason shook his head. "I find that kind of hard to believe. In all seriousness, you bring a lot to the table. You've got her number." He picked up the mason jar. "And a reason to contact her."

"I already thought of that."

"Toss in some of the Mayfield charm. You'll win her over."

Danny laughed. "I hope you're right."

7

False Alarm

"BETSY, WOULD YOU PLEASE HEAD OVER TO THE DELI?" asked Susan.

"Sure," Betsy said with false cheer. She really didn't want to face John.

"Great, I'd like a ham and Swiss on marble rye, lettuce and spicy mustard. Oh, and a bag of salt and vinegar potato chips, please."

Betsy looked up from arranging hand-knitted scarves on a rack. "How can you like those chips? They make me pucker," she said and demonstrated.

Susan shrugged. "I don't know. I bought them by mistake last time and decided I liked them after about ten chips into the bag. Took me a while to decide. Some things just need a chance."

"Like Danny Mayfield needs a chance?"

Susan straightened the stack of braided rugs. "Are you ever going to give up on that?"

"Never." Betsy bent over and picked up another scarf knitted by residents of Whisper's Edge, the Cricket Creek retirement community. "These are really pretty."

"Oh I know." Susan nodded. "I don't take many items on consignment but the profits from the scarves go to Toys for Tots and Teens."

"Is Pete Sully from Sully's Tavern playing Santa this year?"

"I think his son Clint has taken over the job for good," Susan replied.

"Handsome boy, that Clint. I'm so glad he moved back from California and married Ava Whimsy. Her toy store is such a delight. I love that everything in the shop runs on imagination and not on batteries. There's way too many electronic gadgets out there for my liking."

"Yeah, Ava grew up on a farm just down the road from me," Susan said. "Times were tough for farmers then and so her father made all of the toys for Christmas. She used to babysit me on rare occasions when my parents would go into town for dinner. She plays Mrs. Claus every year. Which reminds me that we need to get some snacks for the upcoming Christmas Walk. I think I'll have hot mulled apple cider."

"Good, I know I'm staying away from spiked eggnog."

"Speaking of . . . you need to head to the deli. I'm starving. Have you practiced your fake sneeze lately?"

Betsy groaned inwardly at the thought. "Susan, I don't think I can pull it off. Would you be a sweetheart and get our lunch? I just can't face John. Or better yet, I could walk down to Wine and Diner and pick up something," she said hopefully. "How about some stone soup?"

"You can't avoid John forever."

"Really? You're doing a pretty bang-up job of avoiding Danny Mayfield."

"Danny doesn't own the deli next door. Pull up your big girl panties and get over there."

"I wear thongs."

"Are you kidding?"

"Of course." Betsy sighed. "Okay, I might as well get this over with," she grumbled, and her heart started to race. With any luck Stephanie would take her order and she'd get out of the deli without seeing John.

"Take some money out of petty cash," Susan said before heading over to help an older couple looking at an entertainment center converted into a liquor cabinet.

Betsy took her time buttoning up her coat. She considered herself a bold and brave person but when she took a step out onto the sidewalk her damned knees were knocking. Why in the world had she blown a kiss at John Clark? "Well, here goes nothing," she muttered, and pulled the door to the deli open.

Betsy inhaled a deep breath of yeast-scented air. The line to the counter was several customers deep so with any luck John would remain in the kitchen filling orders. The chalkboard advertised bean soup as the soup of the day and in spite of her nervousness her stomach rumbled at the thought of a hot bowl of soup with a slice of crusty bread for dipping into the savory broth. Being a single working mom had left her little time to make homemade soups and stews. She'd cooked simple dinners for Aubrey and any baking had been from a box. Cooking had been a necessity and Hamburger Helper and Manwich sloppy joes had been her go-to quick favorites.

Betsy's phone pinged, giving her something to do rather than look for John. She smiled at the text from Aubrey: *Cramming for finals. Can't wait to get home for the holidays. Miss you, Mom.* Betsy typed back: *Miss you too! Good luck with your finals! I can't wait to give you a huge hug.* She added a smiley face and her eyes misted over. Missing Aubrey felt like an ache squeezing her heart. She put a hand to her chest and swallowed hard. She could not start crying right here in the damned deli! She took shallow breaths and moved forward with the line, thinking she should abort this mission. Her phone pinged again. *Found some amazing recipes on Pinterest. We will try them out!*

Grinning, Betsy shook her head and typed back: *You will try them out and I will eat them.*

By some miracle that Betsy couldn't comprehend, Aubrey had turned out to be an amazing cook, and when she got old enough she would have dinner waiting for Betsy when she got home after a long day. Aubrey simply had a knack—or maybe she'd grown weary of boxed dinners and slice and bake cookies. Betsy smiled, thinking that Aubrey was such a good kid. Even though Betsy's marriage had ended in disaster, she wouldn't change having her lovely daughter for the world. Aubrey sent another message: *Deal! Love you!*

Betsy stood there and read the message again, suddenly overcome with emotion. Sniffing, Betsy typed back: *Love you a bushel and a peck!*

A tear escaped from the corner of Betsy's eye and she quickly swiped it away. Oh damn, she did not want to start full-on sobbing in John's deli. Usually she wasn't much of a crier, but menopause hormones were playing havoc with her moods. Okay, she seriously needed to make her escape. With a quick look over her shoulder, she saw that she was the last person in line. Two people remained in front of her. Maybe she could take slow steps backwards until she reached the door and then scurry outside. She swallowed hard, knowing it was decision time.

No . . . this was silly. She dropped her phone in her purse, thinking that she needed to get her sorry-ass self under control. The crying over Hallmark card commercials, pictures of puppies, and a text message from Aubrey needed to stop. Lifting her chin, Betsy inhaled a shaky breath. Now that she was next in line, she saw that Stephanie was behind the counter. She could see through the open window that John's dark head was bent over a task. Good, so he hadn't spotted her in line.

Oh, but just seeing him made her heart beat faster. *Oh God.*

And then Betsy remembered the whole fake sneeze she was supposed to perform to redeem herself from the kiss blowing incident. The memory of embarrassing herself so thoroughly brought a fresh wave of unwanted emotion bubbling up in her throat. Normally she was difficult to embarrass but Betsy felt a flash of heat travel from her cheeks to her toes. She loosened the knit scarf from around her neck and wished she could shed her coat. A hot flash coupled with humiliation packed quite a punch. Why oh why had she agreed to do this? When a pitiful moan escaped her throat, she disguised it with a cough.

Well, this really sucked.

Hit with sudden inspiration, Betsy pulled out her cell phone, thinking she could pretend to get a call and make a quick exit. Of course her phone decided to play hide and seek in the bottom of her big purse. She frantically dug around without success.

"Hi Betsy, what will you have today?"

Betsy blinked at Stephanie, drawing a blank. In a panic she looked up at the overhead menu and ordered the first two combos. "A number one and number two."

"Dessert? John just added a few dessert items to the menu. We're offering a free sample of peach cobbler."

"Oh . . . uh, sure."

Stephanie smiled. "Coming right up."

"Thanks." Betsy attempted to smile back and watched Stephanie walk into the kitchen. So far John had failed to look up from his task and she could see him walking back and forth in the kitchen. Maybe she'd get lucky and go unnoticed. Oh, but then she wouldn't get to fake sneeze. But then she saw John stop and put items in a bag. His back was to her so she inhaled a deep breath ready for her performance when her nose started to tickle. Oh no . . . seriously?

Betsy tried to hold the oncoming sneeze at bay because when she really sneezed it was super loud and usually two or three in a row. Pinching the bridge of her nose, she held her breath for so long that she felt light-headed but successfully thwarted the sneeze. Thank God. She released her breath, blinked, and then let out a rip-roaring sneeze that rocked the rafters. And then she did it again. Of course she drew the attention of John and then remembered she was supposed to tip her hand forward as part of the sneeze. She did, but she'd paused, making the gesture look like another blow of a kiss.

Oh. Dear. God.

John's eyes widened, as if wondering if he should return the gesture. He walked closer to the window. "God bless you."

"Thank you." Where was Stephanie when she needed her? "I sneezed."

"I know. I don't randomly say God bless you." Grinning, John leaned his arms on the shelf where he placed the orders. Damn, he looked good in a snug blue T-shirt sporting the Ham Good Sandwich logo.

"No, I mean when I sneezed, I do this silly thing that looks like I'm blowing a . . . kiss. So I thought I should, you know, clarify."

"Ah . . . interesting."

Betsy shrugged. "Sometimes it gives the wrong person the . . . uh . . . wrong idea." Wait, did she say that correctly?

"Or the right person the right idea." He raised his eyebrows and held her gaze.

Betsy frowned, wondering how to respond. "Did Stephanie take a break?" Sometimes changing the subject was the only recourse. She learned this while raising Aubrey. Distraction was the key.

"She asked to take a break to go shopping. Lunch rush is over so I said she could go. I'll have your order up in a minute."

"Oh, good," Betsy said, trying to remember what she'd ordered.

"I'll bring it right out."

"Thanks." Betsy looked up to see what she'd be

eating for lunch. Ham and roast beef double decker with Swiss cheese and a side of potato salad. A number two was ham salad on whole wheat with a potato pancake. Damn, she wanted bean soup and she'd gotten Susan's order wrong. Oh well . . .

A moment later John came out with two white bags and placed them on the counter. "Here you go. Oh and I added dessert. Be honest and let me know what you think of the peach cobbler. It's still warm."

Betsy nodded. "Thanks." She should turn away but she couldn't stop looking at him.

"Anything else you need?"

A couple of non-food suggestions popped into her head. "I think I'm good."

"I'm sure . . ." he said slowly. Was he staring at her mouth? Surely not.

"Sure about what?" tumbled out of her mouth, low and suggestive. She cleared her throat.

"I'm . . . I'm sure you want your lunch." He pointed to the bags she'd forgotten to pick up.

"Oh . . ." She reached to pick up her food.

"Wait—would you like to come into the kitchen for a moment?"

Her heart hammered so hard she thought the big buttons on her peacoat would pop off. "Why?"

"I want to get your honest opinion on something."

Betsy's brain screamed *no* but she nodded. "Okay, but what if someone comes in?"

"A bell dings when the front door opens. We're fine. Come on." John came around and opened the door leading to the back of the deli. She followed him in and looked around at the spotless kitchen. Soup simmered on a six-burner stove, smelling homey and delicious. A big pan of cobbler cooled on a stainless steel table and to the left were two big slicers.

"Impressive." Why was her voice so damned breathless?

"Thanks." John smiled and then just looked at her

for a long, heated moment. "This is where all of the magic is created."

Betsy felt another rush of warmth and knew it wasn't a hot flash. She tugged at her scarf, thinking it had to go. "It's warm in here." Her statement was meant as an observation but sounded suggestive again.

"It sure is. Why don't you take off your coat? There's a hook right over there on the wall."

"Good idea." She removed her peacoat, wishing she'd worn something more stylish than a plain red sweater and black jeans today. She needed to give her boring wardrobe a serious overhaul.

"The reason it's hot is because the oven is on. Excuse me, I've got to check something." He walked to the stove, bent over, and opened the door.

Wow, he wore his jeans well. "Well, if you can't stand the heat get out of the kitchen, right?"

John nodded slowly. "True."

"I'm guessing you can stand the heat." Betsy noticed how blue his eyes were, thinking it wasn't fair that he looked so delicious in a simple T-shirt and dark denim Levis.

"You would be right." His dark wavy hair appeared a bit rumpled, as if he'd recently run fingers through it, and Betsy wanted to protest that she could take over that particular job for him. The dark stubble shadowing his cheeks and jaw had just a hint of silver. She felt a strong pull of desire and swallowed hard.

"So . . . what did you want my opinion about?" Betsy knew she was playing with fire by being alone with him but at the moment she didn't care. Her pulse raced and she felt a sense of anticipation that made her feel young and alive . . . almost reckless. She remembered her toast with Susan about not being a scaredy-cat. Fear took a flying leap out the window and she took a bold step toward him. She knew he couldn't be interested in a relationship with her but it was about damned time she lived in the moment.

"Did you mean it when you blew me the kiss yesterday?"

"I . . ." Betsy nibbled on her bottom lip. "Might have had a wee bit of spiked eggnog." She put her thumb and index an inch apart.

"You didn't answer the question."

She winced. "Do I have to?"

"You don't have to do anything you don't want to do."

"I sure wish I'd gotten that memo a long time ago."

John tipped his head back and laughed. Betsy liked the deep, rich sound.

"Would you believe it was a sneeze that looked like I was blowing you a kiss?"

John laughed harder. "No . . . Wait a minute. Was that seriously your plan to throw me off?"

"No. It was Susan Quincy's plan, also fueled by spiked eggnog, I might add. Why I decided to go through with it is a complete mystery. I was about to abort the misguided mission when my nose betrayed me and I sneezed for real. And if you repeat this to anyone I just might have to kill you."

John's laughter died down and he looked at her. "I'm glad."

Betsy felt her heart turn over. "About what?"

"I'm glad that I chose the moment to look out the window when you and Susan were twirling around catching snowflakes. The scene was quite . . . enchanting." He bestowed her with a warm smile. "And so was the unexpected kiss."

"Enchanting?" No one had referred to her in such a romantic way and it caused her heart to flutter.

"Absolutely."

Betsy shook her head. "John, I was a single mom who taught driver's ed to reckless teenagers. I wore khaki pants and a blue polo shirt to work every single day. I'm a no frills kind of girl, not a princess," she said, thinking of the young socialite he'd been married

to. What the hell was she doing back here in his
kitchen? Living in the moment was a really bad idea.
She inhaled a deep, shaky breath. "I can't do this." But
when she turned to walk away, John stepped forward
and put gentle hands on her shoulders.

"Can't do what?"

At the touch of his hands Betsy felt a long pull of
desire that made her want to walk into his arms. Strong
arms that tested the short sleeves of his shirt. The look
on his face seemed sincere and the wall around her
heart cracked just a little bit. She looked down so he
wouldn't see the vulnerability, the longing in her eyes.
"This . . ." she whispered.

"I really do find you enchanting." He tucked a lock
of her hair behind her ear. "Give me a chance, Betsy.
That's all I'm asking."

Betsy swallowed hard, knowing it was a risk getting
involved with John Clark. A risk she didn't know if she
should take. "If you're playing me, I'll snap you like a
twig."

When John chuckled softly she dared to look up at
him. He had her by nearly a foot and it made her feel
dainty and feminine. "Is that so?"

"Hey, I might be a little thing but don't underesti-
mate me."

"Oh believe me, I don't." Before she could verbalize
a protest . . . okay she wasn't going to protest, John
pulled her closer. Having her body pressed against his
broad chest brought another long wave of desire throb-
bing through her veins.

"What are you doing?" Oh damn he smelled good.

"This." He dipped his head, gave her a tender, sweet
kiss that had her fisting her hands in his shirt. His lips
were warm, firm, and when his tongue lightly danced
with hers, Betsy clung on for dear life. She was drown-
ing in the kiss, melting against him like saltwater taffy
on a hot summer day.

Betsy rose up on tiptoe and wrapped her arms

around his neck. She delved her fingers in his hair and nearly groaned. He deepened the kiss and she felt as if she were floating . . . Oh wait, John was carrying her somewhere. She wanted to ask what he was doing but that would require removing her mouth from his and so she refrained. He carried her over to the stainless steel table and for a second she thought he was going to do one of those steamy swiping everything off of the table moves and then push her down to make wild love to her . . .

And then she came to her senses—well, a little bit anyway. "What are you doing?" she mumbled against his lips, wanting to keep some contact.

"Why do you keep asking me that?"

"I don't like surprises."

"You'll like this one."

"John . . ." she began, but he put a gentle fingertip to her lips.

"There aren't any chairs in here and I wanted to feed you something amazing," he said in a soft, sexy voice. "Well, I hope you think it's amazing, anyway. Give me your honest opinion."

"Okay," she said, still clinging to the making-wild-love fantasy just a bit.

"Close your eyes."

"Is this some kind of test to see if I trust you?"

"No, but I hope you do."

"I'm not a fan of having food put in my mouth before I look at it first."

"Please?"

Betsy was about to refuse but when he smiled she was a goner. "Okay . . . but remember that snapping you like a twig thing."

"I won't forget. Okay, now close your eyes and don't peek."

"All right." Betsy sighed but then crossed her arms and obeyed. She could hear him puttering around and wanted to open her eyes but she'd sort of promised.

She could not believe she was actually doing this. Susan must be wondering what in the world had happened to her. Actually, it was Susan's damned fault she was sitting in John Clark's kitchen . . . well, in a roundabout way, but still. "What if you have customers out there?"

"I didn't hear the bell ding."

"You were preoccupied."

"Do you always talk this much?"

"Yes." She could hear him walk closer and her body responded with a hot tingle that zinged all the way to her toes.

"Open wide," he requested in a low, sensual voice.

Was this really happening? Betsy nodded and tried to calm her racing heart. This was like some forbidden dream she shouldn't be having, but if she suddenly woke up she was going to be royally pissed. She opened her mouth and felt a spoon pass her lips. Sweet, cold cream touched her tongue followed by silky smooth, dark chocolate. She couldn't hold back a moan. She rolled the flavor around in her mouth and then like an eager little bird, she opened for more.

"You like it?"

"Mmmmmm . . ." She nodded slowly and licked her bottom lip.

"Having your eyes closed makes you focus on the taste and texture. It's rich chocolate mousse."

"It's a party in my mouth. My taste buds are doing a happy dance."

"I wasn't sure I had dessert making skills in me but once I got started I couldn't stop."

"Well you do, so don't even think about stopping."

"I won't." John laughed. "More?"

Betsy licked her bottom lip and nodded. "Keep the chocolate mousse train rolling down the track."

"Your wish is my command."

8

Sweet Sensation

JOHN DIDN'T KNOW THAT HE COULD BE SO AMUSED and so turned on at the same time but he sure as hell liked it. Being this spontaneous was out of character for him and his heart thudded but he was pretty sure he was pulling this flirtation off with flying colors. Still, he spooned another generous bite of velvety chocolate into Betsy's mouth and was rewarded with a groan that make him think of other delicious ways to give pleasure. "More?"

"Do you really have to ask?"

Laughing, John dipped the spoon into the chocolate mousse, making sure to get some of the whipped cream. He took a bite for himself. "You're right, this is amazing."

"You didn't try it already?"

"No."

"So I was your guinea pig?"

"Yes, do you mind?"

"No, I am hereby offering my services as your official taste tester. I will work for desserts."

"Good, you're officially on my payroll." John smiled

and gave her another silky bite. For a long time, his life had felt like the aftermath of a tornado and he'd been focused on picking through the rubble left behind. But after coming back to Cricket Creek, he'd started reconnecting to his roots and reexamining the meaning of his life. He couldn't remember ever feeling this relaxed.

"Good."

With a chuckle he gave Betsy another spoonful and studied her pretty face. Her auburn hair was windblown and her makeup was minimal, giving her a natural, fresh look that he found appealing. Her delicate bone structure defied her feisty nature and she had a full, cupid's bow mouth simply begging to be kissed again . . . and again. She had light lines around her eyes and a freckle here and there, and he wanted to kiss each one of them.

John found her completely enticing. In fact, he wanted to kiss her again right this minute. Funny—John wasn't usually a spur of the moment kind of guy. He usually thought things through before acting but this living in the moment thing felt like being set free. He was kind of floored that Betsy actually came back into the kitchen with him, not that he was complaining.

"Are you going to keep me waiting?"

"Anticipation is half of the fun," he said and gave her another bite, including a generous dollop of whipped cream.

"This is just so good."

"I value your opinion." John smiled, but he also knew Betsy didn't want to be attracted to him and he understood why she might be hesitant. She'd probably regret the kiss and this little taste test later, but John wasn't going to let her slip through his fingers. He'd take it slow but he wanted to get to know Betsy Brock. When she licked a bit of whipped cream from the corner of her mouth he inhaled a deep breath. Good God. Going slow wasn't going to be easy.

"Are you going to make me beg for more?"

John laughed, realized he was holding the spoon in his hand while he stared at her mouth. "What if I said yes?"

"Oh John, pul-ease give me more . . ." She drew out the word and folded her hands in prayer.

John scooped up more mousse but halted when he heard someone clearing their throat.

"Um, am I interrupting something?"

John looked over at Stephanie. "We, uh, I, uh, asked Betsy to give the mousse a try for me."

Betsy's eyes opened wide and she looked as if she'd just got caught with her hand in the cookie jar. "Oh!" She tried to wiggle from the table and slid, landing on the floor off balance. She stumbled forward and fell into John's arms.

"Right." Stephanie grinned and jammed her thumb over her shoulder. "I'll just go out and refill the condiments." She turned on her heel. "Let me know when the coast is clear."

Betsy covered her face with her hands. "Is there no end to the ways I manage to embarrass myself?"

John wasn't sure if she was joking or serious. "Betsy . . ." he began, but she looked through her fingers and took a step backward. Her cheeks were as red as a beefsteak tomato.

"I'm sorry. I don't know what got into me. I know I can't blame the eggnog this time but this was a mistake."

"Why?" John wanted to take a step closer but refrained. She looked ready to bolt. "We weren't doing anything wrong."

"I know, but . . ."

"But what?"

She looked at him with troubled eyes. "Oh come on, we're from two different worlds."

"We're both from Cricket Creek, Kentucky."

"Oh John . . ." Betsy shook her head. "You know

what I mean. You're smart and highly educated. You probably get most of the answers right on *Jeopardy*."

John shrugged. "Oh . . ."

"Do you?"

"Okay, I'm a nerd. My parents were professors. Believe me, I would love to be able to hit a baseball as well as I know ancient history."

"What do we have in common?"

"It's clear that we're attracted to each other."

Betsy swallowed hard and gave him a long, measuring look. John's heart pounded with hope but she finally shook her head. "That's not nearly enough."

"It's a good start," John said quietly, but he could tell by the look on her face that she wasn't buying it.

"Susan must be wondering if I got lost. I need to get back to the shop."

John nodded, wondering what he could say to change her mind. He decided to get straight to the point. "I'd like to take you out to dinner sometime soon."

"No."

"Give me a valid reason why not."

Betsy raised her hands skyward. "I already did."

John watched her go pick up her jacket and hurry out the door. He stood there feeling rejected but then grinned when he noticed that she'd forgotten her knitted scarf. Good, he had a reason to pay her a visit. He wasn't about to give up on Betsy Brock without a fight. He put the scarf up to his nose and inhaled the light floral scent. Rachel had been fond of expensive perfumes, but he found this much more enticing.

A moment later Stephanie walked in.

"Are you going to sleep with that scarf tonight?"

"No, that would be weird," he said, but she shrugged. "Wouldn't it?"

"I don't think so. I dated a guy in college I was really into and he left his sweater behind one night. I slept with it for days." She gave him a dreamy smile as if remembering him. "Peter Foster."

"The one that got away?"

"Maybe." She sighed. "Hey, I'm really sorry I . . . interrupted. I didn't mean to chase Betsy away. She ran out of here like the hounds of hell were after her."

John shoved his fingers through his hair. "Guess I messed that up."

"Hey, you know she's into you, right? Betsy gets all flustered every time she sees you."

John nodded. "Yeah, but she's fighting it tooth and nail."

Stephanie pulled a package of napkins from the supply closet. "I know what she's thinking. She's a small town girl and you're a big shot."

"More like I'm a big screwup." John blew out a short laugh. "Thought I needed to leave Cricket Creek to prove something. Then I married a younger woman totally wrong for me, which messed up her life too. I worked constantly and lost myself along the way."

Stephanie walked over and gave him a fist bump. "Welcome to the club. I thought I had something to prove too. I was probably a lot like your ex-wife. Married a handsome, powerful, older man." She frowned. "He treated me like a possession and not a person."

"I didn't do that to Rachel." John scrubbed a hand down his face. Or did he?

"Hey, we screwed up. I should have known better."

"Me too."

"You got it right. We got lost along the way. But now we need to find ourselves back."

John smiled. "You've got the right attitude."

"I've read a ton of self-help books. Like, every book in the self-help section. I know hundreds of inspiring words of wisdom."

"Is it working?"

"A little." Stephanie's smile held a hint of sadness. "I was shallow and self-absorbed and got exactly what I deserved from James Clayborn."

"And what was that?"

"Nothing. Not one thing." She raised her palms upward. "His prenup was ironclad."

"I thought you said you were in interior design."

Stephanie rolled her eyes. "I pretended to work in the office of his furniture store. I basically flitted around doing a whole lot of nothing."

"You have a college degree. It was on your resume."

"In fine arts." She shrugged. "Oh John, I coasted through life without a care in the world. Everything came easy: grades, friends, sports . . ." She arched an eyebrow. "Boyfriends," she said, and the look on her face made John wonder if she was referring to one in particular. "I never learned to appreciate what I had."

"So how did you meet your ex-husband?"

"I met James in Lexington while I sold furniture at his store. I'd just graduated from the University of Kentucky and couldn't land a job with my general degree. John swept me off my feet and then pulled the rug out from under me. But in the end it was my own damned fault."

"So now what?"

"Good question." She tilted her head sideways. "I've been humbled. I've gone from a six-bedroom home to an efficiency apartment."

"What about your family?"

"My parents were opposed to the marriage from the beginning, so I've got no sympathy there." She made a zero with her thumb and index finger. "Nor do I want it," she added, but a shadow crossed her face, making John wonder if she was being totally honest. "I turned my back on a lot of people who mattered for a lot of stupid things that didn't matter one bit."

"I get that too. Lucky for you that you figured it out way sooner than I did."

"You're giving me too much credit. I was a starter wife. Apparently thirty is the cutoff age for James Clayborn or I would likely still be married. I thought the man adored me, even though he paid very little attention to me. I had myself convinced that I was happy living that hollow, shallow existence. I was so stupid."

"What an ass," John couldn't help saying.

"Yeah well, live and learn. But enough about me. Let's get back to you."

"Okay," John agreed, even though he didn't particularly want to.

"What are you going to do about Betsy?"

"You get straight to the point, don't you?"

"Part of the self-help program."

John looked down at the cup of chocolate mousse. "I'm not a man to give up easily."

"There's the spirit. Now all you need is a plan."

"A plan? I don't know much about wooing a woman."

"I walked in on you feeding Betsy chocolate mousse from a spoon. I'd say you're a natural in the wooing department."

"Really?"

"Uh . . . yeah."

"Well, I didn't have to woo Rachel. She saw what she wanted and took it. So, what do you suggest?"

"Well, for starters you need to train me to do more of the management around here and work less hours." She tapped her chest. "I'm capable."

"I believe you."

"And of course that would require a raise."

"Did you plan to lead to this?"

"Self-help books." Stephanie snapped her fingers. "Worked like a charm."

"I think you should write one."

"Excellent idea. Actually, I've been meaning to ask you to give me more responsibility. When spring hits, Main Street will be packed. And then when baseball season begins, we'll be swamped. It's bad enough now during the holidays, but when people want to eat in the park we'll be busy constantly."

"I found that out last year," John agreed. "But it was

my first summer and now I have a regular clientele along with tourists."

Stephanie nodded. "See, you need me."

"I got the impression this was only a temporary job for you."

"To be honest, I thought so too, but if you're willing to give me a chance perhaps my thinking will change. Give me a shot and let's see what happens. What do you say?"

"Okay, deal. But you also have to give me advice on wooing Betsy. You know, girl things."

"No problem, boss." The bell over the door dinged. "Looks like we have a customer," she said and hurried out to the counter.

John thought over what Stephanie said while he waited for the order to be placed. She was smart and capable. He was also considering opening up another deli in Restaurant Row, a great location overlooking the Ohio River just outside of town. He smiled, thinking that in the past couple of days his life had gotten a whole lot more interesting.

And hopefully would only get better.

9

Stuck on You

SUSAN RANG UP HER CUSTOMER AND THEN WALKED over and turned over the sign on the front door indicating she'd be back in thirty minutes. She liked having lunch with Betsy and it gave them time to chat and brainstorm ideas. After stopping to straighten up a messy display, she headed to the break room. But instead of eating, Betsy was sitting completely still with her arms crossed over her chest.

"Something wrong?" Susan asked.

"That's putting it mildly."

"Oh." Betsy had a knack for being dramatic but by the look on her face, something had really upset her. "Is Aubrey okay?"

"Yeah, just cramming for finals. She'll be home next week and will be on break for nearly three weeks. I can't wait."

"Then why so glum?" Susan asked as she sat down. She opened the bag and pulled out a sandwich. She unwrapped it. "Wow, it's not like John to get an order wrong."

"He didn't."

"Oh, you forgot what I wanted? No big deal. This looks really good and I'm hungry."

"No." Betsy shook her head slowly.

"You thought I might want this instead?"

"No. I panicked, okay?"

"Panicked? Oh . . . the sneeze!" Susan leaned forward, making the giant Christmas tree on her fringed sweater jingle and blink.

"How does that sweater even do that?" Betsy asked.

"A battery pack. The ornaments flash when I move." She wiggled her shoulders, making the abundance of bells jingle and jangle.

"That sweater has got to go."

"It's the newest addition to my growing collection. Never mind about the sweater from hell—tell me what happened."

Betsy started telling her tale, pausing now and then to take a bite of her ham salad sandwich. With each addition to the story, Susan's eyes widened.

"Are you kidding me?"

"You've said that five times now."

"I'm just . . . blown away."

"How do you think I feel?"

"I don't know, Betsy, how do you feel?"

Betsy picked up her spork. "These don't really work as a fork, but they're kinda funny." She opened the lid on the plastic cup and wrinkled her nose. "I don't even like potato salad."

"No problem." Susan handed her the potato pancake. "We'll trade. When you grow up on a farm you pretty much learn to like everything. But I'm not talking about the food and you're avoiding the question. I'm talking about you being spoon-fed chocolate mousse by John Clark. Did you bring any of it with you, by the way?"

"No, but I think there's peach cobbler in there."

"Excellent. Wait, this means we have dessert at our

disposal every day. Maybe not so excellent. We must use our willpower or we will both start to waddle."

"Um, hello, I obviously have no willpower." Betsy moaned. "Oh, damn it all to hell and back! How in the world did I allow this to happen? I want to throw myself on the floor and have a total cussing-up-a-storm toddler kind of meltdown."

"I'm pretty sure toddlers don't curse," Susan said.

"I bet I did."

"Please don't throw a tantrum." Susan wasn't sure if Betsy was serious but she wasn't taking any chances. "Now, back to the discussion."

"I went over there with the intention of throwing John off, not throwing myself at him!" She cradled her head in her hands. "Ugh!"

"Sounds to me like he's totally into you, just like I said from the very beginning."

"And he's totally wrong for me, just like I said from the very beginning. So this has to end. Now."

"You can't know that!"

"That's what John said."

"And?" Susan asked.

"I said if he hurt me I'd snap him like a twig."

"No you did not."

"I did, and I meant it."

Susan opened wide and took a bite of her double decker. "Wow, the mayonnaise on here is delicious. I bet John makes his own." She took a sporkful of the potato salad. "You don't know what you're missing."

"Are you talking about the potato salad?"

Susan put her spork down. "Listen, we made a toast not to be scaredy-cats."

"Yeah well, I think I'm winning that challenge."

"You are winning, so why stop now?"

"I'm not going to dinner with him, Susan. What would be the point?"

"Um, to get to know him."

"I don't even have anything to wear!"

"That's easy enough to remedy. We can head over to Violet's Vintage Clothing and hook you up."

"No." Betsy flapped her potato pancake back and forth.

"Yes! You must be thinking about it or you wouldn't have been wondering what to wear."

"I don't know why you're getting so high and mighty with me. I don't see you announcing your date with Danny Mayfield."

Susan put her stacked sandwich down and tilted her head to the side.

"I don't like that look on your face."

"What look?" Susan tried for innocence.

"It's that look of challenge. You get me to do things I didn't know I wanted to do all the time. When I said I was considering going red you told me to go for it." She pointed to her head. "Now look."

"It suits you. And now I'm challenging you to go shopping with me and get a kick-ass outfit."

"Ha, coming from someone wearing a blinking Christmas tree that jingles all the way. That thing looks like a walking fire hazard."

Susan lifted her chin. "I've been thinking about updating my closet too."

"To impress anyone in particular?"

"No . . . I'm just ready for a little change here and there. And we do have the holiday season upon us. Let's close a little bit early and go shopping. Then we can walk to Wine and Diner tomorrow for wine down Wednesday and half-price wine and flatbread wearing new outfits. I haven't been out in ages and I hear customers talking about the wine bar there all the time. What do you say?"

"The last time we drank it got us into loads of trouble."

Susan shook her head. "We'll be sensible this time," she said, although she was getting damned tired of being sensible. Thoughts of Danny would not leave her

head and it was getting on her nerves. "Maybe if we get
all dressed up we might, you know . . ." She leaned one
shoulder forward.

"Get hit on?"

"Yeah. The best way to get Danny and John out of
our heads is to get interest from someone else." She
took a bite of the potato salad and then licked the
spork.

"Look, Susan, I have good reasons not to go to dinner with John. He's totally wrong for me in a million
different ways. But you and Danny would make such a
cute couple. You're frustrating the hell out of me by
not giving the boy a chance."

"You know I have my reasons."

"Yeah, stupid reasons, so they don't count."

Susan opened up the container of peach cobbler
and took a bite. "Oh this is wonderful. The crust melts
in my mouth. Okay, let's just get the shopping out of
the way and go out and have some fun tomorrow.
Deal?"

"Deal. Anything to get you out of those doggone
sweaters. Now give me some of that cobbler."

Susan took another bite of the dessert and passed
the rest over to Betsy. "Oh, would you do me a favor
and drive down to Whisper's Edge and pick up some
handmade ornaments? The proceeds will go to the
Toys for Tots and Teens."

"Sure," Betsy said.

"Thanks. We seem to be a bit slow today so I can
handle the showroom myself for a little while." She
wrapped up the second half of her huge sandwich and
put it in the small fridge in the corner.

"Okay, I'll get on over there. Anything else you
need while I'm out?"

"I don't think so." Susan dusted off her hands. "I'm
going to get back out there and get a tree ready for the
ornaments. I have one in the storeroom. I think I'll
string some lights around the windows too."

Betsy stood up. "That would be a nice touch." She put on her peacoat but then frowned. "Hmm, I wonder where I left my scarf." She looked at Susan. "Oh no . . ."

"Let me guess, you left it at the deli?"

Betsy nodded slowly and then groaned. "Oh, why did I let the man spoon-feed me chocolate mousse? And kiss me?"

"Maybe because you wanted him to."

Betsy buttoned up her coat. "You are not helping."

"I think I am. So are you heading over there to get your scarf?"

"No way. I'll just buy another one. I am never going into that deli again as long as I live."

"Suit yourself," Susan said, but she was pretty sure John would return the scarf anyway.

"I intend to!" Betsy hurried out the door in a huff.

Susan waited on a few customers browsing for Christmas gifts and then went into the storeroom for the artificial tree that she'd put together last week. Of course the tree was more cumbersome than she'd realized and she struggled to get it through the door of the storeroom. "Why did I put this together in here? Silly me." She gave the tree a hefty push but the fat bottom branches got snagged on the doorframe and she was pretty much stuck.

"Well, there's more than one way to skin a cat," she muttered, then wondered where in the world that saying came from in the first place. She hoped it didn't have anything to do with actually skinning a poor cat. It was her nature to ponder such things and she decided she'd have to do some research later. "Or get a life," she muttered while she pushed. Getting nowhere, she decided she should crawl beneath the branches and pull from the other direction, or perhaps put the tree on its side and slide it through on the floor. "Maybe if I give it one last shove," she said, thinking she should have waited for Betsy to help.

Turning her head to the side, Susan reached inside the branches for the trunk and gave the tree a hard push. To her delight, the tree gave way, but much quicker than she'd anticipated. "Oh my gosh!" She stumbled through the doorway and fell forward, landing in a heap of prickly branches.

"Eeeek!" Susan let out a shriek of surprised pain, and with a lot of blinking and jingling she rolled sideways, taking the tree with her. "Ouch, ouch . . . ouch!" She wiggled, trying to dislodge her arms, but she was somehow stuck. "Great. Just great."

"Oh my God, what are you doing?" shouted a deep male voice. "Susan, are you hurt?"

"I've been attacked by a tree." Susan tried to disengage herself but the plastic pine needles clung to the bells and lights on her crazy Christmas sweater. She looked sideways to see Danny hovering over her. "I think I've gotten myself in a bit of a sticky s-situation. Please don't p-post this on Facebook."

"Seriously, are you hurt?"

"I don't think so, but it's rather uncomfortable to say the least. I'm being poked everywhere. Even my shoelaces are stuck."

"How did this even happen?"

"I tried to force the tree through the doorway. Unfortunately, I succeeded."

10

Pretty in Pink

"OKAY, I'M GOING TO GET YOU OUT OF THIS STICKY SIT-uation you've managed to get yourself in. Just hold still."

"This feels like déjà vu. Sort of."

"I'll have you out of there in no time." He hoped, anyway.

"Thank you," she answered in a pitiful tone that tugged at his heart. "You've made it a habit of coming to my rescue."

"I don't mind."

"I feel so s-silly s-stuck to a tree."

"Here we go." Danny put his hands around her waist, thinking he could simply lift her up, but she remained tangled in the tree. "What in the world . . ."

"My bells are stuck," she said. "That's the whole p-problem."

"Your bells?"

"They're kind of big."

"Um, what are we talking about here?" Danny wondered if *bells* was some kind of girl-parts slang he hadn't heard of, but he'd never heard his sister refer to her bells.

"On m-my sw-sweater." She moved her shoulders and they jingled. "They're everywhere, even on my sleeves."

"Oh, bells . . ."

"That's what I said. There's also fringe and lights . . . it's a tangled-up mess."

"Okay, well I'm going to reach around you and try to untangle the mess."

"Please don't mention this to anyone."

"What, that you've taken tree hugging to a new level? My lips are sealed," he said, trying not to cop a feel while setting the bells free. She went very still. "I'm not trying to . . . you know."

Susan nodded her head.

"So if I do . . ."

"It's okay."

Danny worked for a couple of minutes, not getting very far. Of course his fingers fumbled a little bit and he was trying not to touch her breasts, making the task nearly impossible.

"Don't take this the wrong way, but what are you wearing under the sweater? One of those cami things?"

"Only a b-bra."

"Well, if I can't get you untangled I'll have to tug the sweater over your head. Or maybe you can try to do it."

"The b-bells on the cuffs of the sweater are preventing me from moving much."

Danny might have found the situation funny if he didn't know how uncomfortable and embarrassed she was feeling. Her stutter was becoming more pronounced and while he found it completely endearing, he knew that she did not.

Being pressed against her was stirring up desire, and if he wasn't careful she would figure that out and he'd be pretty damned embarrassed too. Danny inhaled deeply, trying to clear his head from thoughts he shouldn't be thinking, but the coconut scent of her shampoo and the softness of her dark curls in his face only made his situation worse.

"How is it c-coming?" Susan asked in a small voice.

"I set three bells free. I think one fell off. Some of the branches on the tree are missing so you're stuck on some exposed hooks."

"Well, this was a thrift shop find. I knew some of the branches were missing. Oh boy . . ."

Danny felt her shoulders move and she started to shake. At first he thought she was crying but he realized she'd started to laugh.

"Do things like this happen to you often?" God, he wanted to bury his face in her hair.

"All the t-time, I'm afraid."

"Oh, there goes another bell. How many are tangled?"

Susan shook her head. "I have no idea. The tree is full of bells. I'm stuck like Velcro. We could be here a while. Or I could stand up and walk around with a tree stuck to me. That would really be in the Christmas spirit."

Danny laughed while he set one of her arms free. "Where's Betsy?"

"On an errand. Was anybody in the shop when you came in?"

"No."

"Thank goodness." She let out a sigh of relief but it sounded so sexy that he wanted to brush her hair aside and start kissing her neck. To his horror he was becoming increasingly aroused. He moved his fingers faster, freeing the bells as quickly as he could.

"Your sweater is flashing."

"Don't tell anyone I flashed you," Susan said and laughed.

"I promise." Danny joined her laughter. He remembered how sweet and funny she'd been on their prom date. Her sense of humor had been as unexpected as the undeniable attraction he'd had to her. He'd never been around a girl who'd made him laugh so hard. In his teenage experience, girls had mainly been worried about how they looked and what they said rather than just having a good time, but Susan had been so . . . real.

Danny unhooked another bell from a tiny bent branch. "I think we're getting there."

"I'm going to miss you, O Christmas tree."

"Really? I could stop and put a star on your head."

"No!"

"Thought so." Chuckling, Danny freed the last bell and scooted away.

"Oh, that was rather horrible." Susan sat up and pulled plastic pine needles from her sweater. "A few of the bells bit the dust." She gave him a shy glance. "Thank you."

"Maybe you should have me on speed dial."

"I think you'd soon grow weary of my mishaps." She winced. "Just ask Betsy. It's kind of a daily occurrence."

"I can assure you that I would not." Danny shook his head. "Here . . . you missed a few." Scooting closer to her, he reached over and gently pulled a few pine needles from her dark curls. His knuckles grazed her cheek. She had very soft skin and damn if he didn't want to dip his head and kiss her.

"Thank you," she said breathlessly. "I must look a fright."

"You'd look pretty no matter what." He smiled. "Even wearing a Christmas tree."

Susan frowned slightly and remained silent, as if she didn't know how to take his compliment. "You're such a nice guy, Danny."

"Well thank you, but do you think I'm just being nice?"

"Well . . ."

"I came over here with the excuse that I needed the recipe for the cookie mix in the jar, but really I just wanted to see you and ask if you'll go out to dinner with me tonight."

She answered with a small, rapid shake of her head without meeting his eyes.

"Why? Is there something about me that you don't like? Am I being too forward?"

"No, of course not."

"Then help me understand why you seem to want to avoid me."

"B-because I . . . *know*." She looked at him with a distraught expression.

"Know what?" Danny racked his brain for something he could have possibly done for her to look at him that way. "Hey, I know I had a reputation for being on the wild side but I've calmed down. I haven't broken a bone in a long time," he added with a slight grin, but she remained serious.

Susan sucked in her bottom lip, looking so sweet and vulnerable that Danny ached to draw her into his arms. She somehow managed to look gorgeous with tousled hair and wearing that silly sweater. When she tucked a lock of hair behind her ear, he noticed her elf hat earrings and would have smiled had she not been so upset.

"Please tell me. I think it's only fair that I know what it is about me that bothers you. Because I'll tell you this much. I had a great time with you at the prom. I wanted to ask you out again but you always headed in the opposite direction when I walked your way, so I eventually gave up."

Susan's eyes widened. "Oh . . ."

"How can you be so surprised? Susan, I still remember that goodnight kiss—it blew me away."

She tilted her head to the side as if in surprise. "I . . . oh . . ."

Danny shoved his fingers through his hair. "If this attraction is only one-sided, let me know and I'll back off."

"No." She tugged at one of the bells and her sweater started to blink as if in response to his statement. "It's . . . not."

Danny felt relief wash over him. "Then what's the problem with me?"

"Nothing. I didn't know that you liked me."

"I thought I was pretty clear about that."

"Danny, I know that you only t-took me to the prom because your mother asked you to. I overheard my mom talking to your mom on the phone. I was a p-pity date."

"Aw, man." Danny scrubbed his hand down his face.

Susan gave him a small smile. "I was horrified. There was no way I could look you in the eye after I found out." She lifted one shoulder. "But I did have a really nice time."

"So this is why you've spent the past ten years avoiding me?"

Susan nodded slowly. "Yes. I was so embarrassed. I mean, imagine how I felt. Having you ask me was like a dream come true, but it was all fake. And I wondered if anyone else knew the truth and was making fun of me."

"No. I didn't tell anyone, Susan." Danny wanted to scoot closer and take her hand, but he didn't want to break the spell of her opening up to him. "Listen, I always thought you were so pretty and sweet. Asking you to the prom wasn't something I didn't want to do. It wasn't a pity date and I had a great time too. When you avoided me I thought you just didn't like me."

"Oh, not true." Her cheeks flushed a pretty shade of pink.

"So how about we make up for lost time?" This time Danny risked scooting closer. "Say you'll have dinner with me tonight."

When Susan hesitated he thought she would refuse, but she finally nodded. "Yes."

"Sweet." Danny felt like cheering. "Is Wine and Diner okay with you?" He would have suggested the brewery but he knew they would draw a lot of attention there and he wanted something more intimate.

"I love the food there."

"Awesome. I'll pick you up around seven? Is that a good time?"

"Sure," she said, but frowned.

Danny stood up and offered his hands to help her to her feet. When she accepted his assistance, Danny wanted to pull her into his arms for a long kiss, but the bell dinged, alerting them that someone was coming into the shop. Instead, he gave her a light peck on the cheek. "Call me if you get into another sticky situation."

"I will."

Danny nodded, reluctant to leave now that she was warming up to him. But he'd promised Mattie that he'd help out at the bistro and he was already late. He put the tree in a standing position. "Do you want me to carry this somewhere?"

"I have to make space in the showroom. But thanks."

"I'll see you tonight."

Susan gave him another shy smile that he found both sweet and sexy. He walked through the show-room with what had to be a goofy grin on his face. After he pushed the door open and walked out into the brisk afternoon breeze, he did a fist pump into the air. He had a date with Susan Quincy.

Tonight could not come soon enough.

11

Just One Kiss

WHEN SUSAN SPOTTED BETSY STRUGGLING WITH A big, heavy box, she hurried outside to help her into the shop. "Looks like the residents of Whisper's Edge have been busy."

"Yeah, busy having fun. Those folks know how to have a good time. They were having happy hour when I arrived. Dancing and singing to Christmas carols. Can't really vouch for what these ornaments will look like."

"Happy hour? It's only three o'clock."

"I don't think they care about what time of the day it is. I get the feeling they pretty much do what they want whenever they want to do it. I'm considering moving there."

"Um, you're hardly ready for a retirement community."

"Yeah, well their social life beats the hell out of mine. Just sayin'. Hey, why do you have a weird look on your face? I only had one whiskey sour and it was forced upon me."

"Really?"

"Sort of. As in, it was placed in my hand."

Susan chuckled. "Well . . . I have a bit of a crisis on my hands." She helped Betsy carry the box to the back of the shop.

"Are we out of candy canes again?"

"No." Susan rolled her eyes while they carefully lowered the box to the floor. "It's bigger than that."

"Spill, girl."

"I might be going out to dinner with Danny Mayfield tonight."

"Might be?"

Closing her eyes, she inhaled a breath. "Okay, I am."

"Well butter my butt and call me a biscuit!" Betsy did a little happy dance. "How did this come about?"

Susan explained the tree debacle. "It was horrible."

"I swear, only you could Velcro yourself to a tree."

"Well, it was the bells on the sweater that did it."

Betsy fisted her hands on her hips. "I love your mama but those sweaters are a danger to your well-being, as you just found out. All that blinking and jingling. I prefer the pretty, flowy clothes you usually wear. Way less dangerous, I might add."

"Apparently so." Susan laughed but then shook her head. "I still can't believe that I said I'd go out with Danny. Am I setting myself up for heartache?"

"I highly doubt it, but if you ask me it's worth the risk anyway."

Susan played with the fringe on her sweater. "But what if I'm boring and he falls asleep in his soup?"

"You're not boring! And Danny doesn't think so or he wouldn't have asked you to go out with him. Embrace how awesome you are. Don't you have a Pinterest page that tells you all that encouraging stuff written in those little boxes?"

"Yes, do you?"

"Aubrey keeps telling me but I don't know how all

that stuff works. She insisted that I get a smartphone but the phone outsmarts me every time I try to do simple things, like take a picture. And this FaceTime stuff?" Betsy raised her arms skyward. "Who wants to see this mug on their phone, anyway? But let's get back to you and your awesomeness. I can feel that you have more to tell. Come on, girlie."

"Well, Danny also said that he really wanted to take me out again after the prom. I told him that I knew the truth about why he asked me in the first place."

"So much for your pity date theory."

"Well it was, at least at first."

"Any teenage boy who would do his mother a favor scores high points to begin with. And the fact that you two hit it off is just the icing on the cake." Betsy snapped her fingers. "And so you've wasted all of these years avoiding the cutest boy in Cricket Creek. Susan Quincy . . ."

"Well, I'm still nervous. I haven't been out on a date in too long to remember. So we have to close early and make a beeline for Violet's and find something pretty for me to wear." Her heart started to thud. "Maybe I should have waited until I do could an entire makeover . . . Oh, why did I agree to do this tonight? I am totally not prepared."

"It's only dinner, sweet pea. You'll do just fine and dandy. And for the record, you don't need a makeover. You always look pretty. Now, do you want me to hold down the fort for a while and meet you there or come with you right now?"

"Oh, you have to come with me." Susan looked around and shrugged. "It's been slow. Closing a couple of hours early is okay. By the way, when Aubrey is here she can help us out if she wants some extra spending money for Christmas."

"Oh she'd love that. Thanks, Susan."

"Having her help out will give me time to do some shopping of my own. I can also be on the lookout for more inventory for us to sell. I sure wish I knew who made that rocking chair I bought a few weeks ago. I think handmade furniture would go over really well in Cricket Creek."

Betsy nodded. "I agree. We have people looking for furniture all the time."

"I'll have to put some research into it." Susan looked at the bare tree branches. "I'll have to get up early and decorate. I'm curious to see the Whisper's Edge ornaments."

"Just be careful of attacking trees and whatever you do, don't touch the elf on the shelf."

"Right, you keep moving the elf," Susan said.

Betsy raised an eyebrow.

"Don't you?"

Betsy shrugged. "Maybe it's a little bit of holiday magic."

Susan laughed as she went to grab her purse and coat. "Don't forget that you're doing some shopping too," Susan reminded Betsy. "I'm going to hold you to going out tomorrow, so don't think you're off the hook because of my date."

"I guess," Betsy replied slowly as they walked out the door.

"What do you mean, you guess? You shared a hot kiss with a handsome man and I've got a date tonight. I think something magical might have happened when we danced in the snow." She locked the door and looked at Betsy.

"Yeah, it was called bourbon."

Susan laughed. "It just seems like things have gotten interesting ever since that afternoon. I prefer to think it's a special Christmas spell."

"And you've been watching way too many Hallmark Christmas movies."

"Maybe." Susan shrugged as they stood at the curb, waiting for the light to change to green. "I mean, I'm super nervous with a million butterflies in my stomach but I'm excited too, in a good way, you know?"

"I am so glad, Susan. You're beginning to blossom and it's so wonderful to watch."

"You should give John a chance."

"Oh, I don't know . . ." Betsy reached in her pocket and pulled out a glove. "Only one. Where do all of the lost gloves go?"

"With the lost socks and hair ties. But seriously, you should."

"Yeah, I suppose." She smiled briefly but Susan could see the flash of fear in Betsy's eyes.

"Is that a yes?"

"Maybe . . ."

Susan wondered if Aubrey's father put that fear there. She wanted to ask but didn't want to spoil the mood.

"Main Street is beginning to look a lot like Christmas," Susan said, admiring the colorful window displays and wreaths hanging from the lampposts. "It's hard to believe that just a few years ago Main Street was struggling to survive. It's so wonderful to see Cricket Creek thriving again."

"It sure is. This little town was on the ropes until Noah Falcon came back and built us a doggone baseball stadium." Betsy shook her head. "Now we have a recording studio and a venue for weddings that brings in people from all over the place. It's amazing what can happen when a caring community comes together."

"Oh I know." With the stately old brick buildings and mature trees, Cricket Creek really was a picture-perfect small town, simply oozing charm. While Susan longed to travel and explore, she knew that Cricket Creek would always be her home. She couldn't imagine living anywhere else. "Christmas just has that certain special feeling, you know?"

"Yeah, panic," Betsy replied.

Susan fell into step with Betsy, giving her a glance to see if she was serious or joking around. "Is that how you really feel?"

"Not so much anymore. But when Aubrey was little I couldn't afford much in the way of presents. I always hated that I couldn't give her everything on her list." She blew out a sigh. "My daddy left my mother when I was little and so she didn't have much either. Brady left me when Aubrey was only two so I wondered how I would make ends meet."

"I'm sorry, Betsy. Who does that?"

"Eh, I managed."

"Did Brady say why he wanted to leave?"

Betsy looked straight ahead and for a moment Susan didn't think she would answer. "I got pregnant with Aubrey while Brady and I were just dating. We were married by the justice of the peace and got off to a rocky start. Brady didn't want the responsibility of a child or marriage. So he . . . bailed."

"That sucks."

"Well, I guess in the long run, it was better than being in an unhappy marriage. I eventually got a divorce on the grounds of desertion and he did have to pay child support. I mean, yeah it was horrible that he just up and turned his back on me, but how can you leave your baby girl?" She shook her head. "Aubrey is the light of my life. As you know, having her go off to school has been tough. And recently she's been talking about going into law, meaning even more years of school."

"I know, Betsy. My parents were so protective of me and my mother sure didn't want me to move off the farm and into town. But finding my independence was the best thing for me."

"Yeah, the empty nest thing translated to an empty life for me. At least your mom has your dad." They stopped at the next street corner. "Oh, would you just listen to me bellyache. I need to count my blessings. Christmas is just a bit of an odd time emotionally."

"It's perfectly fine to vent your feelings. I know you can't say these things to Aubrey."

"No, and my mother doesn't understand. She loves

me in her own way but she was glad when I moved out. But enough of that. I'm so proud of my little girl. I wouldn't change a thing and she knows it."

"Well then maybe you need to jumpstart your own life again. Truly consider giving John a fighting chance. Forget about all of that different world garbage. We're all just people. And he grew up in Cricket Creek. He might have become a big-time attorney but his roots are here in Kentucky."

"That's only part of my hesitation." Betsy shrugged and they started walking across the street. "I guess in my experience men just up and leave. I suppose that's why I never put my trust in one again."

"That's not fair to the good guys out there, and especially not to you," Susan said as they reached Violet's Vintage Clothing Shop.

"True, and I don't want Aubrey to have that kind of jaded opinion about relationships, but I've raised her to be independent and not depend on a man for money or happiness. Look, I want to believe in love too, Susan, but getting hurt like that sticks with you. I just want Aubrey to be realistic and choosy."

"Nothing wrong with being choosy," Susan said as she opened the door. "And she sure can be. Smart, gorgeous, and fun, just like her mama."

"Well hello, ladies!" Violet said with a big, welcoming smile. Susan guessed Violet to be somewhere in her early seventies but she had a timeless sense of style and radiated beauty. With her silver hair pulled up in a French twist and deep red lipstick, she had an Audrey Hepburn elegance coupled with Southern sass. As always, Violet was dressed to the nines and today she wore a long black velvet skirt and a cream-colored silk blouse.

"Hi, Violet." Susan walked over and gave the sweet store owner a hug.

Betsy gave her a hug as well. "You look lovely, as always. What's your secret to staying so young?"

"Laughter keeps my heart pumping strong. Music

soothes my soul. I try my best not to sweat the small stuff, keeping stress and worry out of my life. People today move at such a fast pace." She shook her head. "I like to move more slowly and enjoy small pleasures."

"Excellent advice," Betsy said. "In other words, stop and smell the roses."

"Precisely." Violet waved her delicate hand in an arc, causing the gold bangle bracelets on her wrist to jingle. "I'm stocked up with some beautiful things for the holidays, both old and new. What brings you two here on a blustery afternoon?"

Susan unbuttoned her jacket, revealing her sweater. "I need a wardrobe update."

Violet's eyes widened. "Oh mercy. But you have such a lovely sense of style, Susan."

"Oh, I wear these because it makes my mama happy. And they are a conversation piece." She moved her shoulders, causing blinking and jingling.

"I can believe it. Well, I haven't seen you in a while but I guess the Christmas season has your shop busy."

"More so on the weekends but yes," Susan replied.

Betsy looked around. "Actually, we both need a wardrobe update. Do you have a rack of petite clothes?"

"Of course." She smiled at Susan. "And tall as well. My shop has something for all shapes and sizes. And if you find something that needs altering, I have someone who can do that for you too. So let the shopping begin! Oh, and be sure to check out the shoes at the back of the shop. It's the Heels for Meals charity. They're all donated and one hundred percent goes toward the soup kitchen over on Third Street and for shut-ins unable to leave home."

"We will certainly do that," Susan said.

"As you know, the fitting rooms are behind the curtain. If you need anything, let me know. I have some great jewelry that I just bought at an estate sale that I know you'll love. It's in the glass case. Let me know if you want to try some of it on."

"Thanks, Violet," Susan said and turned to Betsy. "Are you ready? I don't have much time before I need to do my hair and makeup."

"Wait," said Violet. "Is this a special occasion?"

"I have a dinner date," Susan whispered and felt a bit of a blush heat her cheeks.

Violet clapped her hands together. "Wonderful! I'm surprised you're still single—someone as lovely as you? Do I know this lucky young man?"

"Danny Mayfield."

"Oh, he's a handsome one. You two would make an adorable couple." Violet tapped the side of her cheek. "Oh . . . I have a dress that you must try on. It's a midnight blue empire waist and will bring out your coloring perfectly. And I've got a whole section of Betsey Johnson clothing and accessories. Her line is feminine and whimsical. Kind of a retro look with a modern edge. I think you'll love her style, Susan. Betsy, the petites are over there in the far corner. I have a few outfits I think you'll like too."

"Thanks, Violet. I'll just browse," Betsy said. "We need to concentrate on Susan's date emergency first."

"The two of you can put on a fashion show," Violet said. "I'll put a few of my choices in the dressing rooms for you both."

"That would be fun!" Susan laughed, but she felt as jittery as the one time she'd tried a Red Bull and then weaved ten rugs, washed her car, cleaned her apartment, and baked a cake.

Susan started pushing through the clothes on the Betsey Johnson rack, wondering if the styles were too over-the-top for her to pull off. She chuckled when Betsy complained about the lack of choices for petites.

"Short people get the short end of the clothing stick," Betsy grumbled. "At least Aubrey got some height from her daddy. It's the only danged thing he gave her."

"Betsy, you might be vertically challenged but you

have a nice figure," Susan said. "There's got to be something here that would look amazing on you."

"Yeah, if those *What Not to Wear* folks got ahold of me they'd toss out my entire wardrobe of khaki pants and boring blouses."

"I often wonder what Stacy and Clinton would think of my closet." Susan sighed. "I miss that show. But you know I have a hard time tossing anything out. I would have played tug-of-war with my clothes and won."

"That would have been a sight to see. And like Violet said, other than your mother's ugly sweaters, I've always thought you have a great sense of style all your own."

"Really?"

"Yeah, you do your own thing."

"You're right, but it didn't help my social life in high school. I just never could fit in," Susan said but smiled. In truth she'd never thought much about the latest trends. She'd preferred flowy bohemian and retro styles purchased here at Violet's and at thrift shops around town. Flashy Forever 21-type mall stores just weren't in Susan's comfort zone. Because she was so tall, she usually wore ballerina flats and riding boots and stuck to sandals and flip-flops whenever the weather permitted. Her mother had once called her an old soul, and she supposed the description fit her style and personality. "Finding anything?" Susan glanced over at Betsy.

"A few outfits have some potential." Betsy held up a soft green silk blouse and scrunched up her nose. "Too colorful?"

"No, the color will go well with your auburn hair."

Betsy tilted her head. "I don't know . . . it's kind of fancy."

"At least try it on."

"Okay." Betsy draped it over her arm and started looking again.

Susan pulled a polka dot baby doll dress off the

rack. "Oh would you look at the ruffle trimmed angel sleeves?" She held it up to her body and turned toward the full-length mirror on the wall. "I think it would hit just above the knee on me."

"You love hippie clothes," Betsy said. "I used to pull it off back in high school but now I think I'd look silly."

"No you wouldn't."

Violet walked out of the dressing room and clasped her hands together. "Susan, I was just going to pull that one for you! Rather demure but sexy in an understated way. I have a pair of shoes that would be perfect. I'll go get them."

"Thanks!" Susan picked out a dainty black lace dress. "Too fancy?"

Betsy shrugged. "You could wear a cute denim jacket over it and tone it down a bit."

Susan nodded. "Oh, I love that suggestion. I have a gorgeous antique pin that would simply make the outfit. My jean jacket is one of my favorite things. I have three of them in different styles."

Violet brought over several pairs of chic flats. "Aren't these adorable?"

Susan nodded. "Oh, I love the pair with the cat face embroidered on the toe!"

"Me too," Violet said. "And this one with the almond closed toe and rhinestone bow can be worn with skinny jeans or leggings and would go with the blue dress I picked out. This pair is rhinestone and satin. I have several colors in that style."

"I love them!"

"With your height I know you prefer flats."

"I do," Susan said but thought to herself that Danny was tall enough that she could get away with heels. "Well, I'd better start trying on dresses. Betsy, isn't this fun?"

"Yeah, fun for someone tall and slinky like you. Me? Not so much."

Violet shook her silver head. "Oh pffft. I'll have you in a spectacular outfit in no time at all. You're as cute as a button but need something sassy to fit your personality. I love your hair, by the way."

"Thanks. Carrie Ann Spencer did the color at A Cut Above, right down the street," Betsy said. "I wanted a little change and she talked me into going big."

"I just adore Carrie Ann," Violet gushed. "I'm so glad that she and Easton Fisher fell in love. What a romance! Of course, everyone in Cricket Creek but those two knew for a very long time that they were much more than friends. I'm just glad they finally came to their senses."

"Sometimes it takes a while to finally wise up." Susan shot Betsy a pointed glance.

"Are we talking about me or you?" Betsy asked.

"Both of us, I'd say."

"Okay, girls. Time for the fashion show!" Violet sat down in a high-backed red velvet chair. "I will give my honest opinion." She folded her hands and gave them a lift of her chin, looking very regal. "Let's get this show on the road."

Susan twirled around like she was on a runway, making Violet laugh. Betsy, on the other hand, walked out in a no-nonsense manner, complaining about her short legs, her big hips, and lack of ample cleavage.

"You have a nice butt," Susan said.

Betsy turned to get a better view of her backside. "Do you think so? Maybe I should start doing squats."

"No doubt."

"That I should do squats?"

"No, that your butt is perfectly fine as it is."

Betsy shook her head. "All it took was one kiss and I'm out buying clothes and worrying about the size of my butt. I just bet Danny and John aren't staring in the mirror at their asses."

Violet started laughing from her perch on the velvet chair. "This is worth the price of admission."

"Meaning free," Betsy said.

"Oh yes, but I'd pay." Violet got up to help Betsy arrange the collar on a cowl-neck sweater.

Thirty minutes later Betsy had a bag bursting with clothes. "You've created a monster," she grumbled to Violet. "And I feel like I'm just getting started."

Susan settled on the polka dot doll dress and then decided to get the black lace one as well. "I'll take the cat flats and the ones with the rhinestone bow too."

"Oh, so cute!" Violet said and hurried over to ring the items up. "I know you're in a bit of a hurry. I'm so excited for both of you girls. I want a full report later in the week."

"Well, we're going to Wine and Diner for happy hour tomorrow," Susan said. "You should join us."

Violet appeared surprised at the invitation. "Oh . . ."

"Come on, it will be fun," Betsy said. "There's music and a dance floor."

Violet waved a dismissive hand. "I'm seventy-two. That ship has sailed."

"What ship?"

"The love boat," Violet said, but the color in her cheeks said that she had an interest.

"Are you kidding? Romance is alive and well at Whisper's Edge," Betsy said.

"I've thought about moving there. I just don't know if I could part with my house. I can walk to the shop now and the retirement community is on the river."

"Well, we'd love you to join us," Susan said as she swiped her credit card. "Keep it in mind."

Violet handed Susan her shopping bag. "Thanks, sweetheart. I'll think about it. Have fun with Danny Mayfield. He's such a nice young man, and from a good family."

On the walk back to the shop Susan chatted with Betsy about which outfit to wear. "Oh my goodness, I only have a little over an hour to get ready!"

"I think you can manage," Betsy said with a chuckle.

When they reached the shop Betsy gave her a hug. "I'm heading on home. Sugar, I know you're nervous but just be yourself. That's all you need to do."

"Oh thanks for everything, Betsy. I promise to be myself."

"Unless you can be a unicorn, then always be a unicorn."

"You crack me up." Susan tipped her head back and laughed. "I'll remember that." She unlocked the door and took a deep breath. The comforting scent of potpourri mingled with lemon furniture polish and the earthy old wood. The familiar smell always brought a smile followed by a sigh of contentment. With quick steps, she headed for the stairs to her loft. She tried to remain calm but her heart thudded and she felt short of breath when she reached the landing. Needing to calm down, she sat down in the rocking chair. Closing her eyes, she leaned her head against the smooth wood and rocked until her pulse slowed and her breathing returned to normal. "I've got this," she whispered, and stood up to get ready for her second date with Danny Mayfield.

12

This Magic Moment

DANNY TAPPED HIS FINGERS ON THE STEERING wheel while stopped at the second light on Main Street. While he hadn't been on a date in a fairly long time, it wasn't like him to be this nervous. He'd tried on three shirts and changed his blue jeans to a black pair that he thought looked dressier. He polished his best cowboy boots and decided to wear his leather jacket rather than his casual Carhartt. Rusty had looked at him as if he'd lost his ever lovin' mind.

Susan sent him a text message telling him to come around to the back entrance that led up to her loft, so he turned into an alley that led to the small parking lot around the back of her building. After killing the engine, he questioned if he'd slapped on too much aftershave and should have styled his hair with some gel.

And what about his breath? He'd downed a shot of bourbon to take the edge off and now he worried that he smelled of whiskey. "Damn . . ." Danny dug in his pocket for gum but then didn't want to be chomping on it when Susan answered, so he sat there and chewed it and then spit it out before getting out of his truck.

"This is insane," he grumbled but then chuckled, because it was a good kind of insanity. He knew this was only a dinner date, and with a reluctant companion at that, but for reasons he couldn't grasp, going out with Susan felt like the beginning of something good that he'd been missing in his life.

Danny finally got out of his truck and headed over to the back entrance. He walked up the steep flight of stairs but stood there for a minute, kicking himself for forgetting to buy flowers. "Ah, damn!" He put his fist to his forehead, wondering how late he would be if he hightailed it up to Flower Power and bought a fresh bouquet of roses. He looked at his phone and decided he could make the round trip in fifteen minutes. "I've got this." He turned around and was halfway down when he heard the door open.

"Danny?"

He turned around and looked up at Susan. She looked amazing in a polka dot dress that looked like a throwback to another era. His brain took a holiday and he simply stood there . . . staring.

"Are you leaving?" She frowned down at him.

"Of course not."

"But you've turned around."

"I . . . forgot something."

"Hey, it's okay." She inhaled a deep breath and started to close the door. "You don't have to make something up."

"No!" Danny took the steps two at a time and stopped the door from closing with his shiny boot. "Susan, please, let me in."

The door opened slowly and she stepped aside for him to enter. "Be honest, you were leaving."

"Yes, but—" He started to explain his need for flowers but decided to use action instead of words and pulled her into his arms. When he dipped his head and kissed her, he smothered her gasp of surprise. She put her hands to his chest as if to push him away but then melted against him. Danny felt the same pull of attraction he'd felt back in high school, only stronger because he wasn't a teenager with raging hormones but an adult with deeper feelings. This kiss touched him on an emotional level that had him pulling her even closer. He remembered the sweet girl but he was drawn to the lovely woman she'd become.

To his surprise, Susan wrapped herself around him and kissed him back with a fiery passion that defied her shy nature. Her lips were warm and pliant and with her height she fit just right against him. When her fingers slid into his hair, he slanted his mouth over hers and deepened the kiss. She responded with a sexy moan that had him pressing her against the wall, kissing her like there was no tomorrow.

Finally, he reluctantly pulled back and tucked a lock of her silky hair behind her ear. "I was leaving to go and get you flowers. I was in such a hurry to get here I completely forgot to stop."

"Oh . . ." She sucked her bottom lip between her teeth and damn if it wasn't the sexiest sight he'd ever seen.

"I'm sorry I dragged you into my arms without any warning."

"You are?" she asked in a surprisingly flirty tone.

"Not at all, but I thought I should say that."

She smiled.

"And here I thought I would have to work up the nerve to kiss you at the end of the evening. It was like starting with dessert first."

"Life is short, you might as well," she said.

"I like the way you think." Danny took a step back. "You look amazing by the way."

"Thank you." She blushed at the compliment but didn't look away. He knew that she'd lived a sheltered life and he wanted her to have the confidence that she deserved.

"Would you do me a favor and do a slow twirl for me?" He made a circle with his finger.

"Really?" The blush deepened.

Danny nodded. "Please, if you don't mind."

"Okay." Susan did a slow turn in the polka dot dress. She held her arms out and her full sleeves looked like the wings of an angel. The skirt billowed and caressed her long legs, whisper soft and gently sexy.

"Oh wow . . ." Danny had thought he preferred heels on a woman but Susan's bejeweled flats looked so dainty and feminine that he wanted to scoop her up and carry her off to bed. The hot kiss had him wanting so much more, but he told himself to cool his jets. "I know this sounds really corny, but you take my breath away."

"I think it sounds really romantic." She tilted her head to the side. "Thank you. And I'm glad you approve, because I closed up the shop early and hightailed it up to Violet's Vintage Clothing and bought this dress for tonight."

"The dress is perfect and I'm flattered that you went to the trouble just for me."

"Thanks. I prefer retro to tight and slinky. I like to do my own thing." She lifted one shoulder. "I guess that's why I never really fit in."

"I love the look, Susan. Those shoes are really cool. Why fit in when you can stand out?"

Susan lifted one foot, laughing when she nearly lost her balance. "Whoa, standing is hard," she said and laughed.

Danny reached out to steady her.

"I was always a head and shoulders above the rest . . . literally," she added with a light chuckle. Her laughter trailed off when she met his gaze without wavering. For a few seconds time seemed suspended. Unable to resist, he dipped his head and captured her sweet mouth in a tender, lingering kiss. Smiling, she reached up and slowly swiped her thumb over his bottom lip. "My lipstick . . ."

"Sorry, I kissed it off."

"I'm not sorry," she said, but she glanced away this time. "Did I just say that out loud?"

"Yes, and I'm not really sorry either," he said, making her laugh.

Susan pointed to her face. "I took extra pains with my hair and makeup and had to do it all in record time. I even used an eyelash curler that I'm afraid of."

Danny laughed, loving her candor. "Well then, I'll confess that I changed my shirt three times and my pants once. I worried about everything from my hair to my boots."

"I approve of everything from your head to your toes."

"Thank you, Susan." Danny smiled and had the urge to pull her back into his arms but he didn't want her to think he was too forward, especially after the spontaneous, hot kisses. "Are you ready to head to Wine and Diner?"

"I am. I know it's cold out but we can walk if you like. Main Street is decorated so pretty."

"I think walking would be refreshing." He seriously needed to cool down anyway.

"I'll just grab my coat and purse."

Once they were outside Danny asked, "Do you mind if I hold your hand?"

Susan smiled. "I think after kissing we're definitely up to the hand in hand stage."

"Good point," Danny said and took her hand.

"Your hands are warm."

"And calloused, sorry."

"Don't be. It just shows how hardworking you are."

Danny squeezed her hand. He couldn't remember the last time he'd held the hand of a pretty woman, and it felt nice. "I know this is our first . . . wait, second date, but it feels like I've known you for a lot longer. You have an amazing way of putting me at ease."

"Really? You seem laid-back to me."

Danny shrugged. "I am most of the time. Mason is the moody brother. Or at least he used to be. I like things on an even keel, even though Mason will tell you I have a wild side."

"Really?"

"I've calmed down. I was always the one doing a flip from a cliff into the lake and going off the path with my four-wheeler. Mom would blame Mason when I got hurt since he had the not-so-great job of keeping me and Mattie in line."

"I think I'd be more outgoing if I'd had siblings. It had to be fun to have both a brother and sister and grow up around a marina."

They stopped at a streetlight. "Yeah, I'm lucky that we're so close. Of course, we have our moments, and I still love to tease Mattie, but we've always enjoyed hanging out with one another." He blew out a sigh. "Now that we're all so busy we don't get together as often as I'd like. I was just talking to Mason about it when he stopped over at my place while I was doing some woodworking. Working at the bistro and brewery isn't the same as just having fun with them, though. We need to have a bonfire sometime soon. Would you like to come?"

"Oh, that sounds great."

"Good," he said and wished he'd invited her to the marina when they were back in high school. "It's a date." He brought her hand to his mouth and kissed it, something he didn't think he'd ever done before but it felt so right. Susan somehow brought out a tender, romantic side that he didn't really know he had in him.

They started walking when the light changed. "Isn't Main Street so beautiful all decked out for Christmas?" Susan commented. "It just seems so alive, you know?"

Danny nodded slowly but didn't answer.

"What?"

"I guess I haven't paid all that much attention."

Susan stopped in her tracks, making him pull up short. "Don't tell me you're not in the Christmas spirit."

"Okay, I won't."

"Meaning you aren't."

He shrugged. "Not so much."

Susan's eyes widened. "Are you serious? You don't like Christmas?" She looked at him like he'd said he hated puppies.

"I don't know." How could he tell her that Christmas made him feel left out without sounding like a whiner? "I mean, I don't *dislike* it."

"Would you be annoyed if I try to change your opinion?"

"Does it mean I get to spend more time with you?"

"Yes."

"Then I'm all in."

"Yes!" Susan did a fist pump. "Before you know it you'll love Christmas as much as Buddy in *Elf*."

"Oh wow." Danny laughed. "I draw the line at the elf suit," he said. If anyone could get him in the Christmas spirit, it would be Susan Quincy.

Danny took her hand and they started strolling again, stopping here and there to admire the window displays. Grammar's Bakery had a huge gingerbread house covered in intricate icing and gumdrops surrounded by a candy cane fence.

"Oh, that had to take forever to make," Susan said, stopping to get a better look. "I just love the scent of gingerbread, don't you?"

"Yes, I sure do. My mom makes gingerbread cake with sorghum and serves it warm with a huge dollop of whipped cream."

"Sorghum has such a deep, rich flavor. I love dripping it on homemade cornbread baked in a cast-iron skillet."

"Mm. Good thing we're headed to dinner because you're making me hungry. So I guess you're a good cook?"

Susan tilted her head. "Comfort food, nothing fancy."

"My kind of girl."

Susan gave him a shy smile and then stopped again in front of A Touch of Whimsy, a toy store that only carried handmade toys. "Oh check out the doll house! Isn't it just adorable?" She got closer to the window. "Would you just look at the detail?" She sighed. "I always wanted one when I was little but we couldn't afford anything like this."

Danny nodded, adding another woodworking craft to his list. "Perhaps you should ask Santa? Or are you on the naughty list?"

"I think I've been a pretty good girl." Susan laughed. "This is so much fun. I've been too busy to take the time to get out on Main Street and walk around. When Betsy's daughter comes home from college I'm going to hire her for the holiday season so I have more free time to enjoy the holidays."

"Good, you can save some of that free time for me." Danny would have walked right by all of the decorations without so much as a second glance. "Remember, you have a Christmas spirit challenge on your hands. Are you up for it?"

"Oh no doubt. I think it's already working just a little bit. Am I right?"

Danny nodded. "Your delight in the decorations is impossible to resist." Christmas music drifted out of speakers and a light dusting of snow still covered the grassy areas. Seeing Main Street through Susan's eyes brought back a little bit of the holiday sparkle.

Within a few minutes they arrived at Wine and

Diner. "After you." Danny held the door open and followed Susan inside his favorite restaurant. "I'd like to go over to the wine bar side if you don't mind." The diner part of the restaurant was lively with families but Danny wanted something more cozy and intimate.

"No, that sounds nice."

Danny put his hand to the small of her back and headed through the doorway where the seating was casual. A gorgeous mahogany bar. "Let's sit near the window where we can look out over Main Street," he said. "The Christmas lights will turn on in just a little while."

"Ah, do I detect another bit of spirit already?"

Danny couldn't resist her smile. "Maybe. Here, let me help you." He held her coat while she shrugged out of the sleeves. Her hair brushed over his fingers, whisper soft. He swallowed hard to prevent a groan.

"Thank you." She slid into the small booth.

Danny hung his leather jacket on the hook next to her coat and joined her. Their knees touched and Danny felt a warm flash of awareness. He noticed her quick intake of breath and wondered if she felt the same way. "I haven't been here in a while. I'm glad Jessica added the wine bar to the restaurant. We don't have enough of this sort of venue here in Cricket Creek."

"I agree. This is so relaxing."

A fat candle flickered on the table, casting a soft glow into the dimly lit room. In the far corner a crackling fireplace filled the room with the scent of burning wood. The romantic vibe had Danny wanting to reach across and take Susan's hand and rub his thumb over her soft skin, but he decided to wait until later in the date to make a subtle move.

"Oh nice, live music," Susan said with a nod toward a soloist setting up his stool and microphone, getting ready to sing. Glasses clinked and patrons talked in low tones, in keeping with the laid-back atmosphere.

"Sweet," Danny agreed and picked up a cocktail menu sitting on the table. "Would you like to start with something to drink and an appetizer?"

"Sure." Susan nodded and picked up her own menu. "Oh, they have Broomstick Brewery ales on tap. Mason's brewery sure is taking off."

Danny nodded. "Yeah, he took a hobby and made it into something great. I'm proud of him."

"I imagine you played a big part in getting the brewery off the ground."

"I did," Danny said, but felt that familiar twinge of regret that he was the only sibling without his own business.

"The Mayfield Marina means a lot to the community. You should also be proud of your efforts to keep it up and running when hard times hit Cricket Creek," she said, as if somehow reading his mind.

"I'll get you out on a boat when the weather warms up," Danny said, letting her know that he wanted this to go beyond a dinner date. He wanted to get to know her.

"I'd like that. I might not have gotten to spend a lot of time at the lake or river but having grown up on a farm, I'm an outdoorsy kind of girl. And we have a big pond on the farm so I'm a strong swimmer. I've never been to the ocean but it's on my bucket list of things to do."

"You're too young for a bucket list."

"Not really, because it's already miles and miles long. I'll have to start sometime soon."

A young woman with a long, swinging ponytail came over to the table and gave them a big smile. "Good evening, folks. My name is Sherry and I'll be your server. Can I start you off with a drink and something to nibble on?" She looked at Susan.

"I'll have a glass of your house Chardonnay."

"Okay, and you?" She turned to Danny.

"I'll have the Spellbound," he said. "Susan, do you

want to try the appetizer sampler? It's got a little bit of everything."

"Sure."

"Coming right up," Sherry said with a bright smile and hurried away.

"You'll have to tell me some of the things on your list," Danny said. "I'm pretty fearless so if it includes things like noodling and cliff-diving, I'm in."

Susan raised her eyebrows. "Um, neither of those adventures made the cut, I'm happy to say." She tapped the side of her cheek. "I do have a hot air balloon ride and parasailing on the list. Oh and swimming with dolphins!" She leaned back when Sherry brought their drinks.

"I'd like to experience all three of those things," Danny said, and the thought ran through his mind that he'd like to do just about anything she had on her list, and then add a few things of his own.

Susan took a sip of her wine. "I've been an armchair traveler for a long time. I've got tons of travel books and magazines. I'm sure you're not surprised that I'm an avid reader. I'm the poster child for nerd." She pointed to her head.

"You're a very pretty nerd," he said.

"Thank you . . . I think."

"Nerds rule the world. I'm a reader too. Mattie has a bookstore at her bistro. Every book is a dollar and all of the proceeds go toward a local literacy program here in Cricket Creek."

"That's really wonderful, Danny. I haven't been to the bistro but I heard it's so good."

"We have to remedy that. Mattie would really like you," he said just as the giant tray of appetizers arrived.

"Wow, I don't think I'll need any dinner after this." Susan accepted a small plate from Sherry.

"Enjoy!" Sherry said. "Anything else I can get you two?"

"Thanks, I think we're good for now," Danny replied.

"Okay, I'll check back in a few minutes."

Susan put a few items on her plate and took a bite of a cheese stick, laughing when the warm cheese made a gooey mess.

Danny reached over and helped her get control of the stringy cheese.

"Can't take me anywhere," Susan said with a low chuckle. She twirled a long strand of mozzarella around her tongue.

"Well, I want to take you everywhere. Even in a hot air balloon."

Susan licked a dab of marinara sauce from the corner of her mouth. "I just might have to hold you to that."

Between the beer, the music, the great food, and mostly the company, Danny felt a sense of relaxation and contentment mixed with the heady excitement of attraction. He loved the dainty way she ate a chicken wing and the sexy sound of her laughter. Her shoulders moved to the beat of the music and after a second glass of wine she sang along a little off-key. He found her quick smile and gentle manner completely adorable. When she excused herself to go to the ladies' room, Danny noticed a few lingering male glances at her and felt a possessive stab hit him in the gut. Danny couldn't recall having this kind of reaction to a woman this quickly. He'd been thinking about her ever since he'd helped her out at the shop the other day, and he was falling for her hard and fast.

When Susan walked back toward the table, Danny caught her gaze and she smiled. Heady warmth spread through his body, like he'd just taken a shot of smooth bourbon. He'd been right. Tonight was the start of something good.

13

Taking the Cake

JOHN REMOVED THE PINEAPPLE UPSIDE DOWN CAKE from the oven and put it on a rack to cool. "Stephanie, would you like to sample my latest creation?" He pulled his oven mitts off and glanced in her direction.

Stephanie stopped filling the salt shakers and fisted her hands on her hips. "No way! John, I've gained five pounds since I started working here."

"Just one little slice?"

"Nope." She raised her palms. "I am staying away from the cake. I'll have to say that the pineapple smells amazing and leave it at that."

"You don't know what you're missing."

"Yes, I do." She sighed but then brightened. "I know . . . why don't you take a warm, fresh-from-the-oven sample over to Betsy?"

"I don't know . . ." John pulled a frown. "I tried to call her twice and she didn't answer. She also didn't come in for lunch today. I can take a hint."

"Maybe she was busy."

"Yeah, busy avoiding me."

"Since when do you give up this quickly, Mr. Fancy

Pants attorney?" Stephanie arched one eyebrow and gave him a little sassy head bop. "Huh?"

John leaned back against the counter and folded his arms across his chest. "Never."

"Then why now?"

John sighed. "I failed at marriage. Nothing scares me more than failure."

"You don't have to get married. Just get out and have a little fun."

"Well, I guess I'm also trying to overcome Rachel's betrayal. I know I had it coming but still . . ."

"Oh please! You didn't have it coming," Stephanie said sternly. "Nobody had cheating coming."

"You're right." John lifted one shoulder. "But I was way too full of myself. I deserved to get taken down a notch or two and humbled."

Stephanie made a sound of exasperation. "Okay, look, I'll tell it like it is. You might have had the arrogance to marry a woman much too young, and yeah, neglected her for your career. But cheating is never acceptable for any reason whatsoever." She wagged a finger. "I was on the flip side of the coin as a throwaway starter wife. I got married for all the wrong reasons too, but I didn't have that kind of treatment coming either. It took me way too long to figure that out because I kept blaming myself. Are we damaged?" She rolled her eyes. "Carrying some serious baggage? Yeah, but it's time to dust ourselves off and start all over again." She brushed off her shoulders with her fingertips and then nodded in his direction. "Go ahead. Do it."

"You're kidding, right?"

Stephanie jutted out her chin and pointed to her face. "Do I look like I'm kidding?"

"No." John smiled as he dusted off his shoulders. "Feel better?"

"Yes, actually."

Stephanie nodded firmly.

"If you ever decide to quit working here you could give inspirational speeches."

Stephanie raised her index finger. "Not a bad thought. After I write that book about putting the pieces of my broken life back together. Hey, I know what you mean about feeling humble. But humble feels a whole lot better than used. Trust me, if I ever get married again it will be for all the right reasons."

"So, now that you're dusted off, are you going to get back in the dating game?" John asked.

"Not anytime soon." Something vulnerable flickered in her eyes. "I need to sit on the bench for a while but I will . . . eventually, after I get my act together."

"Are you taking your act on the road?"

"Ha." Stephanie laughed. "Nope, I thought Cricket Creek was a sleepy little town that I needed to leave for bigger and better things. I was wrong. I'm realizing how much I missed this town, especially Main Street."

"I'm glad to hear it," John said, thinking that he'd seen a change in Stephanie in the relatively short time he'd known her. "And you know I feel the same way. What were we thinking?"

"Good question." She shook her head. "I think the bigger the mistakes, the more we learn in the long run."

"Self-help book?"

"Nope." She gave him a wry smile. "Experience. So, are you going to take the cake over to Betsy or cower in the corner?"

"Damn, you're tough."

"I wasn't, but I'm working pretty damned hard on it," Stephanie said with a grin. "Is the cake cooled off enough to cut?"

"Probably. I need to invert it onto a plate."

"Do it. Let's get this ball rolling." She made a twirling motion with her index fingers.

"I need your help." John handed Stephanie a plate. "Hold it over the skillet and I'll flip it over. The skillet is heavy so I'll have to be careful."

"Okay," she said, nibbling on her bottom lip. When they successfully had the fragrant cake on the serving plate, Stephanie cut two generous slices and slid them into to-go containers. "You can take one to Susan too so it won't seem too obvious." After putting the containers into a white paper bag she eyed the remaining cake and groaned. "I just might have to take a tiny piece home with me."

"You won't be sorry."

"Yes I will, when the cake calls my name all night long. I'll eat a bite at a time, thinking there's less calories that way than eating it all at once. It's a game I play with myself."

John laughed but didn't pick up the dessert.

"Here, are you going to take this or not?" She thrust the bag in his direction.

John looked at the bag like it was a snake ready to strike. "I spoke to crowded courtrooms and tough judges. Why am I so nervous over something this simple?"

"Because you're attracted to Betsy but afraid of rejection and getting hurt. Classic."

"You're spot-on, once again."

"Self-help book called *Life After Divorce*. Chapter ten was all about moving on."

"But you haven't exactly done that yet."

"No." Stephanie closed her eyes and swallowed hard. After inhaling a deep breath, she recovered and smiled. "I'm getting there. I'm not where I want to be but I'm sure as hell better off than where I was." She made shooing motions with her fingers. "I'll wrap things up here and close the shop. Go. Let them eat cake."

"Okay . . ." John walked over to the hook on the wall and grabbed his coat. Armed with the cake, he headed over to Rhyme and Reason. A cold blast of winter air hit him in the face and cleared his head. His heart hammered like he was about to give a closing argument but he took a breath and pulled the door open. The scent of pine and cinnamon had an immediate calming effect on his racing pulse. He smiled, thinking that aromatherapy had merit. Susan chatted with a customer who was looking at a display of delicate china teacups and didn't notice him come in. Betsy was nowhere in sight. John thought about leaving the cake on the counter and bolting. The white bag had his logo on it so they would know where the cake came from, but he heard Stephanie's stern voice in his head and squared his shoulders.

John finally spotted Betsy in the far corner of the showroom, hanging decorations on a fat-bottomed Christmas tree. She looked cute in skinny jeans, black leather boots, and a silky green blouse that seemed to flow over her skin. Her auburn hair was swept up in a loose bun with stray tendrils kissing the back of her neck.

Betsy's back was to him and as he walked closer he could hear her humming along to Elvis, who was crooning "Blue Christmas" from a record player perched in the corner. She backed up and tilted her head at the placement of a silver star and then moved it higher. Leaning over, she picked another ornament up out of a box, shook her head as if questioning its odd shape, and then hung it on a back branch. With a grin, John noticed that the top branches were bare since her short stature didn't allow her to reach that high.

John walked up behind her as she stretched to hang a glittery gold ball above her head. "May I help?"

Betsy shrieked and took a step backwards, landing against John. He looped his free hand around her waist, keeping her from tipping sideways. She gave another little yelp and struggled out of his hold. She pivoted, sending gold glitter everywhere, and looked up at him with fire in her eyes. "Just what do you think you're doin' sneakin' up on me like that?"

"I didn't sneak," John protested, trying not to laugh.

"You most certainly did," she accused him, but it was difficult to take her seriously with gold glitter sprinkled in her hair.

"Sorry, I didn't mean to scare you."

"I wasn't scared. I was startled." She eyed the bag he held with interest. "I didn't order anything."

"This is a gift." He held up the bag and wagged it back and forth.

She eyed him suspiciously. "What's in there?"

"Pineapple upside down cake, made in a cast-iron skillet, as it should be."

"Oh, that's my . . ." she started to say and then clamped her lips together.

"Your favorite?" He arched one eyebrow.

"You're putting words in my mouth."

"I can put cake in your mouth." He meant for the offer to be a joke but had a vision of feeding her. Judging by her blush, Betsy was thinking the same thing. "Then should I give this to someone else?"

"I didn't say that either," she responded in a softer tone.

"Then what are you saying, Betsy?"

"That I'd be a fool not to accept the cake."

Her answer brought his attention to the lips he'd been thinking about all morning. The lips he'd kissed and wanted to kiss again.

"Did you add the pecans? Some people don't."

"Absolutely."

Betsy reached for the bag but John pulled it just out of her reach. "Seriously? Did you really just do that?"

He smiled. Betsy brought out a playful side that must have been buried deep inside of him and it sure as hell was fun letting it out.

"You do know that I can wrestle that cake from you, no problem." Betsy tapped her cute boot on the hardwood floor and tried her best to look intimidating. She failed.

"How can I be scared of someone with glitter in her hair?"

Betsy laughed. "These ornaments were made by the residents of Whisper's Edge." She held up a candy cane that looked rather phallic.

John laughed. "Oh wow."

"The ornament making party involved spiked punch."

"I'm not surprised." John cleared his throat. "How about dinner with me tonight and this will be the dessert?" He pointed to the bag.

Betsy paused long enough to give him hope. "I have plans tonight."

"Oh, okay." John felt his stomach plummet. He had to ask, "A date?"

She hesitated but then said, "I'm going to Wine and Diner with Susan."

John let out the breath he was holding. "Oh . . . half-price wine night." He handed her the bag. "I'll see you there."

"Oh, so you were already going?" Betsy asked breezily, but she appeared a little bit disappointed. "Not that it's any of my business."

Did she think he was going there to hit on women?

"Forget I asked that," she said before he could reply.

"I can't forget anything about you."

"You're a smooth talker."

"I'm just being honest."

"So, were you going there already?"

"I just asked you to dinner, remember?" John felt a surge of joy that she might be jealous. "So I wasn't going, but now I am." Before she could back away he leaned over and gave her a light kiss, lingering just enough to have her wanting more. Hopefully, anyway. "I'm going to make crème brûlée this weekend."

"For the deli?"

John paused, gathered courage, and then decided to take the plunge. "No, just for you. And with your permission, I'll feed you a bite or two."

Betsy's jaw dropped, just as he thought it would, but then she recovered. "Ha, you wish."

"I do." John smiled, turned on his heel, and walked back through the shop. Susan spotted him and waved. He waved back and walked outside, whistling along with Elvis. "No, it is not going to be a blue Christmas," he said to himself.

Still whistling, he popped back into the deli to give Stephanie a full report.

"Well done, young Grasshopper." Stephanie leaned her broom against the counter and gave John a high five.

John folded his hands and bowed. "You have taught me well, oh queen of self-help."

"I'm happy to put all of my newfound knowledge to good use."

"Master, heal thyself."

"I'm a work in progress." Stephanie laughed. "I want to hear all about your Wine and Diner adventure tomorrow."

"Thanks," he said, but when he headed for the kitchen she raised her palms in protest.

"I've already told you that I've got everything under control. Go on home and get all prettied up and have some much deserved fun with your feisty little redhead."

"Fun?" he asked with a slow shake of his head.

"Yeah, you know, that thing where you laugh and have a good time?"

John gave her what he knew had to be a blank look. "Honestly, I can't remember the last time I let my hair down. I hope I recall how," he said but then frowned.

"What's wrong?"

"Even as a kid, I've always been about hard work and keeping my nose to the grindstone. My parents preached that I needed to be the best." He scrubbed a hand down his face. "It just hit me that I can't recall how to let my hair down because I never have."

"Like . . . ever?"

"Never."

"No keg stands in college?"

John tried to imagine himself doing a keg stand. "That would have been a complete fail."

"Whoa . . ." Leaning against the counter, Stephanie

raised her eyebrows. "Oh come on, what did they do back then . . . panty raids?"

John had to laugh. "I'm not *that* old."

"Oh, well how about streaking? Food fights?" She snapped her fingers. "Toga parties?"

"Where did you get that information from?"

"*Animal House.*"

John laughed again. "No to all of the above. I was too busy being at the top of my class for any shenanigans." He sighed. "I know, boring. I was always too afraid of disappointing my college professor parents. Anything less than perfection wasn't acceptable."

"Well, you said your parents sold you their house and are on a cross country adventure in an RV."

"It's hard for me to imagine them on the road like that but yeah."

"Well, I think it's about time you cut loose and had a house party. I'm guessing you've never had one."

"You guessed correctly."

"It won't be quite as fun as if the house still belonged to your parents but I think a toga party is in order. What do you think?"

"I think I would need a party planner."

She pointed at her head. "You're looking at the best. Being a trophy wife meant being an expert at entertaining. I'll be happy to assist you. For now, you need to get over to Wine and Diner before some other guy starts hitting on Betsy."

John realized that Stephanie didn't get out any more than he did. "Do you want to come along?"

"Are you kidding? And cramp your style?"

"I don't have a style to cramp," he said.

"I think you are capable of having way more fun than you realize. You've just kept your inner teenager repressed."

"More like I need to discover my fun side," John said, wondering if he would bore Betsy to tears. One

of the things Rachel had tossed in his face was that he
was a complete bore.

"I think Betsy Brock is just the person to bring the
fun side out in you."

"I hope you're right."

"Remember, full report," Stephanie said. "Now
skedaddle."

14

Flying Solo

SUSAN CRANKED UP THE SOUND ON HER FAVORITE
Billy Joel greatest hits album and belted out "Big
Shot" while she put on the finishing touches of her
makeup. "Oh . . . drama." Leaning back, she checked
out her face in the bathroom mirror, hoping she hadn't
gone overboard. "I like it!" she said out loud, proud of
her winged eyeliner and smoky eyeshadow. She'd
tamed her dark curls with some magic product she'd
purchased at A Cut Above, deciding to let her hair
hang loose instead of pulling it up into a bun.

"Okay." With a satisfied nod she glanced at the time
on her cell phone. "Oh no, got to get a move on." She
wanted to arrive at Wine and Diner by six-thirty and
she'd used up almost all of her thirty minutes getting
ready after closing the shop at six o'clock. Since she
knew she would have a couple of glasses of wine, she'd
decided to walk, and now she had to rush to get there
on time. Rushing gave Susan anxiety and so she took
a deep breath and decided to text Betsy and let her
know she would be a little bit late. Betsy's house was in

the opposite direction but also within walking distance so they'd decided to meet at the restaurant.

"I should have known," Susan said when she read Betsy's answer, which said that she was running late as well. While Betsy made it to work on time most days, she always came blowing in the door like a fierce wind, hurrying to make it by nine o'clock. Early wasn't in Betsy's vocabulary.

Susan hurried into her bedroom and put on the black lace dress she'd purchased at Violet's, slipped on her jeweled flats, and then added a soft red shrug over her shoulders. After spraying on her favorite perfume she put on her coat and grabbed her purse. "My phone!" With a groan, she hurried into the bathroom and retrieved it, frowning at the time.

Susan closed her eyes and stood perfectly still for a moment, trying to calm down. She knew that the time wasn't the only thing causing her anxiety. Getting dressed up and going out to a stylish wine bar wasn't something she was used to doing and she was out of her comfort zone. What would she do if someone approached her and offered to buy her a drink? She kept reliving moments of her dinner with Danny, and the thought of flirting with another man didn't appeal to her at all. "But he's not my boyfriend," she whispered to herself. Her mother used to tell her not to put all her eggs in one basket. She chuckled. "But Danny is such a good egg." Susan opened her eyes. "All right, enough." She wondered if people would think she was one taco short of a combo if they knew how much she talked to herself. "But it calms me down," she answered herself and had to laugh.

After wrapping a pretty red knit scarf around her neck she headed out the back door and walked through the narrow alley out to Main Street. The evening air had a serious nip and the cold breeze blew up her dress, making her doubt her decision to walk. Two

blocks later her cheeks felt numb and she picked up the
pace, wanting to be in the cozy restaurant at a table as
close to the crackling fireplace as she could get.

Susan smiled at the memory of walking down Main
Street with Danny. She'd been serious about getting him
back in the Christmas spirit. His comment about wanting to spend more time with her made her feel a bit
warmer in spite of the frigid weather. A few people were
actually out window shopping, carrying steaming coffee
cups from Grammar's Bakery. Some of the shops were
open late, something Susan would do as soon as Aubrey
was home and could relieve her in the evenings.

Susan opened the door of Wine and Diner with the
silly wish that Danny was with her. That way if John
did show up she wouldn't feel like a third wheel. Just
as she thought, the wine bar was packed, but as luck
would have it a couple stood up and left two vacant
seats at the bar. While Susan would rather have the
privacy of a booth, she decided she'd better snag the
two seats and so she draped her coat over one stool and
sat down at the other one.

After ordering a glass of Riesling, Susan shot Betsy
a text message that she'd arrived at Wine and Diner.
Feeling a bit self-conscious, she played with the stem
of her glass, wishing that Betsy would hurry up.

"I think you dropped this," said a male voice near
Susan's ear. She turned to her right and looked at her
scarf. "It was on the floor."

"Oh, thank you," Susan said. The scarf was being
held by the guy sitting next to her. He looked familiar,
and then she realized it was Cole Christian, from high
school. He'd been an amazing basketball player and
she thought he might have played some college ball.
Like Danny, he'd run with the popular crowd. It wasn't
uncommon for her to recognize classmates and for
them not to remember her and so she gave him a polite
smile and turned her attention back to her wine.

After a moment Cole said, "You look familiar."

"Well, it's a small town, so I guess we all look rather familiar."

"Oh, so you live in Cricket Creek. We get so many tourists these days." He gave her a dimpled smile. He was handsome in a Ryan Reynolds kind of way. "I'm Cole Christian." He extended his hand.

Susan gave Cole a firm handshake. "Susan Quincy."

"Oh . . . wait, you own Rhyme and Reason on Main Street. My mother loves your place."

"I do." Susan felt a flash of pride.

Cole tilted his head to the side. "And we went to high school together," he added slowly as if not quite sure.

"We did." Susan nodded. "You were a great point guard. You played in college too, right?"

"Yeah, thanks. I played some division one college ball."

"I thought so."

Cole shrugged. "I wasn't good enough to go any further but I coach at Cricket Creek High School. You like basketball?"

"I do," Susan said, and he raised his eyebrows. For some reason people usually seemed surprised to learn that she enjoyed watching sports.

"I'm so tall that I'm often asked if I played, but I'm afraid I don't have an ounce of athletic ability."

"You look more graceful, like a dancer."

Was he flirting? "No, I'm afraid I have the unique superpower to trip over my own shadow."

Cole laughed. "I'd like to prove you wrong by dancing with you after the band starts later on."

Susan was suddenly stuck for an answer. "I . . ."

"I'm sorry, I should have asked. Do you have a boyfriend?"

"Not really, well sort of, no . . . I guess."

"Hmmm . . ." Cole laughed. "Let me think that answer over while I drink my beer. But I heard a *no* in there somewhere, so I'll keep my hopes up."

"Okay." God . . . Susan wanted the floor to swallow her up. Where was her wingwoman when she needed her?

Cole took a drink from his longneck bottle but then turned his attention back to her a moment later. "Wait, I remember you from my senior English class." He put his hand to the side of his mouth. "Don't judge me but I might have copied some answers here and there. I wasn't much on required reading."

Susan had to laugh and found herself relaxing just a little bit.

"Yeah." Cole nodded slowly. "I also remember you were super pretty but so shy."

Susan was startled by his statement. She'd never considered herself pretty and she certainly didn't think that boys in school had given her a second look.

"You're even prettier now, Susan."

"Oh . . ." Okay, so he was flirting. "Thank you." She averted her gaze and took a sip of her wine, surprised that her stutter didn't kick in.

"And still shy, but it's refreshingly sweet."

"Not as much as I once was. Running Rhyme and Reason has brought me out of my shell. I have to deal with the public."

"Makes sense. You could sell me anything."

"Well then you have to stop in."

Cole chuckled. "Damn you're cute. So who are you sort of, kinda, maybe dating, if you don't mind me asking? A local guy? Some lucky guy that I know?"

"Me."

Susan almost fell off her chair when she realized that Danny was suddenly standing by her side. "Where did you come from?" Her heart did a little tap dance in her chest. He looked so sexy in jeans and a leather bomber jacket.

"I just got here." Danny pointed to the door behind him. "You were talking so you didn't see me approach. I knew you were coming here tonight and I wanted to buy you a drink, if that's okay?" He looked at Cole. "Hey, what's up, Cole? Haven't seen you at the brewery in a few weeks." His tone was friendly but Susan sensed a little bit of tension.

"I've been busy doing some private coaching. This is my last season coaching at Cricket Creek. I'm going to open a private personal training school for kids. I know I can get some Cricket Creek Cougars to work with baseball players during the off season. And I know lots of basketball players."

"Wow, that's a great idea." Danny kept the friendly tone but took a step closer to Susan. "I'll help spread the word for you when you get the idea off the ground."

"Thanks, Danny." He looked at Susan. "Sorry, was I hitting on your girl?"

Susan waited for Danny to correct Cole about her being his girl but he draped his arm over her shoulders. Susan caught a whiff of leather and spicy aftershave and fought the urge to snuggle closer. "No harm. Can't say that I blame you. Susan, do you mind if I take the seat beside you until Betsy arrives?"

"Hey, I'll let you two lovebirds chat," Cole said and then leaned over. "Danny, it was good to see you. I'll pop in the brewery sometime soon."

"Thanks, man. Sounds good."

"And Susan, I'll do some Christmas shopping at Rhyme and Reason."

"Thanks, Cole." She gave him a warm smile.

"Have a seat, Danny." Susan pointed to the empty stool. She felt a tingle of awareness when he scooted next to her. Cole was charming and good-looking but didn't come close to making her feel like she did with Danny.

"I hope you don't mind that I took it upon myself to stop in here tonight. I just couldn't resist seeing you again. But I don't want to interfere with your evening out." He took off his jacket and draped it over the back of his barstool. "I shouldn't have been so . . . possessive. I hope you're not angry."

"No, I'm flattered." Was he jealous?

"Good." He gave a warm smile that made her want to lean over and kiss him. But then again everything made her want to kiss him. "You okay on your wine?"

Susan nodded. They were so close at the crowded bar that her arm pressed against his.

Danny ordered a glass of Merlot.

"I didn't realize you liked wine."

"There's a lot you don't know about me . . . yet." Danny lifted his glass toward hers.

Susan picked up her glass and tapped it to his.

"To getting to know you better."

"Cheers." Susan took a sip of the cold Riesling and felt a heady rush that had nothing to do with the alcohol. She gave Danny a smile that she knew was less shy. She realized now how silly it had been to avoid him for so long.

"You look absolutely gorgeous, by the way."

"Thank you, Danny." Instead of dipping her head in the bashful way she would have done in the past, she looked into his eyes. "It's been fun ditching the sweaters."

"Well, like I said, I think you look adorable in them. Just be careful not to get stuck to a tree."

Susan laughed. "Oh boy, that was some situation," she said. "Thank you for saving me . . . and for not taking pictures."

"I'll come to your rescue any time of the day or night." He took a sip from his glass and then tilted his head at her, staring.

"What? Do I have a wine mustache?"

"I don't think so." He ran his finger above her upper lip. "It is a bit damp."

"That's why I stick to white wine."

Danny laughed. Leaning close to her ear he said, "I have a confession to make."

Susan raised her eyebrows. "Really?" Her heart thumped in anticipation.

"I wanted to see you . . . but I also knew guys would be all over you and . . ." He shrugged and gave her a rather sheepish look. "I couldn't get that off my mind. I have no right but like I already confessed, I'm feeling a little possessive." The low timbre of his voice made a hot shiver travel down her spine.

"Well then, I'll confess that I'm glad you're here. I would have asked you to come but I didn't want to appear too eager. I don't know the rules of dating."

"How about we make our own rules?"

"I like that suggestion," she said, feeling a rush of excitement. "And what are they?"

"We can make them up as we go, starting with you can call me or invite me to anything. And I want you to appear eager. It's good for my ego."

Susan laughed. "Easy enough."

"Your turn."

"Hmm . . ." She took a sip of wine and then looked at him. "Do you have a Christmas tree?"

"Ah, no." He winced.

"I'd like to put one up with you. I'll provide the ornaments and we'll string popcorn."

"That's not a rule."

"A request, then."

"Okay, when?"

"How about this weekend? Betsy's daughter is going to help out at the shop so I have more free time to enjoy the holidays."

"I bartend at the brewery on Saturday night, so how about Saturday afternoon if you can get away? I know you have the Christmas Walk on Sunday evening, right?"

"Yes. I hope you'll stop by. We'll have cookies and mulled cider."

"I'll be there for sure."

"Saturday afternoon should work fine," she said, trying to keep the breathlessness out of her voice. "I'll have to let you know for sure, though."

"We can chop a tree down together."

"That sounds fun!" She pictured them in the snow-covered woods walking hand in hand, laughing while searching for the perfect tree. Picture postcard romantic . . .

"Do you think Betsy is going to show up?" Danny asked.

Susan rolled her eyes. "She's always late but I thought John would already be here by now."

"Maybe they're together."

"I should check my phone. I might have missed a message." She reached in her purse and nodded. "I did miss a message. Oh wow, she said Aubrey surprised her by just arriving so she's going to spend the evening with her if I don't mind flying solo."

"Well, you're not solo, if that's okay."

"Perfectly," Susan said and texted Betsy back. "She said that she told John too." Susan glanced at Danny. "Hmm, but she wants to know if he's here anyway." She lifted one shoulder playfully.

"Interesting. What do you think?"

"That she's such a cool lady. I really enjoy working with her and we've become friends. I think she and John would make a really cute couple."

"I don't see what's holding them back."

Susan didn't want to divulge too much information. "Betsy's been hurt in the past, so it's hard for her to give someone her complete trust."

"Makes sense." Danny nodded and then took a sip of his wine. "My friend Avery Dean went through a painful breakup and it took him a long time to get over it."

"I remember Avery. He dated Ashley Montgomery." Ashley was a queen bee and never gave Susan the time of day. Susan had always thought that Avery was way too nice for Ashley. "I was floored when I heard they ended their engagement. But he and his wife Sophia came into the shop not too long ago. They're just adorable and Avery seems very happy."

"He is, not that I get to see him very much. Everybody is too busy to get together. Sometimes I miss the old days," he said and signaled the server for another round.

"My good old days were pretty low-key," Susan said. "I'm having more fun now than when I was a teenager."

"Maybe I just need to grow up," he said with a grin, but Susan noticed something a little bit sad about his admission. "Mattie and Mason both have a family and a career. I guess I need to get on the stick." The grin remained but he seemed serious.

"Given the chance, what would you like to do?"

"Good question," he said. Susan had the feeling that he knew but was reluctant to divulge it to her. Instead he offered her the small bowl of pub mix.

"Thanks." She dipped her fingers into the bowl, searching for the sesame sticks.

"Would you like something to eat?"

"Just something to nibble on would be nice. I was going to have the antipasto platter with Betsy. Not too heavy since we indulged in the fried foods last night."

"Sounds really good to me," Danny said and placed the order.

"Are you sure?"

Danny smiled. "I guess you think I only eat wings, burgers, and pizza?"

"No, but the selections on the antipasto platter are pretty intense in flavor. They go so well with wine."

"Well, I helped Mason with the menu at Broomstick Brewery. There are certain foods that pair well with different ales, just like with wine. Craft beer drinkers have a very discerning palate."

"I never thought of that."

"Yes, the menu at the brewery has suggestions of

what ale to drink with some of the food. I'll have to take you there soon. Hey, or if you'd like to come by Saturday night after our tree adventure, I'll try to knock off early and we can hang out."

"Oh . . . maybe." Susan wished that she had a group of girlfriends she could call to go out with her. Then she could swing by the brewery, get all giggly, and flirt with Danny.

"Hey, it's cool if you have plans."

"I don't . . . Wow, that sounds lame to admit I'm free on a Saturday night." She accepted a small plate and linen-wrapped silverware from the server.

"There's nothing lame about honesty. What do you usually do on a Saturday night?"

"Work on something crafty or do inventory in the shop after hours. Later I'll read, maybe watch a movie or a ballgame. Sometimes I visit my parents out on the farm and stay for the weekend, doing some canning or gardening in the summer. During the day I putter around at estate or garage sales for items to repurpose. Are you sleeping yet?"

Danny shifted so the server could place the platter on the bar in front of them. "Sounds to me like you've got a lot of interests. And none of it sounds the least bit boring or lame."

"And I think you're being very kind but that's okay." Susan put a few olives, salami, cheese, and crackers on her plate.

"You think so? Let's see . . . Well, I love woodworking, so I'm crafty. Check. I also like to read and often get books from Mattie's bookstore. I like mysteries, crime, and sometimes horror when I'm in the mood. Check again. I'm a big movie buff and of course I love sports. So double check. I'm an outdoors kinda guy, so gardening or hiking or just about anything on your farm would be up my alley too. Check. I don't go to many estate sales but I think it would be a lot of fun." He gave her a smug smile and then popped a cherry tomato in his mouth. She watched him, wondering how chewing could be so sexy.

"So, I'm not as boring as I think I am?"

Danny put some crusty bread in the dipping oil and handed it to her. "I don't think you're boring at all."

Susan took a bite of the delicious bread and felt a bit of the oil run down her chin. She laughed and dabbed at the oil with her napkin. "I told you that you can't take me anywhere."

"And you know how I felt about that. Hot air balloon here we come. And I'm going to get you out on the water come springtime."

"I'm a pretty strong swimmer. We have a nice-sized pond on the farm. But I haven't been around boats much."

"I'll teach you everything you need to know. And I always insist on life jackets." He grinned. "Then I'll tug you around on a tube pulled by my cabin cruiser."

"Slowly, of course."

"Of course," he responded in a tone that said he was lying.

"Sounds like fun," she said, although her heart pounded at the thought. When was the last time she'd done something so carefree and exciting? Um, that would be . . . never.

"I promise you that it will be, so put tubing on your miles-long bucket list."

"Will do." What would it feel like to be flying across the water on a sun-filled day? Susan reached for a slice of rolled-up salami, thinking that if they were still together in the spring, by then Danny Mayfield would officially be her boyfriend. *Holy cow . . .*

"What are you thinking?"

Susan played with the cocktail napkin. "That life is kinda crazy. Random. Do you agree?"

15

The Yellow Brick Road

"No." DANNY SHOOK HIS HEAD FIRMLY. "NOT AT ALL." He swiveled in his stool and leaned one elbow onto the edge of the bar. "I think that everything happens for a reason. Sometimes we're just too preoccupied to know what the reason is and totally miss it. Or it takes looking back to see what the future should bring." He took a sip of his Merlot and waited for Susan to respond but she frowned as she thought his statement over. He didn't usually have such serious conversations with anyone other than family, and that was usually about their issues and not his own, but he felt at ease with Susan.

"Give me an example," she said.

"Okay." Danny nodded toward the window. "Hey, our table just opened up. You get our drinks and I'll bring our tray after I settle up with the bartender."

Susan draped their coats over her arm and picked up the wineglasses. "I'll meet you there."

After paying the bar tab Danny joined Susan in the more secluded spot. "I love that sweet smile of yours. Hope it's just for me."

"It is." She made a sweeping gesture with her palms up. "It's for calling this table ours."

"It just sort of came out of my mouth. I hope you don't think I'm being too forward. I show up here . . . chase guys away." He shook his head. "I know I need to slow my roll but my brain won't listen." He speared a cube of cheddar cheese with a red-tailed toothpick. "I need to fill my mouth with food and keep quiet." He laughed to let her know he was joking.

"Oh no you don't. I want to hear some examples of why you think things happen for a reason, and aren't just random."

Danny swallowed the cheese and then put more food on his plate. "Mattie and Garret Ruleman are a prime example. Mattie is the middle sister so Mason and I were totally protective of her but we also gave her a rough time . . . always teasing her, making her into a tomboy. She had this thing for my friend Colby and asked Garret Ruleman to help make her more feminine. Since his mom is a famous fashion model, she thought he could help her with clothes and pointers on makeup."

"And instead of her ending up with Colby, *they* fell in love." Susan smiled. "Now that's seriously romantic."

Danny leaned forward. "Crazy? Yes. Random?" Danny shrugged. "I personally think it was meant to be."

Susan lifted one shoulder and then slowly swiped a celery stick through artichoke dip.

"When Garret left for London," he continued, "my little sister, who had never been out of the country, flew all by herself across the pond to England so she could be with him."

"Ah, so she made it happen, then."

"No doubt." Danny tapped his chest. "But it was because she listened to her heart and went after what mattered most to her. Like I said, I think some things are meant to be but only if you listen closely. Am I changing your opinion yet?"

"Yes, but go on because I just love listening to you, especially when you get so passionate."

"You bring it out in me. I'm usually way more laid-back but you're so easy to talk to."

"Tell me some more meant-to-be stories in your family," she said.

"There seems to be a lot of that sort of thing in Cricket Creek, and not just with the Mayfields."

"I guess we're just a romantic town."

Danny grinned. "Let's see. Well, Mason met Grace Gordon when she got lost trying to find the Walking on Sunshine Bistro. She got caught in a thunderstorm and then ran for cover into the building that's now Broomstick Brewery. Random?"

"They're married and have a baby now."

"I rest my case." Leaning back, Danny raised his palms upward.

"Well . . ." Susan licked dip from her bottom lip. "If things are simply meant to be, then why don't they always work out?"

"Mistakes along the way." He gave her a wry smile. "And to teach us to appreciate when the right things come along."

"Are you talking from experience?" Susan asked softly.

The compassion in her eyes told him what a sweet, caring person she was and he reached over and took her hand. "No, I'm still trying to find some direction in my own life."

"I think we all are. Life is a journey, right? There's bound to be bumps along the way."

"I don't mind mistakes. We all make them and learn from them." He chuckled. "My mother always said that I learned the hard way. I just don't want to experience regret." He wasn't quite sure why he was going down this path but for some reason being around Susan made him want to open up and talk about his life. She was the kind of girl he could see himself being with for the long haul, but how could he think about a serious relationship when he didn't have his shit together? And yet it felt so right being with her, telling her these things.

"Perhaps you should follow the yellow brick road?"

Danny held her gaze for a moment. "Yeah, only to discover what I wanted was already right here in front of me?"

"Precisely. Just watch out for the flying monkeys!" Susan shuddered. "They always scared me. And what was in that poppy field anyway?"

Danny laughed. He loved that having a serious conversation didn't squash the fun of the evening. "Yeah, they creep me out. Mattie used to cover her eyes and Mason would chase after her saying he was a flying monkey."

"That's so mean!" Susan said, but she giggled. "It had to be fun having siblings."

"Most of the time," he said and rubbed his thumb over her knuckles. Danny felt a sensual tug with every move she made. Something as simple as licking her bottom lip had him wanting to have her in his arms. He didn't know how much longer he could make it without kissing her again. "But yeah, I'm lucky that we're so close."

Susan sighed. "My parents wanted more children but it just didn't happen even though they tried. I think it's why they were so overprotective of me."

Danny felt a pang of sympathy.

"So, if you hear me talking to myself it's because I didn't have anyone else to talk to while I was a kid. Unless you count my faithful dog, Sammy, who is now in doggy heaven. It's a habit I can't seem to break."

"Don't." Danny chuckled. "I think it's cute. Of course, I think everything about you is cute." Even when she stuttered, but he noticed that she hadn't done that for the past two evenings with him. He hoped it was because she was feeling relaxed around him too.

The music started and so they stopped talking, focusing on listening while sipping wine and nibbling on the tray of food. But every time her knee bumped his or his hand brushed against hers, Danny felt the need to kiss her even more. After a couple of songs, he said, "Would you like anything else or would you like me to drive you home? I'm guessing you walked?"

Susan nodded. "I wasn't sure how much wine I'd have, so I wanted to be safe."

"I've only had two glasses and all of that food so I'm fine. It's pretty cold out there to walk back, even for a few blocks." Even though he'd be more than happy to hug her close and keep her warm.

"Yes, I found out how cold it was on the way here, especially in a dress, so you've come to my rescue once again, Danny Mayfield."

"Well, as a reward I hope you'll invite me inside for a little while since it's fairly early?"

"I was planning on it," she admitted with a shy smile. "I'm enjoying the evening too much to let it end."

"I agree." Danny scooted from the booth and helped Susan into her coat. When she lifted her hair from beneath her collar he caught a whiff of her floral fragrance and nearly groaned. He really needed to get out of the public eye so he could give her the long, hot kiss he'd been dreaming about all night long—no, make that all day long.

Danny was glad that the ride to her loft was short because being this close to her in the cab of his truck was driving him nuts.

"Thank you for picking up the tab tonight," Susan said when they stopped for a red light.

"My pleasure."

"I should have offered to pay." She shook her head. "I wasn't thinking."

"Well, I was sure thinking." He gave her a slow smile.

"About what?"

"Kissing you."

She looked down at her clasped hands. "Still . . . it wasn't a date."

"I wouldn't have let you pay the tab no matter what. That might be the modern thing to do but I won't ever allow it so don't even try."

Susan laughed. "That's so old-fashioned."

Danny shrugged. "I don't care. I believe in what I believe in. Now don't get me wrong, I think we're all on equal ground but my mother brought me up to be a gentleman. I know you can open your own door and buy your own food but I want to do it for you when you're with me. If that's okay?" He reached over and took her hand.

"I might fight you on the always paying for everything part." She smiled. "But I love it that you're a gentleman. My father is too."

He flashed her another smile. "Good."

"You can drive down the alley and park on the apron in the back," Susan said when they reached her building. "My car is in the detached garage."

"Okay. Oh, and if you ever need to pick something up for the shop that won't fit in your vehicle, let me know and I'll go get it in my truck."

"Thank you, Danny. That's so sweet of you."

"Another way to get to spend time with you," he admitted and was rewarded with a smile. "Wait and I'll come around to open your door."

"Okay."

Danny walked over to the side of the truck and opened the door. He put his hands around her waist and helped her out, even though she was tall enough for the big step down. "And please, no lifting stuff that you can't handle," he added with his hands still around her waist.

"Oh, I promise Betsy that all the time. The problem is that I overestimate my strength and usually the weight of whatever I'm lifting. And, well, I have a stubborn streak when it comes to doing things myself. It goes back to being an only child on a farm. I had to do lots of chores on my own so I had to find ways to get things done. But I'll try to behave."

"That's my girl." Danny smiled at her and couldn't resist a lingering kiss even before they got inside her place. "Finally," he said. "But well worth the wait."

"I've wanted you to do that all night long," Susan admitted with a laugh. "Oh look, we're steaming up the backyard." She pointed to the fog their breath was making in the cold air.

"We are!" Danny nodded his head and laughed with her. Then, grabbing Susan's hand, he walked over to the back entrance to her loft. "Let's get you inside where it's warm."

"Excellent idea."

Once they were in her apartment, Danny felt a little bit nervous. He helped her out of her coat and this time he couldn't resist brushing her hair to the side and giving the graceful nape of her neck a warm kiss. With a sigh, she tilted her head, giving him better access. "You smell so nice."

"Mm . . . thank you."

"And you taste as sweet as you smell."

Susan turned around and unzipped his bomber jacket for him. "And you smell yummy too . . . leather and spice. It drove me bananas all night long."

"Really?"

"Absolutely." She gave him a shy but oh so sexy smile and then surprised him when she put her palms on his shirt then slid her hands around his neck.

"Good, we're on the same page." Danny dipped his head and captured her mouth in a long, deep, delicious kiss. She pressed her body closer and delved her fingers into his hair. He knew it was too early in their relationship to be intimate, but it didn't *feel* early after all they'd talked about. Still, he knew he needed to keep his libido under control. His brain understood but his body sure as hell had different ideas.

Danny tried not to imagine what those long legs would feel like wrapped around him but his imagination had already run wild and never looked back. "Ah, Susan."

"What?" She gave him a dreamy smile.

Danny rubbed his thumb over her bottom lip. "I've never forgotten the first kiss we shared."

She lowered her gaze but then looked back at him. "Me neither. Danny, I owe you an apology for the way I avoided you for so long. I was simply embarrassed and . . ." She shook her head and sighed. "I don't know what else to say."

"Maybe we weren't meant to be together way back then. I was a little on the wild side and took too many things for granted."

"You were a typical teenager. I was not."

"Hey, I know. I understand. You were shy . . . unsure, isolated, but we're both different now." Danny paused, wanting her to get better insight into his life. He gently tilted her head up. "While I was away at college and Mason was on tour fishing, my dad tried to hold the marina together and it nearly killed him."

"Oh Danny . . ."

He nodded slowly, tucking a loose curl behind her ear.

"So you put your own life on hold."

"My family is my life, and I wanted to do anything I could to save our marina. Mason and Mattie did too." He blew out a sigh. "But they've managed to move on, while I'm still trying to figure my life out."

"You seem to have your act together to me," Susan said but then frowned. She smoothed her hands over his shirt, as if trying to gather her thoughts. "Perhaps . . . you do so much for others that it leaves too little time for you? Tonight you offered to pretty much be at my beck and call if I need items picked up or

moved. I get the impression you do that kind of thing
a lot."

Danny shrugged and then cupped her cheek, loving
the petal softness of her skin. "The offer stands."

"Thank you. I'll remember that. But Danny, you
run the marina, help out at the brewery and the bistro.
That's a lot for one person."

"Because I'm needed."

"But where's the time for you?" She gazed at him
with such caring and sincerity that his heart ached.

Danny took a step back and shoved his fingers
through his hair. "My family appreciates what I do.
They aren't taking advantage of me if that's what you
think. I help out because I want to."

"Oh I know that, Danny. Your mom and my mom
are still good friends even though your parents moved
to Florida. They've stayed in touch. So even though I
managed to avoid you, your name came up and your
mom spoke of you in glowing terms."

"They had to leave for my dad's health."

"I know that too. Trust me, I'm not being critical."

Danny nodded and cupped her chin. She was just
hitting too close to the bone. "I know. I don't think you
have it in you to be critical or pass judgment." He gave
her a reassuring smile. "Hey, I enjoy everything I do. I
wasn't complaining. I just find you easy to talk to and
I've felt a little bit restless lately."

Susan tilted her head to the side. "Because it's all in
the family but none of it is your passion . . . your creation."

"It's amazing how much you understand about me
in such a short period of time."

"Well, being quiet has made me quite the observer.
I've spent my life watching and listening. You want
something of your own but you don't know how to tell
your family."

He swallowed hard. "I just can't bail on them."

"I get that," she said gently and then seemed about

to say more but paused. "Can I get you something to drink?"

"A water would be great."

"Coming right up. Make yourself at home," she said and a moment later joined him on the sofa. She handed him the cold bottle and then sat down and toed off her shoes.

He looked down. Damn, she had cute feet.

"Oh, sorry, the first thing I do when I get home is kick off my shoes. I'd go barefooted all the time if I could." Her cheeks turned a little bit pink. "The problem is that I'm continually breaking my baby toes." She pointed to the left one, which was crooked. "I run into everything since I'm always moving things around. And I'm a light sleeper, so I get up in the dark and . . . Wow, I'm giving you way too much information. I never rattle on like this."

"I like hearing you rattle on. Keep going. Tell me more about how you started your business."

"You sure?"

"Positive." He enjoyed the soft, lilting timbre of her voice along with just a hint of the south.

After taking a swallow from her water bottle she rubbed her lips together and Danny had to concentrate on what she was saying and not on her mouth. "Telling my parents I wanted to leave the farm and live in town was super difficult. I helped out so much and they were so protective. But I'd tucked away money from selling refurbished and repurposed items from my Rhyme and Reason website and by taking my stuff to thrift stores that accepted items on consignment. By my mid-twenties I knew I had to get out on my own, and when a dear aunt of mine passed away, she left me a big chunk of money that gave me the freedom to buy this building." She looked skyward. "Thank you, Aunt Martha."

"Did your parents try to stop you?"

"Oh sure." Susan nodded emphatically. "Especially

at first. They wanted me to sock the money away and stay on the farm or build a house on the property and just do my website stuff but I wanted to do more. My mother said I could make enough money just 'tinkering around,' as she calls it."

"You tinker very well."

Susan chuckled. "I was so scared. But I took some business courses online and then just jumped right in. That was three years ago." Closing her eyes, she sucked in a breath. "I struggled at first but the shop is finally thriving this past year." She placed her hand on his knee but then quickly pulled it away. He wanted her to put her hand back. Damn, she was cute. "So, do you have something you'd like to do? You mentioned woodworking."

Danny looked over at the rocking chair he built and his heart thumped. "Oh, that's just a hobby," he said casually. but wondered why he didn't want to tell her more.

Susan nibbled on the inside of her lip. "Hobbies can grow into something bigger. Like Mason and his craft beer. Maybe you should think about it."

Danny thought about how Mason had almost lost his entire investment, until Grace Gordon came to his rescue and bailed him out. "It can be risky but you already know that." He scooted around to face her. "There's a reason I brought all of this up."

Susan looked at him with serious eyes. "Okay."

"I don't know that I'm where I want to be on a personal level and so I've avoided getting into a serious relationship." He gave her a small smile. "But you changed that."

"What are you saying?"

"I'm saying that ever since the day you fell into my arms I can't stop thinking about you. I know I'm moving fast, but well, I want us to be exclusive. Walking into Wine and Diner and seeing you with another guy made me realize that I want you to be my girl."

"I wasn't with another guy. Cole was just talking to me."

"I know, and I'll understand if you think I'm being too pushy asking you this so soon. And I wanted you to know that I'm not exactly where I want to be and I sometimes . . . struggle with it a little bit." He shrugged. "But I don't want to wait around until I think the time is right and run the risk of losing you. The truth of the matter is that I want to give what we obviously already have a shot at something more. So what do you say?"

"Yes," she answered softly. Susan swallowed hard and then gave him a sweet smile that trembled slightly at the corners. "I want to be your girlfriend, Danny."

"Ah . . . Susan, you just made my day." Danny pulled her close and kissed her tenderly. She parted her lips, offering him more, and so he deepened the kiss. When she slid her fingers into his hair, he gently lowered her onto the sofa. He loved the way her body felt pressed against his, the soft push of her breasts touching his chest and her long legs entwined with his. His mouth moved to her neck and he could feel the rapid beat of her pulse beneath his lips. With a sexy moan she snuggled closer, and he knew she could feel the evidence of how much he wanted her.

Needing to feel skin, Danny slid his hand beneath the hem of her lace dress. He inched his way up slowly, savoring the feel of her soft skin. He kissed her neck and then captured her mouth with a long, deep kiss. He pulled back and smiled. "You feel so amazing."

Susan answered with a breathy little sigh. And when he reached her thigh, she trembled and parted her legs ever so slightly. Danny could feel her heat and he knew she wanted him as much as he wanted her. His brain warned him to put on the brakes but when she started tugging his shirt from his pants, he simply had to experience having her hands on his body.

Danny hadn't been with a woman in a fairly long time but damn, he couldn't ever remember feeling this kind of hot-blooded desire, this kind of yearning. The feeling was a slow burn, a need that went beyond just sex. His mouth found her lips once more and he slowly ran the tip of his tongue over her bottom lip before sinking into the kiss. He wanted to explore every inch of her, taste her everywhere. And when his fingers brushed the silk of her panties she arched her hips, pressing against where he wanted her most. He pulled back and looked into her eyes.

"Danny . . ." she said in a low, sexy tone.

"Oh Susan . . ." Danny wanted her so much, but he inhaled a deep, shaky breath and placed his forehead against hers. "All I can say is . . . wow. My heart is pumping a million miles a minute and I want you more than I thought imaginable. And my imagination is pretty good. I'm not kidding."

"I know . . . me too, but . . . it's too soon."

"Yeah, you're right." Danny groaned. "I think I might whimper. Would that be weird?"

"Kinda." Susan laughed. "But I'll join you and we can be weird together," she said and then brushed a lock of hair from his forehead. "Thank you."

"For what, baby?"

"For knowing in the heat of the moment that this could have gone much further. Not every guy would have been okay with stopping."

Danny leaned back against the cushions and cupped her cheek in his hand. "This all started with a kiss ten years ago. I'm enjoying getting to know everything about you. I'm willing to wait until the time is right."

"Me too," she said, but she gave him a rather coy smile. "Even though I have to admit that the time was feeling pretty right."

Danny had to laugh. "You're something else."

"You mean that in a good way, right?"

"Absolutely, one hundred percent." Danny suddenly thought he should tell her that he'd made the rocking chair but he was afraid she'd encourage him to make woodworking more than just a hobby and he wasn't ready to make that leap just yet. "I know this is selfish but I'm glad that Aubrey came home early and gave us the opportunity to spend the evening together."

"Honesty is never selfish," she said. "And Betsy has been counting the days until her daughter came home, so it's all good."

Danny dipped his head and gave her a lingering kiss. "You're right, Suzy Q. It's all good and only going to get better."

16

Aubrey

"MOM, WHY ARE YOU LOOKING AT ME LIKE THAT?" Aubrey asked Betsy.

"Oh, sweet pea." Betsy reached across the kitchen table and put her hand over her daughter's hand. "I'm sorry I'm staring. I just can't believe you're really here." She tried not to get emotional but she felt her throat tighten. She took a drink of her sweet tea to hide her reaction to finally having her baby back home. She made a show of pinching herself. "Nope, I'm not dreaming."

"Mom, since when did you become such a softie?" Aubrey asked, but her smile trembled just enough to let Betsy know her nineteen-year-old daughter was more than a little glad to be home.

"Ever since you went away to college. And it doesn't help matters that I'm pre-menopausal. I get hot flashes, night sweats, and I cry at the drop of a hat. And you know I'm not a crier. I'm a tough old broad."

"Ha, you pretend to be a tough cookie. I know you better."

"Speaking of cookies, I bought some of those butter

cookies you love from Grammar's Bakery. Oh and the deli next door to Rhyme and Reason had some amazing desserts." She thought about the chocolate mousse and nearly groaned.

"No you didn't!" Aubrey groaned. "I'm trying not to gain the freshman fifteen. You know all I have to do is smell cookies and I gain weight. I don't have that raging high metabolism like you."

"Are you kidding me? In my opinion, one of the sexiest, most beautiful women to ever live was the one and only Marilyn Monroe, and she had curves, just like we're supposed to have." Betsy leaned over the breakfast table and cupped Aubrey's cheeks. "Could you possibly get any prettier?"

"Spoken like a true mother."

"Well, I've sure missed that pretty face, that's for sure."

"I've missed you too, Mom. I'm sorry I can't come home more often, but classes are hard and I have to keep my grade point average up to keep my scholarships."

"Oh Aubrey, I know. And I'm so proud of you."

"You've told me that a million times."

"Well, I'm going to tell you a million more. My, my, I just bet you have to swat the boys away like flies on butter." She made a shooing motion.

"Oh Mom . . ." Aubrey laughed but then shook her head. "I'm concentrating on my studies, just like in high school."

Betsy nodded her approval but she had to wonder if Aubrey's lack of interest in a serious relationship had anything to do with not having a father figure in her life. "Yeah, but you should at least date here and there. Have some fun too."

"Having a boyfriend would just complicate my life right now." She raised her eyebrows. "Not that there aren't plenty of hot guys on campus."

"I can only imagine." Aubrey had always been

oblivious to how pretty she was, and while Betsy liked that her daughter was modest rather than vain, she was a little bit afraid she wouldn't be able to handle the male attention from college boys. Coming from a small town meant she was a little bit sheltered. With long, strawberry blond hair, striking hazel eyes, and delicate facial features, she'd been turning heads for a few years. To make matters worse, she was long legged and curvy. But she played her looks down, wearing minimal makeup and pretty much living in jeans and sweatshirts rather than catering to the latest fashion trends. "I know you study your tail off but go to some basketball games and do some, you know, college stuff."

"Oh Mom, I will." Aubrey smiled. "Would you just look at you, all sassy with your auburn hair?" She gave her a little head bop. "I thought you were messing with me when you said you went red."

"Carrie Ann talked me into it."

"Right—nobody talks you into anything. You wanted to do it deep down or you wouldn't have. What made you do it?"

"Oh, I dunno." Betsy shrugged. "Mid-life crisis? Empty nest syndrome? Just plumb crazy?" She raised her index finger. "Wait, all of the above."

"Let's just go with plumb crazy." Aubrey tipped her head back and laughed. "Oh Mom, I really missed you. And I do have to say the deep auburn agrees with you. Really brings out your eyes. People are going to think we're sisters."

"Oh, go on with you."

"You look amazing."

"You think so?" Betsy reached up and ran her fingers through her hair. "I always did have a bit of a red tint, especially when I was little. Guess that's where you got the strawberry blond. Nobody would ever think a color that pretty was natural." She shook her head slowly. "Mercy, you are a sight for sore eyes. I just want to squeeze you until your head pops off."

Aubrey laughed but then said, "I knew that me leaving was going to be hard on you."

"Yeah, it hit me way more than I let on."

"Probably because we're such a good team."

"That we are," Betsy said, trying to hold back tears. Aubrey was the center of her world. The first day she'd dropped her off at kindergarten was bad enough, but when Betsy had dropped her daughter off at the University of Kentucky and set her up in her tiny dorm room, it had been by far the hardest day of her life. She'd sobbed all the way back to Cricket Creek.

"I know I acted all big and bad, but the first month was homesick city," Aubrey said. "I almost bailed and came home more than once."

"Oh Aubrey." Betsy put her palms on the table and leaned forward. "Why didn't you tell me?" She imagined Aubrey huddled in that damned small bed in a dorm room she shared with a complete stranger. "You should have come home for fall break."

"I needed to stay on task and power through. You taught me well. You always preached when the going gets tough, the tough get going."

"Oh Aubrey, I knew I should have come for a visit. I wanted to and you stopped me."

"Mom, you work most Saturdays and it's a long drive to Lexington."

"Susan would have given me the time off."

"I know, but I needed to get settled and get over my separation anxiety. Coming home would have made it worse." Aubrey gave her a long look and then chuckled. "You would have seen my struggle and, like, enrolled in school with me or something crazy like that."

"Hey, that's a great idea! And what a great reality show. We could become famous."

Aubrey looked so horrified at the suggestion that Betsy had to laugh. "Just kidding. Well sort of, anyway. At least about the reality show part. Oh, sugar, are you doing okay now?"

"Yeah, don't worry. I've got this." She took a swig of sweet tea. "My roommate Jamie is more of a party girl and likes to play her music loud but I like to study at the library anyway. It's all cool," Aubrey said, and Betsy could tell by her genuine smile that she was doing just fine. "And I do hang out with Macy and Cassie."

"Oh, I miss those girls too. The three of you always got along so well. Glad to hear it," Betsy said. She told herself not to think about Aubrey going back to school but to concentrate on the fact that she was here for three weeks. "And I guess it would have been sad to think you didn't miss me."

"I missed you more than you can imagine."

"Well, I've missed your cooking, even though I've gotten better."

Aubrey laughed.

"We'll do some cooking together. I'll make some cookies while you're here and all of your other favorites too. Plus, we can go to Wine and Diner and River Row Pizza. Grab some wings at Sully's some evening." She thought about mentioning Ham Good Deli but didn't.

"I feel my butt expanding each time you mention all of those restaurants." Aubrey smiled. "Seeing Main Street all decked out for Christmas made me realize how much I love this little town."

Betsy let out a breath of relief. "I was afraid that living in Lexington might give you other ideas. I hope you want to come back to Cricket Creek after you graduate." And she sure hoped Aubrey didn't meet some boy from somewhere else and want to move away.

"Mom . . . get that worried look off your face."

"Worry is my middle name."

"I happen to know it's Gertrude and that Grandma wanted that to be my name."

"You could have pulled off the name Trudy."

"Well, I love Aubrey."

"Ah, from the song by one of my all-time favorite

groups, Bread." Betsy chuckled. "Not a very ordinary girl or name," she sang. "Damn I'm old."

"No, you are *not* old. And I love my middle name, Elizabeth, too." Aubrey tilted her head and smiled. "After you. Pretty name, but I have to say that you are totally a Betsy. Elizabeth is too formal."

"Yeah, funny how names are like that. I knew when I looked down at your pretty face and rosebud mouth that you were going to be unique and needed a special name to go with it."

"Well, I love it."

"Your grandmother was so pissed at me for not naming you after her." Betsy chuckled, but she was glad she'd found the courage to stand up to her mother.

"Yeah, Grandma likes things her own way, that's for sure. But I guess she didn't have it easy," Aubrey said quietly.

"I know she didn't. I try to make her smile, even though it's a tough task." It was sad that the only relative in Aubrey's life had such a bitter attitude. Having lost control of her own life, Gladys Gunther liked to rule Betsy's every move, becoming an overbearing, angry woman as the years passed. Getting pregnant with Aubrey had made her mother livid, one of the reasons Betsy opted to get married and get out of the house . . . a decision she was glad she made even though it didn't work out, because it forced her to earn her own way and make her own choices. When she found out she was going to have a baby, Betsy had made a promise to herself that she wouldn't become like her mother, and had made sure that Aubrey had a life filled with love and laughter.

Aubrey took another swig of her tea. "I don't know why, but nobody can make sweet tea as good as you."

"Made with love."

Aubrey laughed. "Ah, the secret ingredient."

"Always."

"Hey, it's the holidays!" Aubrey raised both arms in

the air. "Let's get our Christmas on! It's my favorite time of the year. The dusting of snow outside is so pretty. Main Street looks like the inside of a snow globe."

"You got it, girl." Betsy gave Aubrey a wistful smile.

"What?"

"I was just telling Susan that I always felt like I couldn't give you enough for Christmas," Betsy said, but when Aubrey's face fell she wished she'd kept her mouth shut. "Not that you ever complained."

"Mom, are you kidding? I was always super happy with my gifts. And I loved baking cut-out cookies and making candy. My memories of the holidays are the best. I wouldn't trade them for the latest toy craze. Seriously."

"Oh, it does my heart good to hear you say that."

"I knew how hard you worked. You've always been a good example."

"I sure did my best." Betsy felt her eyes mist over and then cleared her throat. "By the way, Susan wants you to work at Rhyme and Reason while you're on break if you want to."

"Sweet, I could use the cash. My cost of living grant doesn't include Christmas gifts."

"I thought you'd be interested. I'm sure you can work there during summer break too."

"I'm so glad you like working there, Mom. Susan is so nice."

"She's helped me on days that I was so bummed about missing you."

Aubrey twirled her hair around her finger, nibbling on her bottom lip while looking at Betsy.

"What? Are you rethinking your opinion of my new do?"

"Mmmm . . . no, but there is something somehow different about you, though. More than just the hair." She tapped her cheek. "It's a kind of . . . I don't know . . . a glow or something? Does that sound weird?"

"Oh, I don't know . . ." Betsy felt heat creep into her cheeks. Ever since the kiss with John, she'd somehow felt more alive, and if she was honest she'd been excited to have plans to see him at Wine and Diner, not that she would ever let anyone come between her and her daughter. "Just having you home makes me glow."

"If you say so." Aubrey chuckled but didn't seem all that convinced. They knew each other inside out, so keeping something from her wasn't going to be easy, and yet Betsy didn't know how to approach the subject.

"I do." Still, no matter how hard she tried, she couldn't stop thinking about John. It was to the point where she was beginning to think she regretted not giving the attraction between them a fair shot at something more, in spite of her fear of getting hurt. Of course, the whole he's brilliant thing was a bit intimidating as well. Damn, why hadn't she applied herself more in school? But college hadn't been an option since they didn't have the money and Betsy had no clue what she would have studied anyway. While she and Aubrey shared most things in their lives, she didn't know how to approach the subject of John Clark. And yet she wanted her daughter's opinion.

"Mom, okay, seriously, what aren't you telling me?"

"Why would you ask such a thing?" She tried to appear innocent.

"You just zoned out and had this faraway, dreamy look on your face."

"Aubrey, it's just having my baby back home," Betsy said, feeling a little stab of guilt that she didn't confide in her daughter. "And hey, it's the holidays!"

"Well, like I said, you look really cute. I can tell you even took pains with your makeup."

Betsy lifted her chin. "Well, thank you. I did go up to Violet's Vintage Clothing with Susan and picked out some outfits for the holidays. Susan was on an emergency shopping spree for her date with Danny Mayfield."

"You mentioned they had dinner together. I knew

Danny from when I would hang out at the marina with friends during the summer. He seemed super nice. And even though he was older, all of us girls thought he was so hot." She fanned her face. "We all crushed on him all summer long. And he was always showing off, doing tricks on his water skis and his Wave-Runner."

"Yeah, he sure is a looker, that one."

"Susan is such a sweetie. I can't believe she's still single. What's wrong with the guys in this town? But you know, I could totally see her and Danny as a couple."

"Me too . . ."

"Why do I hear a *but* in your tone?" Aubrey asked.

Betsy shrugged and poured more tea from the pitcher. "Susan is just so shy. Owning her shop has helped her to open up more, though. She's getting better and better at dealing with customers. I've noticed a big change this past year."

"Well, I'm sure you keep things lively and have her in stitches. Hiring you was genius on her part."

"After teaching teenagers how to drive, working at Rhyme and Reason is a walk in the park. But you're right, though. Susan's got a lovely personality and an unexpectedly great sense of humor." She pointed a finger at Aubrey. "And like you, she doesn't know how doggone gorgeous she is."

"Oh Mom . . ."

"Just sayin'." She gave Aubrey's hand a pat.

"I think that someone outgoing like Danny could bring Susan out of her shell even more. Like really blossom, you know?" Betsy said.

"I hope so." Aubrey looked down at her tall glass of tea and stirred the ice around with her straw.

After a few moments Betsy said, "Okay, now I can tell that there is something on *your* mind."

Aubrey pressed her lips together, something she always did when she was deep in thought. "Well . . . yeah."

Betsy felt a little flash of fear. "What is it, sugar?"

After drumming her fingertips on the table for a few seconds she said, "This is kinda weird for me to talk about with you."

"You can tell me or ask me anything. You know that."

"I know," Aubrey said but still hesitated.

"Is . . . is it about sex?" For some reason Betsy felt the need to whisper. She was hardly an expert about sex these days but she'd give it a shot.

"Oh Mom. We've had the sex talk," Aubrey said, complete with air quotes. "Please."

Betsy exhaled a sigh of relief.

"Okay . . . here goes." Aubrey inhaled a deep breath. "You devoted your life to giving me everything I ever needed."

"Of course." Betsy waited, wondering where this could be going.

"I think you should maybe consider . . . well . . ."

"Spit it out, girlie."

"Dating."

"Really?" Betsy felt her eyes widen. She could have been knocked over with a feather. Of all things, Betsy didn't think that suggestion would come out of her daughter's mouth. "You don't say . . ." she murmured, wondering if the timing of this conversation was good or bad.

"Well, sure, why not?" Aubrey extended her palms toward Betsy. "Just look at you. Not only are you super pretty, but you have a lot to bring to the table. You're so much fun to be around, Mom. All the kids in high school loved you. Well, unless you failed them," she added with a laugh. "Then, not so much."

"So, you think I'm a good catch, huh?" Betsy had never thought of herself that way. Standing on the front porch with a baby on her hip while watching her husband speeding away in a cloud of dust had created a lasting impression.

"No doubt, Mom. When it comes to knowing your worth, you are a million times worse than me. To answer your question, yes, you're quite the catch."

"Really?"

"Absolutely!" Aubrey nodded emphatically and put her index finger to her pinkie. "Okay, your house and car are paid off. You've got your pension from the school system and a cool job, so you're financially sound and happy. Look, I don't mean you need a guy to lean on. You taught me better than that." She lifted one shoulder. "But why not get out there and have some fun? Weren't you just preaching the same thing to me?"

"Well yeah, but—" Betsy thought of John.

"But what, Mom?"

"Well . . ." This was her invitation to tell Aubrey about John. As mother and daughter they'd shared just about everything, but this was something Betsy didn't know how to approach. "I don't know." She nibbled on the inside of her cheek.

"Okay . . ." Aubrey tucked a lock of hair behind her ear and scooted forward. "Just hear me out."

"I'm all ears, sweet pea." Betsy nodded, wondering again what this was leading up to.

"Macy Morgan and I were talking about how maybe you and her dad might want to go out to dinner or something."

Betsy's heart thudded in surprise. "Oh . . . Grady?"

"Yeah, he's been divorced for a few years, and now that Macy is off to school he's been pretty lonely. He's super nice and always making me crack up. I think you two should start talking."

"Talking?"

"Yeah, you know, like pre-dating or whatever you used to call it." She blew out a breath. "So, what do you think?"

"I'm curious, did Grady show interest, or is this something you and Macy have cooked up? I remember you two wanting to be sisters."

"Mom! Seriously?"

Betsy shrugged. "I don't know; this is sort of out of the blue."

"Mr. Morgan—well, he insisted that I call him Grady—came to Lexington a couple of weeks ago and took us girls out to dinner. He asked about you and . . ." Aubrey shrugged. "We could tell that he wanted us to pave the way for asking you out. At first Macy and I were kind of like, super awkward about it, but the more we talked about it, the more it makes perfect sense."

Betsy nodded slowly, trying to figure out what to say. Grady was a great guy. He'd been a year ahead of Betsy in high school, athletic and popular. He'd met Melanie, his ex-wife, while in college and word was that they'd simply grown apart, wanting different things out of life. She'd seen Grady out and about Cricket Creek and they'd made small talk. Come to think of it, he might have flirted a little bit when she'd run into him at Sully's Tavern one night.

"So, are you open to it?" Aubrey persisted.

"Oh, I don't know. This is rather unexpected," Betsy said, but Aubrey seemed so excited about the prospect that it was hard for Betsy to deny her a positive response.

Aubrey took a sip of her tea. "I know." She reached over and squeezed Betsy's hand. "Mom, like I said, you've devoted your life to me and now it's time you do something for yourself. I like Grady so much and I can picture you two having a blast together. And he mentioned you knew each other from high school and he's seen you recently."

"He was a year older but we ran around in the same crowd. I lost touch when he went away to college, and then he married Melanie." Betsy lifted one shoulder.

"Macy said her parents are on friendly terms. Her mom started dating a year ago and it's kind of serious, so there won't be any weirdness there."

"Yes, I know she's dating Tom Watson." Betsy nodded slowly. "News travels quickly in Cricket Creek."

Aubrey laughed. "Oh, I know." She bit her bottom lip and waited for Betsy to answer. "So? Come on, Mom . . . give it a shot, anyway. I mean, what is there to lose?"

John popped into her mind. "I . . . I don't know." Betsy took a drink of her tea to stall, and then stirred the straw around. Grady owned his own lawn care service and plowed snow in the winter. Betsy had watched him play softball in the men's league last summer and she remembered thinking he was still attractive. So why didn't the thought of going out on a date with a handsome, single man, who just happened to be her daughter's friend's dad, thrill her to no end? Grady was the kind of guy whom she would fit in with and feel comfortable around, unlike some highfalutin' Harvard-educated lawyer.

Maybe if she went out with Grady, she would get John Clark out of her system. Betsy nodded slowly, wondering if kissing Grady would feel just as exciting as kissing John Clark . . . maybe even more so.

"Yes!" Aubrey said and did a fist pump.

Oh no, Aubrey had taken her nod to be a yes. "I . . ."

"I can't wait to tell Macy! Ahhh! This is so cool. I mean, what if you guys really hit it off? Wouldn't that be super awesome?"

"Aubrey, don't start planning the wedding."

"Oh, I'm not," Aubrey said, but it was clear she could barely contain her excitement. She was literally bouncing around in her chair. "Is it okay if I text Macy right now?"

When Betsy nodded Aubrey jumped up and gave her a huge hug.

"I mean, no pressure or anything," Aubrey said, but then did a little twirl that reminded Betsy of when Aubrey was a little girl. She twirled when she got excited and watching her do so now brought a huge lump to her throat. "But Grady's a really cool dude. Okay, I'm going up to my room to call Macy. This is too big for a text."

"Okay, take your time." Betsy forced a smile. But as soon as Aubrey was out of the room, she cradled her head in her hands. She knew she shouldn't feel guilty about going out on a date with Grady Morgan. She wasn't under any obligation to John Clark. *In fact, this could be a good thing*, she thought and raised her head.

So then, why did she feel so rotten?

17

Over the Moon

SUSAN PUT THE FINISHING TOUCHES ON A DISPLAY OF handmade Christmas stockings and then glanced around the shop for Betsy. The feisty redhead had been acting rather odd all morning long. As a matter of fact, Betsy had been behaving strangely ever since she'd come back from the deli with the wrong order, so her mood must have something to do with John. When Susan tried to get some answers out of her she avoided questions and tried to pretend everything was okay, but Susan knew her friend way better than that.

Susan's stomach rumbled, letting her know it was time for lunch, but rather than get her order wrong again, she decided to take matters into her own hands and go to Ham Good Deli on her own. She went in search of Betsy to get her order and finally spotted her red head above a shelf in the Sock It to Me area of the shop. "There you are. What are you doing hiding back here?"

"I was arranging the sock snowmen that a customer had strewn all over the place. We could use a few more. Do you need me up front?"

"No, I just rang a few people up earlier. The Christmas cookie mason jars are flying off the shelf and so are the handmade scarves. I just finished up the display of stockings and I asked my mother to make a few more rugs in red and green when she gets the chance. I just don't have the extra time," Susan said, thinking that any extra time she had would hopefully be spent with Danny.

"The ornaments from Whisper's Edge are doing well too. I hid the funny ones at the back of the tree but they're selling too," Susan said with a laugh.

"Good! I'll call Savannah and get the ball rolling for the residents to make more."

"Oh, Savannah's one of my favorite people," Susan said. "I heard that the house Tristan built for her is flat-out amazing. When they were in here a couple of weeks ago I could just tell they adore each other." Susan remembered feeling a bit envious while Savannah and Tristan strolled hand in hand through the shop, heads bent together, laughing and clearly so into each other.

"Savannah and Tristan sure were a Cinderella story," Betsy agreed.

"No doubt," Susan said with a nod. She knew that Savannah had been raised in foster care and was homeless when she came to Cricket Creek. She landed a job at the local retirement community and residents treated her like family. Tristan was going to plow down Whisper's Edge and put in a fancy marina and hotel until he fell for Savannah and couldn't go through with it. She pointed at Betsy. "Tristan was a high-powered city lawyer. See where I'm going with this?"

"Yeah, but . . ." Betsy said, frowning.

"There's no such word as *yeah-but* and yet you say it all the time."

Betsy laughed. "I suppose I do."

"Would you mind giving Aubrey a call to give her the list of ingredients for the mulled cider?" Susan asked. "And we need our luminaria bags, sand, and tea lights too. I'll be glad to pay Aubrey for her time."

"You don't need to do that. She loves to shop."

"I insist. I really can't spare you this afternoon and I want to get everything ready for the Christmas Walk this Sunday."

"Okay," Betsy said, but seemed preoccupied.

Susan stood there for a moment, nibbling on the inside of her cheek. "Betsy, is there something wrong? Everything okay with Aubrey?"

"Oh Aubrey is fine and dandy. She should be stopping over here later in the afternoon. She had a mountain of dirty clothes to wash and I let her sleep in this morning." Betsy smiled softly. "Seeing her in her bed all snuggled up was just so wonderful."

"So then why are you acting so strange?"

"Um, maybe because I am strange?"

Susan felt the urge to tap her foot. "I'm not trying to pry but . . . okay I am trying to pry. Something's bothering you. Care to tell me before I go crazy with worry?"

"Well . . ." Betsy rolled her eyes. "I've got myself in a bit of a pickle."

"Okay, hold that thought. I'm going to put a sign on the front door saying we'll be back in thirty minutes. I can tell this needs my full attention. I'll meet you in the break room."

Susan hurried over and arranged the hands on the sign's miniature clock and then headed for the break room. "On second thought, let's go upstairs. I have some spinach salad mix we can share if you like."

"Oh good. I really don't want to go over to the deli today."

"I had a pretty good idea you were going to say that." Susan motioned for the back stairs. "Come on up."

Betsy nodded and a few minutes later Susan had the salad tossed and sweet tea poured into tall glasses. She sat down at the breakfast bar across from Betsy.

After taking a long drink of her tea, Betsy sighed. She toyed with her salad for a minute and finally took a half-hearted bite.

"Are you going to keep me in suspense?"

"I'm not trying to be a drama queen, sweet pea." Betsy shook her head. "But listen to this. Aubrey and her friend Macy Morgan want me to go out on a date with Macy's dad."

"Oh, Grady Morgan?"

Betsy nodded. "Do you know him?"

"My dad drives one of Grady's snowplows if he needs help during big snowstorms. I've met him. Nice guy. Divorced, right?"

Betsy nodded. "Yeah, I knew Grady in high school and I see him in passing from time to time. Susan, a guy like Grady would be right up my alley. I guess . . . do I really have an alley?"

Susan chuckled. Betsy tended to crack jokes when she had something serious on her mind. "Ah, but you're still mooning over John."

"I'm not mooning. I don't moon." Betsy grinned. "Well, that's not entirely true, but that's another story."

"Mmmm . . ." Susan chewed a bite of her salad. "Could it be that you're daydreaming about the whole chocolate mousse experience?"

Betsy turned as red as the grape tomato in her salad.

"Just as I thought," Susan said with a firm nod.

"Mercy, it was slap your mama good."

"The mousse or the kiss?"

"Both. I'll never look at chocolate mousse the same way." Betsy leaned closer and whispered. "He said he's making me some crème brûlée this weekend. Gets me all hot and bothered just thinking about it."

"The dessert or John?"

"Both," she said again, fanning her face. "Susan, what am I going to do? I mean, I inadvertently agreed to a date with Grady."

"Why?"

"Well, Aubrey was so excited at the prospect."

"Did you tell her about John?"

"No."

"How come?"

"Well, what was I supposed to tell her? That I blew the man a kiss while I was tipsy on spiked eggnog? That I followed him into his kitchen, let him kiss me senseless, and then closed my eyes while he fed me chocolate mousse?"

"You closed your eyes? I think you gave me the abbreviated version the first time around."

Betsy shrugged. "Yeah. He said it was to get a better taste of the dessert."

Susan chuckled. "Wow, that man's got some serious game."

"Tell me about it. My bones turned to liquid," Betsy whispered.

"Why are you whispering?"

"I don't know." She raised her hands upward. "What's gotten into me?

"So what do I do about this Grady thing?"

"Do you want to go out with him?"

Betsy appeared perplexed at the question. "Well, it would be someone to compare to how I feel when I'm with John. I mean, let's face it, I'm as rusty as an old tin can when it comes to men."

"You still know how you feel."

"That's just it. I don't know how I feel."

"I think you do, Betsy."

"I know full well that Grady is someone I would have more in common with. He's more of a down-home guy. And Grady wasn't married to a much younger woman."

"But your heart doesn't care where the man went to college," Susan said. "And he's divorced from his much younger wife."

"Yeah but . . ." Betsy squeezed a snowman so hard that the button eyes nearly popped off. "I don't know! Susan, what should I do? The sensible thing would be to give Grady a fair shot. It's not like I'm dating John or anything."

"But you somehow feel guilty, right?"

"Isn't that downright silly?"

"You think that if he got wind of you going out with Grady it would hurt his feelings?"

"Maybe. I guess seeing John with another woman would be a tough pill for me to swallow."

"Well Betsy, you know that John is completely taken with you."

"Do you really think so?"

"Yes. But you also have every right in the world to go out with Grady. I just get the feeling that you don't really want to."

"Well I mean, I guess I don't really know. I don't want to disappoint Aubrey. And again, I think I'm curious to see how I feel around another man. I was nearly thirty when Bobby left me high and dry. He was a smooth talker. Sure had me fooled. Left me without so much as a slowdown or a look in the rearview mirror. But I need to get past what he did to me."

"Then I guess you've answered your own question."

Betsy nodded but didn't look at all happy about her decision. "How did my simple life suddenly become this complicated?"

"Because your life is changing," Susan said gently. "Aubrey is a grown woman."

"How did that even happen?" Betsy smiled but her eyes misted over. "Why couldn't she just stay my little girl?"

"Oh, she'll always be your little girl. And she will always need you," Susan said, knowing that her own mother had struggled when she left the farm. "But think of all of the joys left to come. Watching her blossom into a young woman will bring you such sweet satisfaction."

"Oh, I know, but it's bittersweet in a way. I miss having her small hand safely tucked in mine. I think the hardest thing as a mother is not being able to fix everything with a Band-Aid and lollipop like when she was little," Betsy said with a wistful smile. "But of course I'll be the proudest mother at her college graduation."

"I'm sure you will be."

"I dream of someday attending her wedding and holding a grandchild in my arms." Betsy looked down at her salad. "Even though I never want to see her get hurt," she added in a tone that was nearly a whisper.

"It's a risk worth taking, though," Susan said, thinking of Danny. "Don't you think?" Although Susan felt more and more confident with him, she too was frightened of getting hurt. "I mean, otherwise we're predestined to miss out."

Betsy toyed with her salad and then finally looked up. "Yes, I know you're right."

Susan smiled. "I keep reminding myself of our toast not to be scaredy-cats. Because I grew up sheltered, I need to make up for lost time. I just need the courage to keep moving forward." She paused and then said, "And so do you, Betsy."

"I realize that my life is going through some changes, both emotional and physical. I'm sure as shootin' not getting younger." Betsy took a drink of her tea. "While I'm perfectly fine with living the rest of my life single, I think I owe it to myself to leave the door open for . . . love. Obviously, Bobby never loved me."

"Or maybe, like you said, he just wasn't cut out to be a family man," Susan said. "He wasn't from Cricket Creek or you might have known him better. I know that him leaving you had to be just horrible but I think it beats living with an unhappy man."

"Absolutely." Betsy sighed. "So once and for all, what should I do about my situation?"

Susan licked the poppy seed salad dressing off of her fork. "I think that if you have dinner with Grady it will help you sort out your feelings for John. But that's just my opinion. You do what you think is best."

Betsy nodded. "I really appreciate you hearing me out, Susan."

"If you do go out with Grady and there aren't any sparks, then you should take a harder look at giving John a fighting chance. Keep in mind that John is back in Cricket Creek by choice, and he seems pretty darned content owning a deli rather than being a big-time attorney. And he sure seems to have his sights set on you."

"I have to wonder if I'm just a challenge for him, though."

Susan chuckled. "Oh you're a challenge all right. But I truly believe you can leave the *just* part out."

Betsy nodded but didn't seem one hundred percent convinced. "I guess there's only one way to find out. All right, enough about me. How are things with cutie pie Danny Mayfield, anyway?"

"I'm going to help him cut down a Christmas tree this weekend." Susan couldn't keep the excitement from her voice.

"Oh wow. That's adorably romantic."

Susan felt the warmth of a blush. "That's why I want to get everything ready for the Christmas Walk on Sunday. I wanted to have Saturday afternoon free, if that's okay with you?"

"I'll get Aubrey to run the necessary errands for you and she can start working tomorrow. That way you can leave early to cut down the Christmas tree with Danny. We'll make sure we're all stocked up and ready for the Christmas Walk Sunday evening."

"Good! Aubrey will be a great deal of help and a lot of fun to have around."

"She will. But you need to get back out there and get more inventory," Betsy said.

"Oh, I know. But estate sales are scarce this time of year and yard sales are nonexistent. I just don't have as many resources during the winter months."

"I understand. I've been getting a lot of customers looking for furniture, though."

"I've been wondering what to do about that little problem." Susan thought of the rocking chair, wishing she had an entire room full of similar furniture. "I'll get to work on more inventory as soon as the holidays are over and we get back to the basics."

Betsy nodded. "Then we'll need to get ready for the spring and summer tourists."

"When Aubrey goes back to school I'll have to consider hiring another clerk to help us out," Susan said. "Business has been so brisk over the past year that one of my recent considerations is leasing the building next door at some point since it's vacant. It sure would be fun to showcase more handmade and repurposed furniture. We just don't have the space here for a lot of really big pieces, or the necessary storage, but the shop next door has the empty loft that could hold lots of bigger items. I know we touched on this a little bit but what's your take on the idea?"

"I think it's a great idea," Betsy said. "Looking to the future and wanting to expand will keep you excited about your shop."

"I would love to have a variety of furniture but focus on rocking chairs. I think they would sell like that," Susan said, snapping her fingers. "I'll have to sit down and take a serious look at my finances to see if it would even be possible for me to expand so quickly. I sure don't want to overextend myself now that my head is above water."

"You could look for an investor. I know if I had the money I'd go into a partnership with you."

"Good idea. I'll start doing some research on it when I get a minute here and there," she said, and then turned her attention back to her salad. Thinking about expansion was exciting but a touch of cold fear also slid down her spine, making her shiver.

"You okay, sugar?"

Susan looked up. "I was initially afraid to leave the

sanctuary of the farm but I'm abundantly glad that I made the leap to being on my own."

"You should be so proud of yourself, Susan."

"I am. I just don't want to move too fast." A partner would be the way to go with the least amount of risk . . . but who could she ask? Susan chewed a bite of salad, thinking she'd best get through the holidays before leaping into more debt.

"There's no rush, you know."

"Oh, I know." Susan nodded. She hoped that someone else didn't lease the shop next door before she had the chance to look more closely into the prospect of expansion. "I just don't want to miss a golden opportunity."

"You'll know when the time is right. And you know you can bend my ear whenever you need to."

"I know, Betsy. Your friendship means a lot to me."

"Same here. Well, now that we settled all of that we'd better get back to the shop."

Susan smiled. "You're right, let's go!"

18

I've Got You, Babe

DANNY STOOD BACK AND GAVE LILY'S MINIATURE rocking chair a nod of satisfaction. "What do you think, Rusty?" he asked the Irish Setter. Rusty seemed more interested in his hambone than a rocking chair. "Well, I think Lily will love it." Danny pictured his little tow-headed niece rocking with her favorite red teddy bear, who she dragged around as her constant companion. Since she was still unable to pronounce her r's, Lily called her stuffed animal Wed Ted.

Lily's infectious giggle always lifted Danny's mood, no matter what kind of day he'd been having. She called him Dandy, making everyone laugh when she said it, and of course Mattie thought it was a riot to call him Dandy as well. If he wasn't careful, everyone in Cricket Creek would soon be calling him by his new nickname.

Danny smiled, thinking of how much he adored Lily and baby Oliver. If he loved his niece and nephew this much, how deeply would he love a child of his own? The thought brought a vision of Susan to his mind, making him sit back on his workbench with a sense of wonder.

"Wow," he said, scrubbing a hand down his face. "Rusty, do you think I'm . . . falling in love?"

Rusty gave him a bored, how-do-I-know look.

"Really, Rusty? You're the lovesick pup who jumped into the river and dogpaddled after Abigail. A little help in the love department would be appreciated."

Rusty gave him a you're-on-your-own wheezy yawn and started chewing on his bone again. "Thanks a lot, pal." Danny shook his head and chuckled at his dog. "I can't stop thinking about her." Not that he wanted to stop. "If thinking about Susan was my job, I'd be a wealthy man, and you'd have a lifetime supply of hambones."

Rusty raised his bushy eyebrows at the mention of hambones.

"Ha, thought that would get your attention." Thinking about Susan brought a huge smile to Danny's face. With a glance at the time on his cell phone, Danny decided he'd better head to his cabin for a quick shower before she arrived to go hiking for a Christmas tree. "Damn, the time got away from me." He'd mentioned to Mason he might be a little bit late for work. He wished he could ask for the night off but Saturdays were busy and he couldn't leave his brother hanging. Danny knew he could be replaced with a simple want ad but he couldn't bring himself to quit the brewery. He supposed that hanging on to helping Mattie and Mason was a safe haven for him, an excuse not to put himself out there and risk failure. Seeing the marina almost go under still spooked him. He knew he needed to get over the feeling of panic but he just couldn't pull the trigger when it came to talking to his family about doing something on his own.

With a sigh, Danny tried to remember when he'd had a weekend to himself . . . and damned if he couldn't recall one. Not that his lack of a Saturday night off was Mason's fault. The tips at the taproom were great and he always had fun behind the bar, even though he was working. But now that Mason had a family, he hurried home after the taproom closed instead of hanging around to play cards or shoot some pool. Danny didn't blame his brother one bit. If he had a wife and child waiting, he'd hurry home too.

Danny ran his hands over the smooth, sanded wood of the rocking chair and could almost hear the light tinkle of Lily's laughter. At just over two years of age, she had a wicked sense of humor and lively personality that never ceased to amaze him. Of course, his sister Mattie had been a rough and tumble tomboy who liked to keep up with the boys, so it wasn't a surprise that Lily was following in her mother's rowdy footsteps. But also like Mattie, his little niece had an incredible, lovable, cuddly side that made it nearly impossible to put her in time-out, no matter what mischief she got herself into. And Garret? Oh, Lily had her daddy wrapped around her tiny finger, and the little imp already knew it.

Danny decided he would paint Lily's name on the back of the chair in yellow, her favorite color. Maybe he'd even make a tiny version for Red Ted to rock in next to her. "She'd sure love that." Danny pushed the chair and as he watched it rock gently, he wondered what having a family of his own would feel like. The thought brought on an unexpected stab of wistful longing. "Something of my own . . ."

Like Mason, Danny wasn't one to show his emotions, but damned if he had to fight a sudden lump in his throat. "Ah, what the hell is going on with me?" he asked Rusty with a shake of his head. He'd heard about the biological clock that women felt but what was this all about? "It's way too soon for a mid-life crisis, right, Rusty? I'm not even thirty yet."

"Woof."

"Ah well . . . who the hell knows?" Danny inhaled a deep breath filled with the scent of freshly sanded wood and then sneezed. Sneezing always made him chuckle. A big space heater cut the chill from the workshop but he suddenly felt the need to zip up his hooded sweatshirt.

Bringing his bone, Rusty trotted over and sat at the bottom of Danny's feet, as if knowing he should be closer to his master. He rested his head on Danny's boot, ignoring his precious bone.

"What's going on with me, boy?" Danny reached down and absently scratched his dog behind the ears. He supposed that the Christmas season was partly responsible for his melancholy mood. What had once been a magical time of the year had dimmed to a mere flicker in the past few years, leaving him feeling detached from the abundant joy felt by the rest of his family.

Knowing he should get ready for Susan's arrival, Danny stood up, but instead of leaving the building, he looked around at the various pieces of furniture. While he felt a sense of pride at the beauty of the painstakingly crafted work, he once again felt the heavy weight of failure. Mason had turned his craft brewing hobby into a lucrative business. Mattie had converted the breakfast and bait shop into a beautiful bistro loved by both tourists and residents of Cricket Creek. "What am I waiting for?" Danny looked around and sighed. "Christmas?" he asked with a small chuckle. He could take pictures and sell the furniture on Craigslist or on consignment at a local shop, but neither thought appealed to him. "Maybe there's some other way," he said and scrubbed a hand down his face, but nothing came to him. "Okay, enough." After whistling for Rusty, he walked toward the door. "Come on, boy. Let's get a move on."

Bright sunshine sliced through the cold afternoon breeze but did little in the way of warmth. His boots crunched through the crusty layer of snow that had melted from milder temperatures yesterday but refrozen overnight. Light flurries danced and twirled around in the clear blue sky dotted with a smattering of white and gray clouds but held little threat of more accumulation . . . at least for now. Danny remembered hearing there was a possibility of accumulation later that night, depending upon which way the impending storm blew. Cricket Creek didn't typically have very harsh winters but this December had started out colder than previous years. When ice or snow hit hard, bread and milk flew off of the shelves and the town came to an abrupt halt.

Rusty trotted ahead of him with his treasured bone sticking out of the side of his mouth, apparently eager to get inside the cabin and into the warmth. "Come on, I'll start a fire," Danny promised, knowing that Rusty would perch on his favorite braided rug in front of the hearth. Mason and Danny had rescued Rusty from the side of the road and he'd lived at the marina ever since, but over the past year Rusty had spent most of his nights with Danny, almost as if knowing that he was needed with him more than Mason or Mattie.

Although Danny had already tidied up, he looked around the cabin, wondering what Susan would think of his place. It was lacking in Christmas cheer, but he felt it still had a cozy appeal. His furnishings were mostly his own creations, except for a buttery soft leather couch that he'd splurged on last year. He kept knickknacks to a minimum but after seeing Susan's loft he thought perhaps he needed to liven things up a little bit. He smiled, thinking he would ask for her help—yet another reason for her to spend more time with him.

After grabbing a bottle of water from the fridge, Danny headed to the bathroom for a quick, hot shower. He'd remodeled the master bath last winter while the marina was slow, adding a vintage claw-foot tub and a huge walk-in shower stall. He looked over at the tub that he rarely used, picturing Susan taking a frothy bubble bath with her dark curls piled on top of her head, exposing the delicate nape of her neck and gentle slope of her shoulders. She'd be surrounded by flickering candles and slow, sultry music would be piped in through the speaker system he'd hooked up. Danny groaned, imagining a big sea sponge squeezed in her hand while she soaped one long leg extended out of the steamy water.

And then he imagined stripping down and joining her.

"Oh boy," Danny said, thinking he might need a cold shower if his thoughts kept going down the same sexy path. Still, he made a mental note to invest in some scented candles, bubble bath salts, and fluffy towels . . . just in case. Tilting his head, he decided he needed to build a few shelves against the far wall to hold any lotions and potions she might want in order to have the best bathing experience ever. Ah, and hooks for warm, fluffy robes. Maybe a heated towel rack?

Danny undressed and turned the large round shower head onto a pelting massage. He lathered up his chest and then washed his hair, turning his face up to the hot spray. His thoughts drifted here and there while the woodsy-scented soap suds slithered from his body. When he finally shut the water off he realized that he'd lingered longer than he should have. He inhaled a steam-filled breath, thinking that he needed to hurry before Susan arrived. Grabbing a towel, he started to dry off, but then heard the chime of the doorbell followed by Rusty's excited, we-have-a-visitor bark.

"Damn!" Wishing Rusty could answer the door, Danny hastily wrapped the towel around his waist and padded on bare feet through his bedroom as the doorbell rang again. In his haste he stubbed his big toe on the corner of the fieldstone fireplace and hopped in a circle of pain.

He recovered and tugged the front door open just in time to witness Susan turning away, carrying a big bulky box in front of her. She started gingerly descending the wide front porch steps, clearly struggling to see beyond

the box. "Susan, wait!" Danny shouted. Rusty barked
his disappointment as well and joined Danny in the
doorway. He clutched his towel tighter. "Don't leave!"
he added, louder.

At the sound of Danny's voice, Susan turned, slipping on the slick stone steps. With a shriek, she missed
the last step and tossed the box into the air. The lid
opened and when it slammed to the ground its colorful
contents flipped upward and spilled onto the grass in all
their Christmas glory. Susan shrieked again and tried
to keep her balance, moving her feet like she was on ice
skates for the first time in her life. She was surely going
to wipe out on the flat fieldstone sidewalk any second.

"Susan! You're on a patch of black ice. Stand still!"

"I'm trying to! Whoa!" With her arms flapping her
feet did a lightning-fast Bruno Mars move.

Horrified, Danny rushed forward, releasing his grip
on the bath towel in his effort to grab her. A blast of
frigid air hit his damp, warm skin, making him shiver,
but he barely noticed. When Susan slipped backwards
Danny caught her beneath her armpits like it was part
of the choreography.

"I've got you, baby, but hold still." Danny wrapped
his arms around Susan in an effort to keep her from
hitting the deck, and he succeeded but only because he
fell first, pulling her down on top of him.

Luckily, Danny landed to the left of the steps but
prickly, icy grass scraped into his bare skin, making
him curse in surprise. Something sharp poked his ass,
probably rocks or a stick, and he realized he'd smacked
the back of his head pretty damned hard. Dimly, he
heard Rusty bark his concern.

"Danny?" Susan wiggled in his grip until she
flopped over, landing on her side next to him.

"Oh my God, are you okay?" Danny asked but
couldn't hold back a gasp.

"I think I should be asking you that question. Good
God, Danny . . . why are you . . . n-naked?"

"Isn't it National Naked Day?" he asked, wondering if he was frozen to the spot.

"Oh, guess I didn't get the memo."

"I was in the shower," he replied as if his answer made sense to why he was nude on his front lawn. Feeling ridiculous, he tried to scramble to his feet but his body refused to obey his urgent command and instead he floundered around like a fish out of water.

"Let me help you up." Susan offered her hand but she slipped and landed right back on top of him.

Danny let out an *ooof* and tried to laugh, but his lack of breath caused him to wheeze.

"Oh my g-gosh. S-sorry!"

"It's . . . oh . . . kay." Danny decided it was high time to make this crazy situation into something good. "But I think you need to warm me up before I get hypothermia."

Susan gasped. "Wh-what should I do?"

"Wrap your warm body around me and give me mouth to mouth resuscitation."

"I can do that." She dipped her head and captured his mouth in a sweet kiss that had Danny forgetting all about the prickly grass, the stick poking his ass, and the hard buttons of her coat pressing into his chest. All he felt was the soft warmth of her lips pressed to his. When she deepened the kiss, the touch of her tongue to his warmed him up more than a roaring fire. The frozen world around him ceased to exist and he wrapped his arms around her puffy coat and melted into the delicious heat of Susan Quincy.

Finally, she pulled back.

"What are you doing? I need more medical attention from your amazing mouth."

Susan chuckled. "We need to g-get you inside."

"Probably, or we might cause global warming. Your kiss carried some heat."

She giggled. "Can you get up?"

"Oh . . ." Danny closed his eyes, realizing he was

totally aroused, and nearly laughed at her comment. He was already quite . . . up. "Would you mind grabbing my towel? I lost it in my failed attempt to save you from falling."

"Well, you certainly broke my fall," she said. "I just hope I haven't broken *you.*"

"Not a chance. I might have played my injuries up for your . . . warmth."

Susan giggled harder. "I can't believe you're . . . *naked*," she whispered as if someone would hear her.

"Don't you dare tell this to anyone," he said, only to have her laugh harder.

"Oh, I do think you've one-upped me with this one. The Christmas tree incident comes close but thankfully I wasn't . . . you know."

"Naked on the front lawn," he supplied.

"Yeah."

"So, I win the dubious prize?"

"Definitely. Pretty hard to beat me in the how-did-that-even-happen situation." Susan nodded, still laughing. She tried to stand but fell back into a fit of giggles, leaving Danny to fetch the towel by reaching forward on his hands and knees. "Great, now I'm mooning my dog." Once he was modestly covered, he stood up and offered one hand to help Susan to her feet.

"Holy crap, I'm cold without you on top of me," he said as they hurried toward the porch.

"We'll have to remedy that."

"Now you're talking." He shot her a wicked grin. Quiet Susan could come up with some good comebacks. "You surprise me with the things you say sometimes. Have you always been that way?"

"I don't always voice what I'm thinking. Sometimes that's a good thing," she said with a laugh.

Rusty sat back on his haunches and looked at Danny as if he'd lost his marbles. His big tail thumped on the porch as he looked at Susan with adoration.

"I know, bud, I feel the same way." Danny turned and gave Susan a quick peck on the cheek.

"Oh, you're both so sweet."

"But I'm sweeter," Danny said. "Just sayin'."

"Well, you did greet me nude."

"I could greet you in the buff every time if you like."

Susan laughed. "I just hope you don't have too many bumps and bruises."

"You can check me out from head to toe and back again," he said and remembered his stubbed big toe. "I will likely need a lot more medical attention."

"A medical massage, perhaps?"

"Definitely," he said as he pushed open the door, making her giggle again. He decided that making Susan laugh was one of his favorite things to do on the planet.

"Yes!" The warmth of the cabin hit Danny like a sweet caress and he hobbled over to the fireplace, holding the towel securely in place. When he shivered, Susan stopped laughing.

"Oh Danny, are you really okay? Did I crush every bone in your body?" She unwrapped the scarf from her neck and took off her coat. "I'm so sorry," she said, and he could hear real regret in her tone.

"This little escapade of mine wasn't your fault. The limp is from stubbing my toe earlier."

"Oh Danny . . ." Susan looked down at his feet with concern in her eyes. "I can sympathize. I run into things a lot. Part of my problem is that I prefer being barefooted to wearing shoes. And of course I'm always moving things around in my loft." She shook her head. "It's a recipe for disaster."

"Well, you sure couldn't have seen the black ice. I should have tossed some rock salt out there earlier," he said, thinking she looked adorably sexy in a dark green V-neck sweater that molded to her sweet curves. Although it was devoid of any blinking lights, she still had a cute, sparkly little candy cane pin to celebrate the season. She wore skinny jeans tucked into black snow boots trimmed with white fur.

"I hope none of your Christmas decorations were broken," he said.

"I have tons of ornaments where that came from. We'll worry about gathering them after we get you warmed up."

Danny grinned. "I'm glad you put a *we* in there."

Susan laughed and he knew the pink in her cheeks wasn't just from the cold air. "*We* is much more fun, don't you think?"

"No doubt. Still, I'm so sorry you fell," he said.

"I can trip over my own shadow, remember? Add ice and it's almost a given that I'll go down. But, am I early?" She put an apologetic hand to her chest. "I know you're bartending tonight so I didn't want to get here too late."

"No, I was in my workshop finishing up a rocking chair for Lily and time got away from me."

"Oh wait . . . you make rocking chairs?"

"Yeah." The excited tone of her voice made him nod, even though he didn't quite want to admit it to her. Stupid, and he didn't really know why he hesitated.

"I know you're super busy but would you consider making some chairs for my shop?"

"I told you it's only a hobby, remember?" Danny replied with a small shrug. Having her know about his furniture would be revealing a vulnerable side of himself that he wasn't quite ready to share, even though he wanted to, and so he felt the need to hold back. "Just something I do to relax." When Susan looked about ready to ask more, he pulled her into his arms and dipped his head for a lingering kiss. He would show her his workshop someday soon, but right now he had other things on his mind.

19

Genie in a Bottle

AT THE TOUCH OF HIS LIPS TO HERS, SUSAN'S QUES-
tion flitted right out of her head like a butterfly
taking flight. Nothing mattered to her except having
her body pressed to Danny's while he kissed her with
a sweet hunger that had her opening her mouth for
more. She held on to his broad shoulders and then slid
her fingers into his damp hair, letting the tendrils curl
around her fingers. The spicy scent of his soap mingled
with the smoke of the crackling fire, filling her head
with desire.

When his towel slithered to the hardwood floor she
nearly giggled but that would mean breaking the contact with his warm, delicious mouth and so she refrained. "Oops."

"Oh my . . ."

He was hard, muscular, and naked.

And he was all hers.

The realization slid softly into her brain and slowly
warmed her body. She wanted to touch him everywhere, explore every inch of his body with her hands . . .
and then with her mouth. Susan had never felt this way,

but the more he kissed her the more her shyness melted away like a delicate snowflake on her warm tongue. Knowing how much he wanted her chased away any inhibitions and her inner sexpot unleashed itself like a genie from a bottle. She slid her hands down over his shoulders and to his biceps, loving the feel of smooth skin over taut muscle. When she pushed her body even closer, he moved his hands downward, cupping her tush and pressing her to him, showing her how much he wanted her. Well good, because she wanted him just as much.

Rusty barked, obviously not liking the lack of attention.

"Really, dude?" Danny said to his dog. "Can't you see that I'm, uh, occupied?"

Susan laughed and then glanced over at Rusty, who gave her a pouty, hey-what-about-me expression and inched forward, tapping his paw on the hardwood floor.

"Woof!"

"I think he just said for us to get a room," Susan said, drawing another chuckle from Danny.

"I just so happen to have one available." Danny angled his head sideways toward the hallway, but then pulled back and tilted her chin up. "We're moving fast again." While looking into her eyes he rubbed his thumb over her bottom lip.

"Apparently, I have a need for speed," Susan said. "Who knew?"

Danny tilted his head back and laughed harder. "You say the most unexpected things."

Susan wrapped her arms around his neck, amazed at how at ease she felt with him, even while he stood there in the buff. "Is that a good thing?"

"Yeah, you keep me on my toes," he said and then reached behind her and scooped her up in his arms. "Now, I'm going to sweep *you* off your feet."

Susan let out a squeal of surprise. "Are you crazy?"

she asked, worried that she was too heavy, but he didn't grunt or anything, thank goodness.

"Yeah, crazy about you, Suzy Q," Danny replied as he carried her with apparent ease. The great room became a blur of beautiful, sturdy furniture as he somehow managed to walk with fast, long-legged strides, barely avoiding lamps and end tables. Afraid she might kick something over, Susan tried to tuck her booted feet closer to his body, without much luck. "You have the need for speed too," Susan said as he moved down the hallway and into his bedroom.

"Oh no, I plan to savor every inch of your delectable body slowly," he promised. He eased her onto an enormous four-poster bed constructed of white cedar logs. Kneeling down, he began tugging her boots off. Susan watched, loving the way his rich chestnut brown hair had started to curl around his ears now that it was nearly dry. The muscles in his shoulders bunched and rippled while he tugged and he fell back on his haunches when the boot popped off.

Susan laughed. "Oh my gosh, I should have told you there's a zipper on the side."

"That would have helped," he said.

"Sorry, but I was preoccupied ogling your body."

Danny chuckled as he pushed back up to a sitting position. "You can look as long as you like."

"That would be a very long time."

"Good," Danny said. He braced his arms at his sides and gave her a killer grin. Fingers of sunlight reached through the windows, giving the room a soft glow. While she knew there wasn't much daylight left, searching for a Christmas tree suddenly ceased to matter. Everything faded into the background while she focused on the man in front of her.

Susan nearly gasped at the sight of Danny's powerful body. Thickly muscled but without that bulky gym rat look, he was a glorious sight to see. He had a light dusting of dark chest hair that she longed to touch.

And then she would trail her hands over the ridges of his six-pack. Susan swallowed hard. "You're . . . one gorgeous man, Danny Mayfield."

"Thank you," Danny responded with a hint of a blush that she found incredibly endearing.

"Surely you know how incredibly handsome you are."

He shrugged. "I know that I like hearing you say so."

"Then I'll have to keep reminding you."

"Mmm, now, if you don't mind, I'd like to sit back and watch you take your clothes off for me. Starting with the other boot." He pointed to her foot. "By the way, it unzips," he added with a grin.

"Okay . . ." Susan whispered, but she suddenly felt horribly self-conscious. When had she ever done a striptease for a man?

Uh, that would be a great big *never*.

Susan's heart beat in anticipation and she wondered if she should go really slow? Swing her clothes around on the tip of her finger? The thought nearly made her giggle and then she realized she was literally shaking in her one boot, mind numbed with nerves.

"Take your time," he said softly.

Susan gave him a smile that thank goodness didn't tremble, although her lips were probably the only thing not trembling. "No need for speed?"

"Not at all. In fact, the slower the better."

Inhaling a deep breath, she felt heat creep up her neck and into her cheeks. She nibbled on her bottom lip and tried to slow the wild beat of her heart. Leaning down, she unzipped her remaining boot and let it slide to the floor with a soft thump. She glanced at Danny, who watched her with intense expectancy. Taking her sweet time, she peeled off her thermal socks, glad that she'd thought to paint her toenails a glossy pink. "Catch." She tossed the socks at Danny with what she hoped was a saucy grin, but her heart continued to beat like a jackhammer and her wild toss was way off the mark. Still, he managed to snatch one of them.

Susan's thoughts started to tumble over one another. What if she totally sucked at this? After all, she wasn't very experienced. Growing up isolated and only dating here and there had left her way down the line on the novice scale, like nearly negative. But just when she started to go into serious doubt mode, her inner sexpot reared her lovely head and whispered, *Come on, girl, you've got this.*

Where have you been all my life? Susan wondered, but then thought it was actually Danny who made her want to toss caution to the wind and make wild uninhibited love to him. Holding his gaze, Susan pulled her snug cashmere sweater up over her head, so glad that she'd recently indulged in new bras and panties. Today she wore a cream-colored satin push up bra and matching wisp of satin and lace. She'd always wished for a fuller figure, but at the sound of Danny's intake of breath, she guessed he liked what he saw. Feeling bolder, she unzipped her jeans, but had trouble peeling them off.

"Let me help," Danny offered and pushed up from the floor.

"Coming to my rescue again?"

"I think this is actually coming to my own rescue this time," he said with a sexy grin. "Just lift your hips. I've got this, baby." He gently tugged her jeans off and tossed them to the floor. "Wow . . ." He gazed down at her. "You're even more gorgeous than I imagined."

"You've been thinking about me?"

"Pretty much nonstop, and when I do stop, I start again."

"Really?" she asked softly, and when he nodded she felt a wave of emotion. She inhaled a deep breath, thinking crying right now would be the worst timing ever. But the thought of him daydreaming about her was just . . . well, wonderful.

"Absolutely. You're . . . just . . . full of grace and beauty. Everything about you blows me away. Just thinking about you puts me in a good mood."

"Oh . . ." she said, and gave him a smile. "What a lovely thing to say."

"It's the truth," Danny admitted and then joined her on the bed. He pulled her into his arms and gave her a deep, hot kiss that melted her bones. She felt liquid . . . weightless, and when he trailed his fingertips over her bare skin she gasped with sheer pleasure. He toyed with the edge of her panties, touching, caressing, but leaving her wanting more. In desperation Susan arched her back, urging him to satisfy a yearning that seemed to start from inside of her and radiate outward in hot waves. Susan wanted, no *needed*, to have her body wrapped around his and feel his skin sliding against hers. Her entire body throbbed with the urgency and she arched her hips, allowing him to shimmy the wisp of satin and lace down her thighs. Rising up to his knees, Danny tossed her panties up in the air, laughing when they landed on a lampshade, dangling like a rock climber trying to get to the top.

"I'm leaving them there forever."

"No you're not!" Susan gasped but then laughed when she saw the teasing twinkle in his eyes.

Susan sat up, reached around her back, and unhooked her bra, allowing the straps to slide down over her shoulders.

Danny leaned forward and kissed the swell of her nearly exposed breasts. The moist warmth of his mouth had her sucking in a breath and when the tip of his tongue dipped beneath the satin, Susan closed her eyes and couldn't hold back a breathy groan. When Danny pulled back she made a sound of protest but then she dimly realized he was tugging her bra the rest of the way off.

She was naked, exposed physically and emotionally.

Part of her still longed to tug the covers over her body but she didn't. Instead, she leaned back against the pillows, her heart racing while he gazed down at her.

"Susan . . ." he said, and she realized how much she loved something as simple as him saying her name. She'd sometimes longed for a more exotic or cutesy name but the low timbre of his voice felt like a soft caress.

Susan swallowed, resisted the urge to grab a pillow as a shield, and instead, let him look his fill. Having always been taller than most girls, she'd been self-conscious about her body, but Danny seemed to drink her in with his gaze, lingering here and there. She felt her nipples tighten and desire like she'd never felt pooled between her thighs.

"God, you're just . . . *wow*," he said when his gaze returned to her face.

"A good wow? Because you know, wow can go either way." She intended to be funny but the slight tremor in her voice gave her away.

"No, an excellent, take-my-breath-away . . . *wow*." He leaned down and gave her a light but lingering, oh-so-sweet kiss. Pulling back, he looked down at her with heavy-lidded eyes full of emotion. "Susan, I'm not one to toss around flowery compliments. I mean every word I say to you. I find you absolutely gorgeous. The vision of you leaning back against the pillows on my bed will remain like a snapshot in my brain forever." Smiling, he tapped his skull.

"Oh . . ." She caught her bottom lip between her teeth. She smiled since he obviously liked what he saw . . . a lot. She'd never stepped foot inside a gym, too self-conscious to work out in front of other people, but being so active on the farm and in the shop kept her toned and fit.

"I love everything about you," he said.

"Show me."

Danny explored her body with his hands, lingering, caressing, driving her desire into an absolute frenzy. When he took a taut nipple into his mouth Susan arched her back and groaned. His mouth was magic, creating a deep, aching need inside her. Threading her fingers through his hair, she leaned back against the plump pillows and let him explore her body. His hot, moist mouth and gentle stroking hands caused her to close her eyes and drown in the delicious sensations. When he oh-so-lightly trailed his fingertips over her mound, her breath caught. She tingled, she burned, and she wanted Danny Mayfield more than she knew was humanly possible.

She needed to tell him, wanted him to know. Opening her mouth, she tried to voice her need, but all that came out was a gasp, a moan, and when he parted her thighs and touched his tongue to her core, she cried out with pleasure. "No . . . I . . . oh . . ." she said, wanting him to stop and then wanting him to never stop. This . . . this was too much and not quite enough . . . a spiraling upward climb, an ache . . . and then an intense orgasm burst open and fell, like colorful confetti raining down upon her.

Susan's pulse pounded, and she felt oh so . . . *satisfied*. She smiled and sighed. She couldn't have moved if she'd wanted to. Wild and wanton took a backseat while she melted against the pillows. "Mmm . . ." She just wanted to curl next to him and revel in the sweet afterglow.

She needed just a teeny little nap.

But Danny had other ideas.

Susan heard a drawer open and realized he was putting on protection. She felt a flash of guilt that she couldn't exactly move one single part of her body. She seriously felt as if she were made of unset Jell-O. "Danny, I can't . . ." she began, but he smothered her protest with a searing kiss that somehow reignited the flickering flame of desire, like a match to tinder.

To her utter amazement, she became intensely aroused all over again. His mouth, the steely hardness, the wide set of his shoulders to which she clung, was like a sexy lifeline. He kissed her senseless and then entered her body with one sure, delicious stroke, filling her with need once more. Somehow completely recovered, Susan matched his rhythm, urging him faster, loving the way he filled her, stroked her, held her against the hard planes of his powerful body. She wrapped her legs around his waist and held on to him, giving herself to him in a wanton way she didn't even know she had in her.

This went beyond physical and touched her on another level of intimacy that she'd never experienced before.

When Susan felt the powerful pulse of his climax, she flew over the edge and clung to him while wave after wave of sweeping pleasure poured over her. Her heart thudded and every nerve in her body seemed to be on high alert. When he pulled her into his embrace, holding her tightly, she was beyond words. In her limited experience she'd found making love to be pleasant, not mind-blowing or romance novel worthy . . .

Until this moment.

Susan could feel the solid, steady beat of Danny's heart against her cheek and she smiled. He kissed the top of her head and held her close, making her feel safe, cherished . . . He was silent as well and she had to wonder if he was feeling any of the same emotions that were soaring through her body like a kite on a windy day. She felt languidly immobile and yet energized at the same time. She wanted to shout with joy and spin around the room, arms akimbo like Julie Andrews in *The Sound of Music* . . . if only she could move.

Oh wow . . .

I'm in love.

The realization hit Susan like a bright white shooting star racing across the sky. Not just *in love* but head-over-heels-no-holds-barred-no-use-denying-it in love.

And it scared the ever-living daylights right smack out of her.

Pow.

Oh no.

What if this was just, like, really good sex to Danny Mayfield? Or maybe this really was just normal sex to him and extraordinary to her. Oh God, what if this was pity sex like the pity date to the prom? Perhaps she'd just set herself up for a really horrible, chocolate binging, whiskey drinking heartache.

"What are you thinking, Susan?" Danny asked gently.

"Nothing." She tried for casual but her voice sounded frightened and small. Where in the hell had her inner sexpot suddenly scurried off to? *Come back! Please!*

"I can hear the wheels turning in your pretty head."

"You have a very good sense of hearing." Susan tried to joke but her voice came out low and breathless. Feeling completely overwhelmed, she suddenly wanted to jump up and race for the hills where, apparently, her fickle inner sexpot had suddenly run off to. She tried to get her emotions under control but failed miserably.

"Apparently so," Danny said. "Talk to me."

"I, um . . ." Susan tried to clear her clogged throat. Don't cry! God . . . crying would just be horrifying. She seriously needed to just . . . bolt. But scurrying away would be really difficult since she was nude, with no idea how to recover her clothes without doing a hunched-over tiptoeing search around the huge room.

"Hey," Danny probed gently. He cupped her chin but Susan couldn't look up at him just yet. "Talk to me when you're ready. I'm not going anywhere," he said with a slightly worried tone that made Susan feel guilty. He hadn't done one single thing wrong but how could she tell him she was freaking out over knowing she was completely, madly in love with him?

"'Kay . . ." Susan nodded and damn if she didn't love him even more for being so wonderfully understanding— or at least for trying to understand something she couldn't even begin to comprehend herself.

This love for him was the kind of heady feeling she never thought she would experience and had only read about in the endless pile of romance novels that she adored. She loved fairy tales and happily ever afters even though she'd been fairly certain that kind of love would never happen to her.

This was stuff movies were made of, so why should she fight it? *Just tell him.*

Wait, were women allowed to say those three little words first these days? Surely . . . but then again, Susan certainly didn't want to profess her love and have Danny feel obligated to say it back. This was too soon, though, right? But if she felt this way, then it really wasn't too soon.

Susan sucked in her bottom lip, thinking.

Don't be a scaredy-cat, went through Susan's head. *You promised Betsy*, she sternly reminded herself. But the problem was that she *was* a scaredy-cat.

No . . . no, I'm not.

Susan tried to calm the wild beating of her heart and to breathe slowly. Inhale. Exhale.

She knew she needed to power through this sudden bout of nervous insanity but neither her mind nor her body felt the need to respond to her desperate commands.

Inhale. Exhale.

Susan only knew that she had to plan her escape before making a complete fool of herself by proclaiming her undying love. Plus, if she attempted to talk she knew she'd stutter like crazy and he wouldn't understand a word she said.

Inhale. Exhale.

How could absolutely wonderful crash into total

disaster so very quickly? Deep down Susan knew she was creating drama where there was none but her befuddled brain refused to listen to reason.

"Susan?" His chest vibrated with the deep sound of his voice.

Inhale. Exhale.

Danny cleared his throat, making her head move around.

Relax.

He inhaled deeply and blew out a breath that stirred her curly hair.

Pretend to sleep . . .

"Sweetheart?"

Oh . . . he called me sweetheart. Shaky inhale. Shaky exhale. Oh how she wanted to kiss his warm chest.

"Are you asleep?" Danny asked, and Susan nearly let out a nervous chuckle. She'd always thought asking if someone was asleep was such a silly question. She forced herself to remain still, even though her neck started to ache from being in the same position and her left leg was growing numb. But the very last thing she wanted to do was to give Danny a stuttering explanation of why she'd suddenly gone into freak-out mode.

Susan knew she was an over-thinker, another product of growing up an only child. With no one else to talk to, she'd had to answer her own questions, which led to a whole lot of pondering, often while sitting outside beneath a tree or walking through the woods gathering wildflowers. She wished she could be more spontaneous and live in the moment.

Perhaps that's precisely what she should do.

20

Ice, Ice, Baby

BY THE SOUND OF SUSAN'S HEAVY BREATHING, DANNY thought she must be sound asleep. While he wanted to stay in bed with her endless silky legs wrapped around him, he needed to get the Christmas tree cut down before heading off to the brewery to bartend. He decided that if she was that tired she clearly needed to rest, so he'd surprise her by having a tree up and in the stand by the time she woke up. He'd leave her a text message and she could join him if she wished. Plus, he wanted to go out and gather up the scattered ornaments and assess the damage to her decorations. But having her head on his chest and her warm body entwined with his felt so amazing that he opted to close his eyes and savor the sensation for just a few more minutes of bliss.

The scent of her shampoo, something coconut and citrus, filled his head, leading to more bubble bath images, and then, better yet, having her join him in the shower. That visual, along with actually having her naked in his bed, had him getting aroused all over again. He nearly chuckled when he thought of how he'd answered the door wrapped in a towel and then the craziness that had ensued, but he didn't want to wake her and so he kept his mirth to himself—barely.

Looking up at the paddle fan, Danny smiled, experiencing several emotions at once. Every moment spent with Susan Quincy seemed to be filled with something unexpected. And Danny's life, he realized, although busy, had become something of an organized routine. His jobs were all predictable, with a sameness that had been making his daily life feel stale. He longed for something to be excited about, to look forward to, and Susan filled that role quite nicely. Even so, Danny knew he needed to have the courage to branch out and do something meaningful on his own, just like she'd suggested.

Danny frowned, though, knowing that Susan had been having some kind of moment before she drifted off to sleep. While he wanted to know what was on her mind, he understood the emotional impact of what was happening between them. He'd been blown away by the intensity of making love to her and he knew she felt it too. This wasn't just about amazing sex. He was falling hard for Susan.

Ah, but he didn't want to scare her away by telling her the depth of his feelings too soon.

Or should he? Maybe she needed to know that he was already looking to the future? Even at this stage of their relationship, he couldn't fathom not having her in his life.

Danny inhaled a deep breath, thinking that he needed to figure out his own path first. She deserved more than someone who drifted between three jobs and failed to have something solid of his own. He wanted a career he could sink his teeth into, to be proud of and passionate about, just like his siblings. Just like Susan. He'd already confessed that he struggled with that but he hadn't planned on falling for her this quickly.

Danny closed his eyes.

Thirty is breathing down my neck like the breath of

a damned dragon. I should have this all figured out by now.

His excuse that his family needed him was valid but only up to a point. Even so, nearly losing the marina had imbedded a fear of failure deep inside his brain. While Mattie and Mason had both pitched in to help save the family business, Danny had been the one who'd juggled the financial end of the books, keeping the worst of the near disaster from his father. When the marina had been hanging on by a thread, he'd made it his personal responsibility to keep things afloat, robbing Peter to pay Paul while presenting a much rosier picture to the rest of the family. To this day, no one else totally realized how very close they'd come to filing for bankruptcy. So after saving the family business, how could he even begin to consider turning the reins over to someone else? Who else would care as much as he did, especially now that Mason and Mattie had a family and businesses of their own?

Danny inhaled another unsteady breath.

Well damn. How can I be the right person for Susan when I'm not the best person for myself yet?

I'm moving too fast.

But I don't want to slow down.

Maybe I need the stability of Susan Quincy in my life.

That light bulb thought slipped into Danny's head and clung like kudzu, but he mentally shook it off. Susan had been right from the start. He'd always been the person who other people needed, not the other way around. He liked coming to the rescue, being the sounding board, the solid factor in the life of his friends and family. Needing someone else made him feel odd and vulnerable, taking him out of his comfort zone.

While Susan had a sweet personality, he felt her inner strength, her passion for Cricket Creek and her shop. Shy Susan had the courage to leave the family farm and strike out on her own. She didn't need his help or rescuing, as much as they joked about it. But he believed that having her fall into his arms hadn't been random but meant to be. He could feel it. But what should he do about his feelings for her? Profess them or wait until he was where he wanted to be in his life?

And what if he was never where he wanted to be in his life? The question scared him more than he wanted to acknowledge.

When Danny heard Susan sigh he oh-so-lightly kissed the top of her head. She had such pretty hair, thick and lush, full of curly waves. He decided he'd love to wash her hair, sink his fingers into the dark, silky tresses, lather up and massage her scalp. He'd never had that kind of fantasy about a woman before, but then again, he'd never felt about a woman the way he felt about Susan. He could picture her eyes fluttering shut while a slight smile tugged at the corners of her mouth. He made a mental note to visit Burst my Bubble, a new bath and body lotion shop that had recently opened up on Main Street.

With a yawn, Danny wondered how he could wiggle free without waking Susan and decided he'd just rest his eyes for a few minutes before sneaking out for the tree. Using his left foot, he pulled at a decorative quilt folded at the bottom of the bed and draped it over them. His mother had provided the abundance of fringed pillows and other odds and ends, telling him that his cabin needed a splash of color, whatever that meant.

I'll just rest my eyes for a few minutes. A little cat nap wouldn't hurt, especially with sweet Susan curled up next to him. The scent of her skin was like aromatherapy and he relaxed, breathing deeply. What would it feel like to wake up to her in his bed every morning? Share the double sink in his enormous bathroom? Cook dinner together? Danny knew he was thinking way ahead of himself but his train of thought kept going right down the track at breakneck speed.

No, slow down. I'm not ready for this. And judging by her earlier silence, neither is she.

"*D*ANNY?"

"Mmmm?" Danny mumbled and snuggled closer to the warm body curled around him.

"Danny? Um . . . I think we have a slight . . . problem."

"Mmmm . . . ?"

"It's . . . dark."

"Dark?"

"Yeah. Really dark."

Danny opened his eyes and inhaled a deep breath, trying to shake the cobwebs from his brain. "Oh, wow . . . wait. Susan, what time is it?" he asked thickly.

"I have no idea. I'm so sorry but we . . . fell asleep," she said, sounding apologetic and worried.

"Baby, it's okay," Danny said, reaching around for his phone and then remembering it must be in the bathroom from when he'd taken his shower earlier.

"B-but what if you're late for work?"

"Mason won't fire me," he said with a reassuring kiss on her head.

Susan nodded but Danny felt a definite shift in her mood from earlier in the day. "But—"

"Seriously, it's okay," he said gently. "I told Mason I might be running late because we were going to cut down a tree and he was completely cool with it. Colby Campbell is going to be there tonight helping out too. They'll be fine without me," he said and realized it was true. He needed to ask for an occasional Saturday off.

She nodded against his chest but her breathing seemed a little swift.

"Susan, are you okay?" he asked, wishing he could see her more clearly in the dim light of the room. The idea that she regretted sleeping with him made his heart sink like a stone to the bottom of the lake but how could he ask her that question?

"Yes." She nodded again but Danny wasn't convinced.

"Did I say something wrong?"

"Of course n-not."

"Then what is it?" he asked softly, a cold fist of fear knotted in his stomach. "Susan?" Danny felt her swallow against his chest and she shifted like she was nervous or uncomfortable. Oh God, maybe she was going to break up with him? "Please tell me. I want to know," he said, thinking that breaking up while lying naked together would be super awkward. "You seem upset about something."

"Oh Danny, I . . ." she began but then trailed off as she couldn't bring herself to say what was on her mind.

"I *need* to know." Tensing his muscles, Danny braced for the worst. "Please."

"I . . . love you, Danny," she said in a low, breathless tone that swirled around his heart like morning mist on the lake. She placed a gentle hand on his chest. "I just had to tell you how I feel," she added with a little tremor in her voice. "I listened to my heart, like you said."

"Oh wow." Relief rushed over him and he released a laugh. "Oh my gosh, thank you, for a moment I—"

"Thank you?" Susan went as still as a statue.

He chuckled again. "No, it's because I thought—"

"Oh my God." Susan swiftly sat up and grabbed for the cover, trying to tug it from beneath him. "You thought that was . . . f-funny?"

"No, I—" He tried again but she wasn't listening this time. "Susan, I'm sorry, I—"

"I'm sorry too! Just pretend I never said it," she said in a horrified rush.

"I can't do that because I love you too!"

Susan's eyes widened but then she shook her head and appeared even more upset. "No! You're just saying that because you feel like a jerk!" She let out a little exasperated grunt and pulled so hard on the quilt that it gave way, sending her tumbling backwards.

"Susan!" Danny reached for her but she did a lightning fast backward roll right off of the bed and landed with a muffled thump, quickly followed by a string of curses that didn't remotely belong together.

"Damned stupid, should have, damned shut . . . oh shit, silly ass promise, damn . . . why . . . shit. Just . . . sh-shit . . . ouch, ouch—"

"Susan!" Danny scrambled over to the edge of the bed and flipped on the small lamp on his nightstand. "Susan, are you okay?"

"No." She rubbed her elbow, rapidly blinking her eyes.

"Baby, what hurts?"

"Everything, but m-mostly my p-pride," she replied with a narrow-eyed glare and wrapped the quilt around her so tightly that it resembled a cocoon with her head and feet peeking out. "I'd like m-my clothes pl-please."

"Susan, seriously, you've got it all wrong."

"Apparently so." She continued to blink rapidly and he knew she was on the verge of tears. Damn, he'd ruined her moment and he knew how much courage it must have taken for her to profess her love.

"Please listen to me," Danny pleaded, but she dipped her head, refusing to look at him. And then the reason for her distress smacked him in the face. "I wasn't laughing at you."

"Well, you sure weren't laughing w-with me." She let out another little growl. "D-damn stupid, st-stutter. Errrr!"

Danny shook his head. "You took me by surprise," he began, but before he could go on she scrambled awkwardly to her feet and hobbled like a sheathed mummy, searching around the room for her clothes. She looked so cute and funny that he wanted to laugh, but he knew that wouldn't go over too well at the moment and so he looked for his clothes as a distraction. He needed to clear this little misunderstanding up fast, but he also needed to choose his words carefully. Should he simply repeat that he loved her too or would she think he was saying it out of pity? "Susan, if you'll just calm down," he said, and she stopped in her tracks to shoot him a glare.

"Calm down?" she asked, and it was then that Danny remembered that telling a woman to calm down was like throwing gasoline on a fire.

Spotting his black boxer briefs, Danny scooted from the bed and tugged them on. He turned around to see Susan picking up her bra but her panties were missing in action.

"On the lampshade," he said sheepishly.

She closed her eyes briefly and then with a long-suffering sigh she hobbled over to the lamp in the corner of the room, nearly tripping several times. Of course, putting them on meant unraveling the tightly wrapped cover and so she looked around until she spotted a door and took short, geisha-like steps in that direction.

"That's a closet."

With a little squeal of anger, she spun around so fast that she nearly turned full circle and then had to catch herself from falling by bracing her hand on the log wall. Because she clutched her underwear in the other hand her action caused the cover to unravel and land at her feet. She stared at it for a horrified second and then with her head held high she marched over to the bathroom with a saucy sway of her hips. *Well damn* . . .

She looked . . . wow, *magnificent*, completely naked with her dark curls tumbling around her shoulders. Unable not to, Danny stared at the delicate slope of her back, her cute tush and shapely legs . . . legs that had been wrapped around him not long ago. Whatever he expected her to do, she nearly always surprised him. He loved her unpredictable nature—it brought spontaneity back into his life. What had become stale felt fresh again, and he knew that being with her would be that way forever.

Danny stood there for a few seconds, stunned, barely flinching when she slammed the door. For some odd reason he found her white-hot anger a complete turn-on, perhaps because he wouldn't have guessed that someone so sweet-natured could get so riled up. Danny suspected that she didn't get angry often but when she did . . . well, clearly it was time to duck and run. He smiled in spite of the situation, thinking he loved her sweetness but also her unexpected fire. As soon as he could explain his reaction, everything would be just fine, and they could have amazing makeup sex. Not that they needed to make up . . . he just needed to let her calm down so they could talk and clear the air. When Susan knew that his laughter was of relief they could have a good chuckle together. He heard things banging around in the bathroom, followed by a muffled curse . . . Well, he hoped so, anyway.

Danny needed to know the time but his phone was on the sink, so he had to just wait. But when Susan failed to come out for a couple of minutes, he decided to give her some privacy.

After pulling on his jeans, he headed out toward the kitchen to check the digital clock on the microwave and to grab a cold bottle of water. Rusty snored softly, still lounging in front of the hearth, stirring a little bit as Danny passed through the great room. *Great watch dog*, he thought, and then glanced toward the floor to ceiling windows. "No way." Danny hurried over to the window and then slowly shook his head. "Holy shit. When did that happen?"

At the sound of Danny's voice Rusty raised his head and trotted over to stand beside his master. "It's a solid sheet of ice out there, bud," Danny said, taking in the beauty of the ice glittering off the outdoor light shining from the roof of his workshop. "Susan and I aren't going anywhere anytime soon," he added and then smiled slowly. "She has to listen to me now, Rusty. She's trapped. Now how's that for meant to be, huh? Thank you, Mother Nature."

21

Try a Little Tenderness

"OH, WOW." IN SPITE OF THE HORRIFYING HUMILIATION of declaring her love and getting a thank-you followed by a laugh, Susan had to admire the beauty of the bathroom. She gazed longingly at the lovely claw-foot tub. She tiptoed over and peeked inside, loving the soothing natural colors of the slate tile. "Amazing." Why she felt the need to tiptoe was a bit of a mystery, but she figured if Danny didn't hear her walking around she might be able to sneak past him and make a swift departure, unnoticed. Funny but during her high school years she'd often felt invisible. Now, she wished being invisible really was her superpower.

When she inhaled the masculine scent of his spicy body wash, a steamy image of Danny standing naked beneath the pelting spray slid into her brain and hovered there. Mmm, soapy and slippery, muscles rippling while he turned his face up to the hot water. The fantasy caused a flush to warm her skin and she cursed her vivid imagination. But her imagination didn't care and carried on with a vengeance.

"No . . . stop!" She backed away rapidly and then caught sight of herself in the big shiny mirror. Dear God, that surely couldn't be accurate. Her hair was a tangled mess, curling wildly around her bare shoulders, and she looked . . . well, like she'd just made wild love and then slept with her legs entwined with Danny's while her head rested on his warm, solid shoulder.

"Well . . ." Susan put trembling fingers to her lips. "Because I did." She remembered the wanton way she'd behaved and cradled her cheeks in her palms. "And then I told him I loved him." She groaned and then leaned against the cold edge of the tiled sink. "What was I thinking?" she whispered. "This whole empowerment thing Betsy and I concocted is way overrated. I need to go back to being a scaredy-cat."

Inhaling a deep breath, Susan looked at the skimpy bra and panties dangling from her fingers and then gazed in the mirror again. She recalled how he'd said she took his breath away and that she was gorgeous. Did he really think so? Or was that one of those in-the-heat-of-the-moment things guys say? Having very little experience to draw upon, she really didn't know the answer, except she really didn't think that Danny was that way. No, he definitely wasn't.

But then how could he laugh at her when she'd confessed her love, for pity's sake? "Who does that?" she asked her reflection hotly, but it just stared back, unblinking. For a shy, stuttering girl who'd weathered her share of humiliation, this one sure did take the cake. Susan was actually floored that someone as nice as Danny could be so callous. His lame "I love you too" only made her even angrier.

But what if he meant it?

"No, don't even go there," she whispered, knowing full well that as soon as she got home she'd be reduced to a really messy, noisy crying jag, cradling a big wineglass while listening to sad Rascal Flatts songs. But for now, her anger was carrying her through her emotional crisis. She seriously wanted to throw something and watch it smash, something she'd never even considered doing before. Of course, smashing something would beget instant regret and she'd had enough of that particular emotion today to last a lifetime.

After using the really cool, high tank, chain pull toilet that she was rather fascinated by, she washed up and then slipped on her panties. Her trembling fingers made hooking her bra a bit more difficult but she finally managed. Now, all she had to do was sneak into the bedroom and put her clothes on. Surely Danny had the decency to give her some privacy, but eventually she was going to have to face the music. Oh, but maybe she could find a way to slip past him, dart out the door to her SUV, and peel out? She imagined fishtailing, spitting rocks as she made her mad escape, and nearly laughed.

"Oh God, I'm totally losing it," she mumbled and then spotted Danny's phone resting on the sink. When the cell phone pinged and vibrated she felt a hot flash of guilt but couldn't resist looking down at the text message. The message was from Mason: *Don't even think of coming in tonight.*

Susan's eyes widened and she put the heel of her hand to her forehead. "Mason fired Danny?" she whispered, thinking it was all her fault for pretending to fall asleep and actually dozing off. She might be angry with him but she certainly didn't want him to get fired. But would Mason really fire his own brother? Probably not, but she looked at the phone and frowned.

For a day that had started out so nicely, it was speeding south at whiplash speed.

After finger-combing her riot of curls, she shook her head at the very little progress she'd made at taming her wild hair and sucked in a deep breath. "Just do it." After opening the door a mere crack, she put her ear there and listened for movement. "Okay," she whispered, and then put one eye at the opening, trying to see. Feeling silly, she opened the door with a quiet whoosh and tiptoed over to where her jeans and sweater had landed in a heap at the side of the giant log bed. She felt the heat of a blush when she looked at the rumpled covers. A couple of fringed pillows had fallen to the floor and Susan had an odd urge to straighten the bed to cover up the evidence. But first and foremost, she needed to get dressed.

With an inward groan, she wished she'd worn one of her gaudy Christmas-themed sweaters instead of the snug V-neck style she'd opted for in an effort to be more alluring. "Guess it worked," she said with a wry chuckle. She tugged on the skinny jeans and was contemplating whether to put on her boots when she heard footsteps heading her way.

Susan froze as still as one of those silver statue guys she'd seen on the streets in Nashville. Her heart hammered so hard that she felt light-headed. God . . . passing out would be even worse than crying, but she suddenly felt like doing both. *Oh, Scotty, beam me up.*

Susan wasn't remotely prepared for the sexy sight of Danny standing there shirtless with his jeans slung low on his hips. He gazed at her without speaking and then reached up and shoved his fingers through his hair. The movement caused a ripple of muscle that made her want to run over to him. Instead, she stayed rooted to the spot. She gave him a slight lift of her chin but her damned lips betrayed her by trembling. She gritted her teeth, willing her body not to crumple into a heap. She wanted to say something flippant but she didn't trust her stutter and so she just stood there, with her jutting Jay Leno chin, feeling rather silly.

"Susan?" Danny asked in a deep voice filled with tenderness that felt like pity to her. Susan always hated when people looked at her with sympathy when she stuttered.

"Yes?" she responded crisply, glad he stayed out of

reach, because if he came any closer she would fall right into his arms, in spite of everything.

No . . . no she would not. *Stay strong* vibrated through her head but her body reacted differently.

"We really need to talk."

"No we don't." Right, she'd professed her love and he'd laughed it off with a polite thank-you. Talking was out of the question. Clearing her throat, Susan said, "Sorry, but I'm heading out. I'm not really in the mood for a chat."

"Luckily for me it's impossible for you to leave."

"Watch me." She lifted her chin even higher but her feet refused to move forward, which was a good thing because with her chin tilted that high she'd surely run into something. And seriously, why did he have to look so . . . scrumptious? Having him appear so composed when she was so rumpled made her want to march over there and mess up his hair. Oh, why hadn't she shoved on her boots so she could stomp right past him and straight out the door? And just where were her socks?

"No, do me a favor and follow me," he said. "I need to show you something that will change your mind about leaving."

"Not likely," she said, but a tiny bit of hope blossomed inside her heart. He seemed very sure of himself.

"Susan, I get why you're upset but you've got this all wrong," Danny began, but she stopped him with a deadpan stare. She wished she could add the arch of one eyebrow but her eyebrows didn't arch. Since sticking out her tongue wasn't an adult option, she just sighed. He appeared ready to say more, in spite of her obvious displeasure, and her heart hammered. "Follow me."

Susan stood there for another agonizing moment, but she figured she couldn't remain in the bedroom forever, and so with an added shrug she scooped up her socks and boots and slowly followed him, trying very hard not to admire his very nice, denim-clad butt.

So what? So he's got a nice butt. Shania Twain's song, "That Don't Impress Me Much," started playing in her head. She knew she was trying to mask her humiliation with a display of anger but she could not stop her pee-vish behavior, even though it was making her feel worse.

How could it be that just a little while ago he'd carried her down this hallway and made wild love to her and now she wanted to scurry out the door in total humiliation? Still pondering her predicament, she reluctantly followed Danny over to the window. Rusty trotted over with them and sat on his haunches right beside her, seemingly oblivious to her inner turmoil. When she didn't pet him he looked up at her with sad dog eyes and so she leaned over and scratched him behind his ears. Rusty made a doggie sound of approval and tapped his paw on the floor for more.

"Look." Danny pointed outside.

"Oh my goodness." Forgetting her anger for a second, Susan stared out at the frozen world of jagged ice and gasped. "It looks like someone took big buckets of water and tossed it everywhere and then it all froze. When did this even happen?"

"While we were sleeping."

For a moment she admired the stark, glittering beauty and then it dawned on her that she was stuck here with Danny. "Is . . . is it supposed to melt anytime soon?"

"Nope, freezing rain changing over to snow overnight," he said without an ounce of the wild panic that was welling up in her chest. In fact, he sounded cheerful.

"Snow?" Susan put a hand to her chest. "How much snow?" she asked with an edge of panic.

"Five to eight inches, which means they really have no idea. But one thing's for sure: We aren't going anywhere anytime soon," he said, and seemed rather pleased at the current situation. "Don't worry, I have plenty of bread and milk and some excellent craft beer."

Susan swallowed hard, thinking this was an insult to injury kind of situation. She gave him a scowl that suggested that the weather was all his fault. "What am I going to do?"

"Hunker down."

"I don't want to hunker down. And I have the Christmas Walk tomorrow."

"Susan, it will be cancelled. You know the drill. Ice and snow pretty much shuts Cricket Creek down. Just enjoy the unexpected break from all of the holiday madness."

"I want to go home."

"You can't drive anywhere," he said gently. "The roads are impassable."

Susan nodded while thoughts started to explode like mini fireworks in her brain. "So now what?"

"Now do you believe me when I tell you that I love you?"

Susan looked at the floor and inhaled a deep breath. Finally, she swallowed and gazed up at him. "I want to believe you," she said softly.

"Well, I have all weekend to convince you," Danny said with a smile.

Susan's emotions were bouncing around like a ball in a pinball machine and she didn't know whether to laugh or cry. If she laughed she'd probably end up crying and he would think she'd lost her marbles and so she dug deep to gather her wits. Finally, she cleared her throat. "So what do we do now?"

"We could hike into the woods and chop down a tree if you like."

"It's dark."

"I have a heavy-duty flashlight. The ice will be crunchy but we can walk through it before it starts to snow. Are you up for a little adventure?"

"No!" Susan shook her head, picturing herself slipping and sliding. She suddenly wanted to be in the safety of her loft, curling up in her bed reading a good book.

"Where's all of this Christmas spirit you've been bragging about?"

"Um, it's pretty much been busted. And that's really difficult to do," she added with an accusing little glare. "Congratulations."

"We need to rescue your ornaments at the very least."

"I think I'll go with the hunkering down plan if it's all the same to you." Susan shook her head again, wondering if there was a spare bedroom and if he had any romance novels lying around. She gave him what she hoped was a nonchalant shrug. "I think the ornaments are probably toast."

Danny sighed. "I wish you would drop the attitude and talk about this misunderstanding. You've got this all wrong, you know."

"I don't have an attitude!" she sputtered with a definite attitude and almost jutted her chin again but thankfully refrained. God, she sounded like she was ten.

It was his turn for a deadpan stare and it made her bristle.

"Okay, so I have a bit of an attitude going on. But I didn't get your reaction wrong, Danny." She considered telling him that she didn't mean it when she'd said she loved him, that it had just popped out of her mouth in the heat of the moment. But honesty was important to her and so she refrained from saving her wounded pride with a great big lie. She loved him and him not loving her back didn't change the fact. "An amused thank-you wasn't the response I was going for."

"You absolutely did get it wrong," he said with just enough heat in his words to give her pause and capture her full attention. "My laughter was from relief, Susan.

Look, you got all weird on me and I thought—" He paused to shove his fingers through his hair. After sucking in a breath, he said, "I thought you had regrets . . . you know, and honestly I worried that you were about to maybe break up with me."

"What? Are you serious?" Her heart pounded while she tried to make sense of what he was telling her. "Break up with you after . . . after we just . . ." She shook her head in disbelief. "That would have been some seriously bad timing, to say the least."

"I didn't say what I was feeling made a lick of sense. Falling in love is really damned scary and is messing with my brain."

"You've got that part right," Susan admitted, with a slight return of her humor. Her own brain was still reeling from this sudden roller coaster ride of emotion. And she'd never been fond of roller coasters. She hated that stomach dropping feeling . . .

Wait, *did he really love her*?

Her legs started to tremble. God, she really needed to sit down, and so she sort of slithered to a sitting position right there on the floor in front of the window. Rusty flopped down and rested his head in her lap and she petted him absently. He gave her an it's-about-time-you-paid-attention-to-me doggie look.

"Okay." Danny sat down beside her with the graceful ease of an athlete, close enough that their shoulders touched. She wanted to scoot away . . . okay no, she didn't. "Yeah, my stupid, ill-timed laughter was from relief that you weren't dumping me."

"The fact that you even thought that blows me away." She shook her head and then looked at him.

"I really do love you, Susan. And the fact that you had the courage and honesty to say it to me . . . well it's just a beautiful thing."

Susan closed her eyes and swallowed. "It was like it just bubbled up inside me and I had to tell you or burst."

"Well, I'm sure glad you didn't burst." Danny chuckled and then took her hand. "That would have been quite a mess."

"Me too," she said with a slight smile and a heart full of hope. "I'm sorry I flipped out on you, though. I'm not really like that, you know."

"Oh, trust me, I realize that." Danny kissed her hand. "But I have to admit that I found it kind of sexy when you were storming all around in the bedroom."

"You did?" Susan felt the heat of a blush in her cheeks. "Well, it did feel . . . I don't know, like I guess, maybe an adrenaline rush to get that fired up. But Danny, surely you must understand how humiliated I felt."

Danny nodded slowly. "I'm so sorry."

"Help me understand what's going on. I'm totally confused."

"Ah . . . it's just . . . I don't have my life together. You know that. I was honest from the beginning about my struggles with finding direction. I thought that things would go slower with us so I would have the time to figure some things out."

"You're one of the most grounded people I know," she said. "You're much more together than you think."

"Susan, you know I work three different jobs. Some-times I feel pulled in too many directions."

"There's nothing wrong with that. You're a hard worker and help so many people, Danny. I find what you do for people to be commendable, even though you know how I feel about you needing something of your own too."

He smiled. "Thank you. But I feel like I'm juggling too many balls in the air and I'm afraid of dropping any of them."

"Oh Danny," she said. She finally had more of an understanding of what he must be going through. The unfairness of it all jabbed like tiny daggers at her heart, making her want to help him in the same way that he looked out for everyone else. But what could she possibly do?

"Hey, I love my siblings and I'm really proud of what Mason and Mattie have accomplished. Of course, I still enjoy working at the marina, but you've been right all along. I want something I can call my own." He patted his bare chest. "And it might sound trite but it just feels like I'm trying to swim upstream, you know?" He shook his head and then looked up at the high-beamed ceiling. "You deserve someone who is invested in a solid career, not a jack-of-all-trades like . . ." He paused again to sigh. "Like me."

"That's not true," Susan insisted, but he remained silent, as if contemplating how to explain more of what he was feeling. She wanted to pull him into her arms and kiss his worries away. "Have you told your family any of this?"

"No . . ." Danny shook his head slowly. "Of course not. I mean, not really. Like I said, they all need me in one way or another. Mason and Mattie might be able to replace me but who would run the marina? I can't put that pressure on my father. He's in pretty good shape and I don't want any of his heart issues to come back. He's got a pacemaker, Susan. He insisted that I put my head on his chest and feel it." Danny shuddered. "It's got this thing that will shock his heart if it stops beating."

Susan squeezed his hand.

"Seeing my strong, robust dad nearly die . . ." Danny shook his head and squeezed his eyes shut. After a moment he cleared his throat. "No way am I going to lay this on him," he said gruffly. "I'm sorry. I shouldn't have brought this up again."

"No, Danny, I want you to tell me everything. We need to understand each other completely and be there for each other no matter what. That's what love is all about."

"You're right. I'm sorry I said that. You deserve to

know everything about me and what makes me tick. But I hope you can understand my reasoning and my fear."

"I do. I have from the beginning. But Danny, things are different now. The marina is flourishing. I still think you might benefit from telling your family how you feel."

"True, but there's still stress involved. I can't take that chance with my dad's health. How could I live with myself if he had to come back at the helm and started having heart issues again? Besides, my parents spend most of their time in Florida. They love the warm weather, and fishing has always been my father's favorite way to chill."

"But there's grandchildren involved now. They just might want a reason to have to stay in Cricket Creek year-round. Did you ever think of that?"

"I know my mom would like that," he said with a hint of sadness. "She confessed as much to Mason. But Mom puts my dad's health first too. We all do."

"Maybe you should at least approach the subject with him," Susan gently persisted. "You might be surprised at his reaction."

Danny scrubbed a hand down his face. "It's just not a risk I'm willing to take."

"Or you could hire someone to do your job managing the marina so you can branch out and try other things," she said. She hoped she hadn't offended him by suggesting that anyone could run the marina as well as he did. "Is there something you're passionate about doing?" she asked, thinking there must be or he wouldn't have this restless feeling. "What about the rocking chairs? I know you claim woodworking is just a hobby that calms you down, but why don't you make a few for my shop? Like a trial run?"

Danny shrugged but something in his eyes said that this was something he longed to do.

Encouraged, Susan continued, "What do you say? I bought a lovely rocking chair at an estate sale but I just couldn't part with it, even though I knew it would bring a pretty penny. I just know they would sell."

"I . . . just can't. I don't mind making pieces for my friends or family as gifts but . . ."

"But what? It's a talent that needs to be shared." She tilted her head to the side. "It's almost as if you're afraid of success," she said hesitantly.

Danny's eyes widened and he let out a chuckle devoid of humor. "Wow, you nailed it. Here I thought the entire time I was terrified of failure, but in reality it's success. Susan, if I make money at doing what I love, then how can I go back to working for my family? No, I'm better off not doing it at all and keeping my woodworking a hobby," he said firmly.

"Okay." Susan nodded, but his admission troubled her. Her mind was reeling at his admission of loving her, but the turmoil she saw in the depths of his eyes affected her in a way that made her sure of how deeply she'd fallen in love with him. Danny Mayfield was a kind, giving person, putting others before himself. But it wasn't at all fair that his own life's ambition had to fall short because of the love and respect he had for his family. There had to be some sort of compromise for him to be able to do both.

"I thought about hiring someone to manage the marina," he continued, "but I can't really imagine anyone other than a Mayfield running the family business."

"I understand. I felt guilty leaving the farm. Like most kids raised on farms, I was doing chores from the time I could walk, and I knew my mother would miss me, especially because I was her only child. We did everything together, from cooking meals to weeding her garden."

"I can picture you doing those things," he said with a warm smile.

"We went through some tough financial times too, and for farmers that stress never goes away. Selling our land or leasing the acreage to a corporation would have solved our financial difficulties but farming has always been more than earning a living . . . it was a way of life. In my parents' blood. I know that's how you and your family feel about the marina. Danny, I really know some of what you're going through."

"Yeah." Danny nodded. "It would have been easier to sell for us too. We had offers but my father didn't want a big hotel or fancy upscale marina to come in and change the heart and soul of the marina, or for the local families not to have the opportunity to use the beauty of the river or the lake up by the cabins. Selling out wouldn't have been worth the pain of losing the marina."

"I get that too. We all pitched in during the lean years, not only to save Cricket Creek but to keep the quaint, small town atmosphere." Susan's family wanted to preserve the Quincy family farm and Susan hoped to someday be successful enough to come to their aid if need be. Opening Rhyme and Reason had been intensely, over-the-top scary. Investing her inheritance and losing it would have been just horrible, but in the end she'd taken the chance. But if the health of her mother or father had been involved, she wouldn't have risked it, so she understood his feelings. "It just doesn't seem quite fair for the burden to rest so solidly on your shoulders, Danny."

He gave her a crooked grin. "Life isn't always fair though, is it, Suzy Q?"

"No."

"Mason gave up his fishing career to come home for my dad. Mattie ran the restaurant, and I knew she had other things she wanted to pursue, but she never complained." Danny smiled. "Who knew my tomboy sister had such a creative side?" he said, and she knew he was attempting to change the subject.

"Oh, I know," Susan said. "Walking on Sunshine Bistro is so amazing. The menu might be a bit more progressive now that it's no longer just a breakfast hangout for local fishermen, but she still makes the best melt-in-your-mouth biscuits and gravy on the planet. Sophia Gordon came pretty darned close when she took over during Mattie's pregnancy but Mattie still takes the prize."

Danny grinned. "I'll pass that along to her. Look, we all pitched in and put our lives on hold and I wouldn't change a thing," he said vehemently. "And they wouldn't have either."

"I know that, Danny, but—"

"Unfortunately, there are no *but*s. I've thought this over a million times," he confessed but then seemed sorry he'd said it. "Look, it's fine," he added, even though the stormy expression on his face defied his statement. "It's not like I hate any of the jobs I do."

"Oh Danny . . ." It occurred to Susan that falling in love also meant feeling the other person's pain.

"No, really. I think I get like this during the slow months of the winter when the marina isn't busy. And now that Mason and Mattie are married with children, our social lives have changed, so I tend to get bored."

"I never had much of a social life, so I can't relate, but I do get it." She leaned her head over onto his shoulder. She wanted to snuggle next to him on the couch, cuddle, hug him tightly, and give him tender kisses. But she knew Danny didn't want sympathy from her right now. Still, she had to say something encouraging and meaningful. "Danny, the marina is such a vital part of Cricket Creek. It's not just about the recreation for the residents, but also the tourism that boating and fishing brings to the town. Running the marina is important," she said, but she felt as if her attempt at reassurance fell woefully short.

"I know." Danny put his arm around her shoulders and squeezed before he looked at her and smiled. But there was a hint of sadness at the corners of his mouth that tugged at her heart. "You know that I'm very proud of the marina, the brewery, and the bistro. I know what all three mean to the Cricket Creek economy. And you should be very proud of your part in the continued revival of Main Street, Susan."

"Thank you." Susan thought of the empty store she was considering leasing but didn't want to talk about her desire to expand right this moment. She thought again that it wasn't fair that Danny couldn't pursue something on his own, and she just bet that if he'd finally talk to his family about it, they would come up with a solution that would work for everyone. Her mother used to say that where there was a will there was a way. She sat there for a moment, absently petting Rusty's head, but her heart thudded. "So . . . where does this leave us, Danny?" she asked, thinking this was the weirdest day ever. "I have to admit that I'm confused."

"For right now I think we need to brave the elements, get out there, and cut down a tree."

Susan decided that an adventurous distraction was the best way to handle things at the moment. They were in love. Surely the rest would fall into place.

"Are you game?" he asked.

"Ha, brave the elements? I grew up on a farm, remember?"

"I remember everything about you, including the first kiss we shared when we were seventeen. It seems like a million years ago."

"Oh Danny . . ." Susan felt a wave of emotion grab her and cling like Velcro. She wanted to tell him that she didn't care what he did for a living or how many jobs he had, but it mattered to him, so in turn it mattered immensely to her as well. He deserved to feel a sense of fulfillment and to use his God-given talent. And she knew his parents would feel the same way if only he would confide in them. She leaned her head against his shoulder.

He loves me.

The words fluttered around her heart like a colorful butterfly and landed with delicate beauty in her brain. The knowledge gave Susan the strength and the power to smile and nod. "Let's go chop down a tree!"

Danny smiled back and said, "Later, Suzy Q. I've got something else in mind first."

22

If You Could Read My Mind

BETSY LOOKED OUTSIDE THE WINDOW OF RHYME AND Reason and nearly shrieked . . . and then she did shriek. "Holy moly, when did this happen?" While she'd been in the back room scooping sand into the luminaria bags, Cricket Creek had been transformed into an ice skating rink. Worried about Aubrey's safety, she hurried back into the break room and frantically searched for her cell phone. "How in the world do I continually lose my doggone phone?" She finally located the elusive phone beneath her sweater and then shook her head, thinking she could have used the landline rather than run around like a chicken with its silly head cut off. "Ew," she muttered, when she pictured a headless chicken.

Aubrey had gone home a while ago to prepare dinner but Betsy wanted to make sure her daughter had the good sense not to go out. Young people sometimes feel the need to brave the worst of weather just to go out on a Saturday night.

"Hey, Mom," Aubrey answered in a sleepy tone.

"Sorry, Macy came over and we both dozed off watching a movie. What's up?"

"Have you looked outside, sweet pea?" Betsy walked back through the showroom and peered at the window, somehow hoping that the ice had miraculously melted. Nope . . . but it sure was pretty glittering off of the bright holiday lights strung across Main Street.

"No. Should I?"

"Yes, it's a winter wonderland."

Betsy heard Aubrey moving around and then shouting to Macy to wake up and look outside. "Oh wow. That's crazy."

"Just stay put and don't even try to go anywhere."

"I won't. Hey, but how are you going to get home? From the looks of it you shouldn't even attempt to walk, much less drive."

"I'm not about to risk a broken bone. I can tell you that much. I'll just have to stay here at Rhyme and Reason."

"Oh Mom, I know how you hate storms. Wait, did Susan get back there yet?"

"I'm guessing she's in the same boat and is stuck at Danny's."

"Ooooh . . . snowed in with Danny Mayfield. There are worse things in life," Aubrey said, and Betsy heard Macy laugh. "Or I guess I should say iced in. Mom, what are you going to do about sleeping?"

"I have a spare key to Susan's loft so I can crash there, I'm sure. Don't forget to charge up your phone in case we lose power. Ice is the worst thing for power lines and tree limbs. Your car isn't parked beneath a tree, is it?"

"No." Aubrey yawned and Betsy could picture her stretching.

"Good. Well, just relax and enjoy the evening. I think *Rudolph, the Red-Nosed Reindeer* is on tonight."

"Oh Mom . . ." she said and then laughed. "Although it's still my all-time favorite."

"Okay, well just stay warm and shoot me a text later."

"I will, and you do the same thing, Mom."

"Hopefully, the road crews will get out and throw down some salt and by tomorrow I can at least walk home."

"Well, Macy just said they're calling for piles of snow on top of this."

Betsy groaned. "Well, at least we're all safe and sound. I knew we were on the edge of a possible storm system but I was hoping it was going to miss us. Have you talked to Grandma?"

"Earlier. I invited her to dinner like you asked but she said she was staying in, so I left it at that. She seemed in pretty good spirits, though."

"Good to hear," Betsy said. You never knew what you were going to get with Gladys Gunther, since her mood could swing at the drop of a hat. "Well, there's plenty of food in the fridge. I stocked up on all of your favorites. You and Macy have a good old-fashioned slumber party."

"Mom," Aubrey said with a laugh, "Macy and I already raided the fridge earlier. You bought all the stuff I loved when I was like . . . five."

"What, you don't still like grape popsicles, Hot Pockets, and Toaster Strudel? Orange Crush?"

"Oh look, SpaghettiOs!" Macy said in the background. "Cap'N Crunch cereal!" she exclaimed with apparent delight.

Aubrey laughed harder. "Yes, I guess I still do. Funny, you bought a lot of stuff that you used to say no to when I was a kid. What's up with that?"

"I was just going down memory lane while at the grocery store. Couldn't help myself. There's Sour Patch Kids and gummy bears in there too."

"Yes!" Aubrey exclaimed but then said, "I hate that you're stuck there and not hanging out with Macy and me."

"I'll be fine," Betsy promised, hoping Aubrey believed her lie. She cleared her throat. "Listen, I'm going to call Susan and make sure she's okay. Looks to me like we don't have to worry about the Christmas Walk tomorrow."

"That's kind of a bummer. I was looking forward to it."

"Maybe it will be rescheduled. But hey, after all that studying, just kick back and do a whole bunch of nothin'."

Aubrey yawned again. "Actually, that sounds like a plan. And you have to admit that it sure looks pretty outside. Maybe we'll have a white Christmas this year."

"More like an ice Christmas," Betsy said, peering outside. "You might want to heat up your dinner soon in case the power goes soon. The flashlights are in the junk drawer. If you burn candles remember to blow them out."

"Mom . . . geez. I've got this."

"Okay well, remember now, charge up your phone, okay? I got rid of the landline." Even though Aubrey had received several scholarships, every cent still counted.

"I know, Mom."

"Right . . ." she said, trying to think of more motherly advice just to keep her daughter on the phone and hear her voice a while longer. "Oh, and there's extra blankets and pillows in the hall closet."

"Gotcha, Mom," Aubrey said with a hint of humor, and Betsy could almost hear her eyes roll. "You do realize I've only been gone a few months, right? The house hasn't changed one single bit."

Betsy had to chuckle. "Well, it's seemed like forever to me, honey child."

"Oh Mom, I love you," Aubrey said with a little hitch in her voice, sounding much younger than her eighteen years. "I'll be honest, it really sucks that you can't come home."

"Yeah, I know. I'm just glad you're there and you have Macy with you. And knowing you're in Cricket Creek instead of Lexington is a big comfort."

"Oh wow, Mom, there's more ice hitting the window again. Macy, come look," she said, and Betsy loved the sudden excitement in her daughter's voice. Aubrey always did love any kind of storm. Getting her to go into the basement during tornado warnings had always been a challenge.

"I love you too, my sweet baby. I'll be fine here at Susan's. If I get bored she's got a stack of romance novels up to the ceiling."

"Speaking of romance, Macy gave her daddy your number, so he might be calling you sometime soon," Aubrey said in a sing-song voice.

Betsy winced. "Oh, okay."

"Isn't that cool?"

"Oh . . . fantastic," Betsy said with a bit of false enthusiasm. She wanted to come up with an excuse, like the holidays were going to be busy and perhaps they should put it off, but she didn't want to disappoint Aubrey and she heard Macy do a little clapping in the background. "Bye now," Betsy said. "Give Macy a hug for me."

"Will do. Bye, Mom. Stay warm."

"I will," Betsy promised, but just looking outside at the ice made her shiver. Aubrey sure didn't get her love of storms from Betsy, who cowered in the corner clutching a flashlight during thunderstorms. Ice? Snow? Forget it.

After ending the call, Betsy shot Susan a text message asking if it was okay if she stayed up in the loft even though she knew Susan wouldn't mind. She would have called but she didn't want to interrupt Susan's time with Danny, even though she was really curious about how things were going. A moment later her phone pinged, giving her the okay to stay. But Susan didn't give any hints on how her tree cutting adventure had gone this afternoon. Hopefully they got the job done before the ice storm hit. Susan said she was snowed in with Danny and was glad they were all safe. "How romantic," Betsy murmured with a smile.

She stood there gazing out the window for a couple more minutes, wishing she could muster up more excitement about going out to dinner with Grady Morgan. She blew out a breath and to her dismay she felt a hint of hot moisture gather at the back of her throat, and the sting of tears in her eyes. She wanted to be home with her daughter and here she was, stuck . . . all alone. The Cat Stevens song "Another Saturday Night and I Ain't Got Nobody" started playing in her head and she sighed, swiping at the corners of her eyes.

"Well Aubrey was right. This sure does suck," she muttered and then wondered if Susan would mind if she dipped into the secret stash of bourbon they'd imbibed not too long ago. "Just a little nip to warm my blood," Betsy said, but then remembered the kiss blowing incident and thought perhaps she should stick to milk and Christmas cookies. But then again, Main Street was already deserted, so how much trouble could she possibly get herself into? She sure wasn't about to twirl around outside in an ice storm.

Betsy gave a long, drawn out sigh and tried not to feel sorry for herself, but didn't really succeed. Nope, not at all. Sniffing hard, she swiped at a big fat tear, telling herself that Aubrey was going to be home for a couple more weeks and from the sound of it she was having fun with Macy. "Just get a damned grip on your sorry self," Betsy muttered, cursing the menopausal hormones that were surely the cause of her sniffling, which pretty soon might become a full-on blubbering session if she didn't get a grip.

In the middle of inhaling another shaky breath, a shrill alarm went off, scaring the ever-living daylights out of her. "What in the world is that?" She looked around, wondering what was wrong. Was it the secu-

rity alarm? She got her karate chop ready, not that she
knew karate, but she'd seen *Kung Fu Panda* so she could
fake it. "Dear God, is the shop on fire?" Had she left
that pine-scented candle burning in the bathroom? Was
the wiring faulty in this old building?

Panic welled up in Betsy's throat and she started
running around in circles, searching here and there for
flames or smoke or an intruder. "Where in the hell is
the alarm coming from?" she shouted, wondering if
she should call 911. She felt as if her entire body was
one big heartbeat. Dimly, she heard a banging on the
front door. "I'm coming!" She hurried over and fumbled with the lock, cursing a blue streak until she got it
to open, expecting to see a fire truck or a SWAT team
at the ready.

"John!" she shouted, glad to see him. "Did you
smell the smoke?"

"Smoke?" His eyes rounded and he hurried inside.
"What smoke?"

"The fire alarm went off," she said, barely feeling
the blast of cold air that swirled into the shop.

"Betsy, the alarm came from the cell phone you're
holding in your hand. Mine went off too, alerting us
that there's a weather emergency and we're not allowed in the streets. More ice and snow is on the way."

Betsy looked down at her phone and swiped her finger across the screen. "Oh . . . well, butter my butt and
call me a biscuit," she finally said, feeling dizzy with
relief. "I didn't even know I had an alarm. But then
again, most of what this phone can do is a mystery
to me."

"Smartphone." John laughed.

"Right, Aubrey said it's user-friendly . . . ha. And
that Siri chick has a snippy attitude. Smart-aleck if you
ask me," she said, and John laughed harder. Betsy
stared down at the thin phone and shook her head.
"For such a small thing, it sure is mighty shrill. But I
should have realized the sound was coming from my

very own hand, for pity's sake. I was just so scared." To her horror tears welled up in her eyes. "It wasn't funny, John. I was terrified."

John immediately stopped laughing. "Oh Betsy, I'm so sorry. I just thought you were joking around as usual," he said, and to her surprise he pulled her into his arms. "I'm such a jerk."

"For once I agree with you." He smelled like freshly baked bread and some sort of sweet spice that made her want to snuggle closer to him. His arms felt comforting, even through his winter coat. After so many years of having to stay strong, being held this way felt like heaven. She suddenly wanted to hang on for dear life.

"Are you okay?" John asked gently.

"I am now," Betsy said, but then horrified at her admission, she quickly added, "You know, now that I know the store isn't burning down and we aren't being robbed, even though I can't remember the last time there was a robbery in Cricket Creek. Mercy, I'm such an idiot."

"You're no such thing." John squeezed her just a bit tighter, making her want to unzip his coat and slide her arms around him and feel the warmth of his body.

Betsy knew she should disengage herself from the security of his arms but she lingered just a little longer. "You smell like a bakery."

"Gingerbread. I was so busy baking that I didn't realize Main Street had turned into an ice skating rink. When I saw your car parked in the lot I wanted to make sure you didn't attempt to drive home."

"I'm not that big of an idiot."

"I repeat, you are not an idiot."

"Thank you, you're too kind. If you keep giving me compliments like that I don't know what I'll do," she said, and when John laughed she enjoyed the rumble against her cheek.

"You're not ugly," he said, and this time Betsy laughed with him.

"Neither are you," she said, and reluctantly pulled away from his embrace.

"Better now?" The concern in his tone was almost her undoing.

"Yes, thanks. I was just having a moment . . . I seem to have a lot of those lately."

"You're entitled."

"Teaching teenagers to drive should make me able to withstand just about anything, but I guess I'm not as tough as I used to be."

"You're too pretty to be considered tough."

Betsy felt a flutter in her chest at being called pretty. Real compliments made her feel almost uneasy and so she didn't answer.

"Is Susan here?"

"No, she took the afternoon off to go over and help Danny Mayfield chop down a Christmas tree. She's making it her personal mission to get that boy into the holiday spirit."

"Not always an easy task."

"Don't tell me you're a Grinch too."

John pulled a face and then shrugged. "When I was a kid my professor parents concentrated on giving me so-called educational toys. I wanted dump trucks and superhero figures and I got telescopes and science experiments and books . . . lots and lots of books. I wanted loud and noisy toys but Santa never came through. And a baby brother would have been nice. I would have even taken a sister."

"Aw . . ."

"And my parents gave each other practical presents, never anything shiny or exciting. Holidays at the Clark house were pretty dull, I'm afraid, even though they tried in their own way. And you know, I never had kids of my own so . . ." He shrugged and Betsy wondered if he regretted not having a family. "While I appreciate the meaning behind the holiday, Christmas for me has always been rather subdued."

"Well, I only had Aubrey but she was noisy enough for three children. Rambunctious little thing. Still is." She shook her head. "I couldn't give her all that much but she loved every single present and made a fuss over the simplest of toys and clothes. I had to do the whole layaway thing and had a Christmas savings account so I could have the fun of shopping with money put away for the holidays, or I would have felt too guilty spending grocery money. I didn't know what it was like to have the freedom of shopping sprees but it made us appreciate the holidays even more, I think." She grinned. "At least that's what I used to tell myself."

"I think you're one hundred percent right." John nodded. They stood side by side at the frosty window, nearly touching but not quite.

"Did you go on big shopping sprees or were you the typical guy and waited until Christmas Eve to start shopping?"

"I had a personal assistant who did all of that for me," he said in a flat tone.

"Oh . . ." Betsy turned her head and looked up at him. He had such a nice profile, handsome but with an edge of sadness that made her want to inch even closer. "Well, I suppose you were really busy." She imagined the expensive gifts he must have given his young, beautiful wife and felt a twinge of . . . something. Jealousy? Envy? What would it feel like to open a lavishly wrapped box and find a gorgeous necklace or ring? Wonderful? No, only if he'd picked it out and the gift had meaning.

"Mmm . . ." John frowned and after a moment he shrugged. "I think I just wasn't all that interested."

Betsy recalled the thrill of watching Aubrey and her mother open presents. Although her mother wasn't much on showing affection, she did brighten up during the holidays. "That's so sad," Betsy said. Whoops—she hadn't meant to voice her thought out loud.

"Yes," he said with a solemn smile. "It was. I think

it's about time to change that situation, though. What do you think?"

Betsy didn't know what to say or what he was getting at. "Change can be a good thing," she said carefully. "I'm adjusting to my daughter being gone but discovering some things about myself."

"I'm on a path of self-discovery too. Interesting that it took me this long to get to know myself and I'm still only part of the way there. I just know that it's more fun to be spontaneous and not be so serious all of the time."

"Well, you're an interesting guy, so you should have a good time getting to know yourself."

John laughed. "You know, you're really fun to be around."

"I had to develop a sense of humor to get me through the tough times." She smiled at him. "Thanks for saying that, John. I really do like to make people laugh. It makes me feel good to bring a smile to someone's face. Rich, poor, young, or old, we all have stuff we're dealing with."

"An excellent observation. For a long time, I was all about myself. Let me tell you, it was an empty existence. Rachel actually did me a favor by cheating on me so I could reexamine my life. What she did was wrong but I wasn't a very good husband." He shoved his fingers through his hair and appeared so troubled that Betsy reached over and put a hand on his arm.

"We all make mistakes. But there always seems to be a silver lining."

"Do you believe that?"

"Yeah, my mistake of a marriage brought me Aubrey. Sounds like your mistake, if you want to call it that, has given you a better outlook on life. If you hadn't gone through what you did, how could you know what you do now?"

"Another excellent observation."

"I'm full of them," she said, drawing another chuckle.

"Well, there was a time when I wouldn't be this open and admit my failings. But I'm a different person now. And I like the changes."

"Thanks for telling me all of this, John."

"And you can ask me anything about my past and my nightmare of a divorce."

Betsy shook her head. "It's not necessary for you to revisit that painful part of your life. But having you open up to me makes me feel a lot better."

"Good, I figured that you might have concerns about my past. I don't blame you."

"We all have a past. I think it's time to look toward the future. What do you say?"

"I say that's a good suggestion." John nodded toward the ice-covered street. "We're stuck, you know." His playful smile made Betsy feel warm all over.

"Now who's the good observer?"

"Well I can tell you, it was scary just walking the short distance from the deli to here. I nearly wiped out twice. But if you want to risk it we could slide over to the deli and I'll fix you a damned good sandwich of your choice and a potato pancake, followed by warm gingerbread slathered with whipped cream."

Betsy remembered what had happened between them the last time they were alone in his kitchen and felt a blush steal over her cheeks and go all the way to the roots of her auburn hair. "Oh . . ." she said, trying to think of a reasonable way to decline. But did she really want to decline? *Yes . . . okay no. A big fat no.*

"I haven't made the crème brûlée," John continued. "You have to come to my house for that particular experience. If you like, I'll let you do the torch part."

"Oh no, handing me a torch would be putting me, you, and your home in danger. The crème brûlée itself wouldn't stand a fighting chance, unless blackened crème brûlée is a thing."

"Not to my knowledge, but some really excellent

recipes evolve from mistakes. But somehow I don't think that one would qualify."

"I think you would be right."

John tipped his head back and laughed. "I'll keep that in mind when you come over."

"Pretty sure of yourself, aren't you?"

He stopped laughing and gave her a more serious look. "Actually, not at all."

"Mmm . . ." This is where Betsy knew she should say she wasn't coming over to his house but she couldn't bring herself to tell him, and so she stood there wondering if she should follow her own advice and take a little risk—okay, a pretty big risk—with her heart. But maybe this little romance could have a holiday movie ending? She sneaked another glance up at John but he was looking back out of the window. "I do find it really interesting that you've taken up baking along with your deli," she said. "Knowing what I did of you in high school, I would never have guessed."

"Well, you could get to know me while I get to know myself." He looked at her with raised eyebrows.

"John . . ." she began, but he kept on talking.

"I recently remodeled my parents' ancient kitchen appliances. I'd love to show it to you."

"Are your parents coming home for the holidays?" Betsy asked, changing the subject while she tried to think of a good reason not to go over and have dinner with him. But all of her good reasons seemed to have taken a holiday.

"No, they're snowed in somewhere in one of the Dakotas right now. I can't remember which one."

"Wait, so you're spending Christmas alone?"

"It wouldn't be the first," he said casually, but something in his eyes told a different story.

"Come over to my house, then," she heard herself say.

"Thank you, Betsy. I'll take you up on your invitation."

"It will just be me, Aubrey, and my mother. Susan

will pop in for a little bit maybe. Nothing exciting . . . oh, and I'm not what you would call a great cook." She winced. "Aubrey does most of the actual cooking and leaves simple things like chopping and whipping to me."

"Interesting, I would have thought it would have been the other way around."

"She got tired of my last-minute boxed dinners and soup and taught herself to cook. She just has a bit of a knack for it. I don't."

"Single moms don't have it easy," he said. "I'm sure she wanted to learn to cook for you even more than for herself."

Betsy's smile trembled a little at the corners. "She's got a kind heart."

"Well, she did get that from you. I'm looking forward to coming over and being of assistance. What about your mother?"

"My mother sits on a stool and observes like a queen on her throne, tossing out constructive criticism here and there until I turn the Christmas music up loud enough to drown her out," Betsy said. She didn't want to rattle on but her lips just kept right on moving while words spilled out. "And wine helps."

"Well, I don't mind pitching in," John said, and Betsy had this vision of him in her kitchen, laughing with Aubrey and making her mother blush. "I'll bring the wine and dessert."

"I don't have any fancy gadgets or state-of-the-art cooking equipment," she said. In fact, her kitchen was on the small side, just like the rest of her modest home. But she was proud of owning her house. It might not be lavish but she loved it as much as she would love a mansion. *Well . . . maybe not*, she thought and chuckled.

"Are you going to let me in on the joke?"

"I was just wondering what you would think of my little brick house."

John tilted his head at her. "Well, let me put it this

way: I lived in a huge house with a four-car garage and I was miserable. I feel much more comfortable in my childhood home in the small town of Cricket Creek. It took me a while but I'm finally beginning to understand what I want out of life and what truly matters," he said with a grin, and his eyes were warm and sincere. His gaze lingered long enough for her to wish he would say more. Say things no man had ever said to her . . . well, said and meant it, anyway.

No . . . don't go there. It's too dangerous. John Clark is out of my league.

"And what would that be?" Betsy asked, and could have bitten her traitorous tongue right off for sounding breathless and hopeful that she might make the list.

"This sounds trite, but the simple things."

"Like?" she prompted, and this time she physically bit down on her tongue. She seriously needed to quit going down this dangerous path of getting to know him better . . . falling for him harder. Wait . . . what?

"A good sandwich."

"Ah . . ."

"Strong coffee with just the right amount of cream and sugar."

"So true. Couldn't start the day without it." *What would it be like to start the day with you?*

He sucked in his bottom lip as if thinking. "Music. Wine . . . a well-written book," he said, still looking out the window.

Betsy waited for him to go on. She realized how much she enjoyed the rich timbre of his voice, with just a tiny hint of Southern twang that had stuck with him. He spoke slowly, giving each word meaning—or maybe she was just hanging on to every word.

"Getting trapped in an ice storm with a beautiful woman on a cold winter's night." He looked down at her and her breath refused to leave her chest.

"Smooth talker," she said, but she was shaken to the core by her reaction. Her usually sturdy knees actually felt wobbly. She didn't know that the weak-in-the-knees thing could really happen to a person . . . especially not her.

John shrugged, still holding her gaze. "You asked a question and I answered honestly. And know I always will."

Betsy's pulse fluttered and she had the wild urge to drag him into her arms and kiss him senseless. Lordy, she felt as if she needed to fan her face. "Honesty is a good thing," she managed to say.

"And you'll always get it from me. By the way, thank you for inviting me to Christmas dinner. You didn't have to."

"I wanted to," she said. She didn't want him to think her invitation was out of pity.

"Good."

Betsy nodded, but she suddenly wondered if Aubrey would object to having John over to their little celebration that had always just been the three of them. But she couldn't take the offer back, especially knowing he'd be all alone. No one should be alone on Christmas Day. Surely Aubrey would understand and approve.

"So do you want to brave the elements and head over to the deli for dinner? Or if you'd rather I can bring dinner to you. I'm guessing you're staying in Susan's apartment tonight?"

Betsy nodded. "I got her permission already."

"Good. At least you're stranded somewhere with a bed."

Betsy nodded. "Oh . . . John, what are you going to do about sleeping?" she asked, and had a really hard time chasing away thoughts of him in bed with her.

"Curl up in my office, I guess." He gave her a look that said unless-you-have-a-better-suggestion, and of course she did. Several.

"You could crash on Susan's sofa, I guess. I'd have to ask her first, but I'm sure she'll be fine with it. In fact, she'll most likely insist." Betsy gazed out the window. "From the looks of things, we're going to be trapped in here for a couple of days if we get several inches," she said, and then felt a hot blush. "Of snow," she added quickly, but her thoughts took another erotic turn. Good Lord, if he could read her mind right now . . .

"Okay, thanks," he said quickly. "Hey, I'll go bring dinner over so you don't risk slipping. I nearly fell twice."

Betsy nodded.

"I'll be back in a few minutes."

"Be careful." She nodded again, wondering what she'd just gotten herself into. She shot Susan another text message and got an immediate enthusiastic okay for John to stay in the loft and she added several emojis . . . hearts, fireworks, champagne. Betsy had to chuckle. "Not gonna happen," she whispered, but then felt another spark of excitement that she just couldn't completely squash, and maybe . . . just maybe, she didn't really want to.

23

Don't Worry, Be Happy

JOHN PREPARED ENOUGH FOOD TO FEED A SMALL army and then took silly, shuffling baby steps on the slick sidewalk toward Rhyme and Reason. He quickly realized that the heaviness of his shopping bag further hindered his precarious balance and he nearly landed on his ass twice. There was no easy way to maneuver on ice and there was more in the forecast. He noticed a wide-eyed Betsy watching his progress from the front door window and when he nearly went down again, she hurried—or rather slid—out to help him.

"Betsy, no, get back inside!"

"John, let me help you."

"I'm slipping well enough on my own. Seriously, get back to safety, sweetheart."

"I can steady you . . . whoa! No . . . I take that back. I can't . . . *ahhh*." She clutched at his free arm and they slid like Snoopy with his arms akimbo, creating a clumsy ice skating dance routine. They skidded right past the entrance to Rhyme and Reason since there wasn't anything to grab on to but frosty air. "This is a total sheet of ice!" Betsy shrieked.

"Tell me something I don't know. You're not even wearing a coat."

"I should be wearing a football helmet!"

"Grab on to the lamppost! Anything!"

"Okay!" Betsy managed to snag her arm around the lamppost and they came to a slippery stop.

"What do you think you're doing?" John asked when they managed to catch their breath.

"You looked like you needed help."

"I don't need help falling. I was doing a bang-up job on my own."

Betsy laughed, clinging to the pole. "Do you think we can make it back to the shop in one piece?"

"Let's give it a go," he said, and they somehow managed to make it back to the entrance together.

"We made it!" Betsy said with triumph. They huddled in the alcove for a moment.

"By the skin of our teeth."

"I always thought that was a funny saying, since our teeth don't have skin."

"True," he said as she pushed the door open. "But I suppose I should be flattered that you risked life and limb to save me."

"Are you kidding? I was saving our dinner."

John laughed as they entered the shop. "I feel like kissing the ground," he said, and carefully put the heavy shopping bag down.

Betsy peeked inside. "My goodness, what all do you have in there anyway? The kitchen sink?"

"No, only delectable edibles," he said, thinking she looked delectable and kissable herself. "And a nice bottle of Merlot made it in there as well. I was worried about that more than the food."

"You keep wine at the deli?"

"Helps my creativity when I'm working on a new

sandwich combo, and more recently, my desserts. Hope you're hungry."

"I'm always hungry. I'm a bottomless pit when it comes to food."

"You'd never know it by looking at you. I think a strong wind could blow you away."

"I'm afraid of storms so there's no chance I'd be caught out in any kind of strong wind. And now I know to avoid ice at all cost. But anyway, I've always been that way. I'd actually like to gain weight but I've learned never to say that to another woman."

"It's probably because of your feisty nature," he said. "I bet you burn more calories standing still than most people do on an uphill treadmill."

Betsy laughed. "I do find it difficult to sit still. Being in a car teaching teenagers to drive all day long was just about the death of me, in more ways than one."

"You helped make the streets of Cricket Creek much safer."

Betsy laughed. "I sure hope so."

"Are you glad those days are over?"

"Interesting question." Betsy shrugged. "In some ways, yes, but in other ways, no. I enjoyed working with the kids and I have to say that I was a good teacher. But I was ready for a change. Working with Susan at Rhyme and Reason provided that for me. It's fun giving old things new life."

"I would imagine so."

Betsy sighed. "I know my daughter grew up way too fast, though. Seems like yesterday she was still in diapers. But it's fun to get to enjoy her as an adult . . . well nearly an adult anyway. I was lucky. She's been pretty easy. Of course, I don't even think about what she might be doing while she's away at college."

"Sounds like she's pretty responsible to me. You must have done a good job raising her."

"All I could do was my best with the hand I was dealt. And love her."

"She's lucky to have you for a mother."

"Thank you. She will always be my greatest accomplishment. I've been struggling with the whole empty nest thing."

John nodded, wondering what it must feel like to have a child, and felt a pang of regret. But he also was relieved not to have a custody battle with his ex. He couldn't go back and change his choices, so regret would just be a waste of energy. He'd also grown up being a worrier, but he'd realized that worry was also a worthless waste of his time. Little by little, he was learning to live in the moment. And as moments go, this was a good one.

"I'll lock the door and we can head upstairs. Susan insisted that you stay, by the way," Betsy said over her shoulder. "She has a big comfy couch, or you can take the spare bedroom and I'll take the couch."

"The couch will do nicely," he said. He'd never take the bed . . . well, unless she was in it with him.

"I've stayed over a few times when we've been working on crafts. She doesn't have a problem with us being here without her, so just make yourself at home. That's what Susan just texted me to tell you."

"She's such a nice girl," John said, and fell into step with Betsy. The light scent of her perfume found its way through the Christmassy smell of pine and cinnamon. He felt a little bit guilty that he was glad for the ice storm that had forced this rather intimate setting. The business over the next two weeks before Christmas meant a lot to the stores on Main Street, and yet he couldn't hold back a smile as they walked up the narrow staircase to the loft apartment. *But still, thank you, Mother Nature.*

Betsy flicked on the lights, illuminating the loft with overhead lighting. "The kitchen is this way. Isn't her place really cool?"

"Wow, I guess this is pretty much what I would expect Susan's place to look like. It's really amazing. I want to stop and look at everything. That rocking chair is exquisite."

"Susan bought it at an estate sale to sell but she just couldn't part with it. She'd actually like to sell more furniture but quality pieces are hard to come by."

"Was it made locally?" John asked while he pulled a mountain of containers from the shopping bag.

"I'm not sure," Betsy replied. "Oh my, you really did pack a feast. Everything smells wonderful."

"Well, I got a weather update and we're going to get socked with more than they even expected. I wanted to be prepared."

"Oh." Betsy frowned and it saddened him that she didn't seem too thrilled at the prospect of being shut in with him for any length of time.

"Are you okay? Do you not want me to be here?" he asked hesitantly.

"Oh no! I was just looking forward to spending the evening with my daughter. Lexington is just far enough away to make it difficult for me to visit. Next year I hope she can get out of the dorm and into an apartment, or maybe share a house with a couple of friends."

"Yeah, I wasn't too fond of dorm living."

"I wouldn't really know about that," Betsy admitted and then ducked her head to put the whipped cream into the fridge.

John couldn't help himself and gently snagged Betsy around the waist. "Come here," he said in a husky voice.

"What are you doing, saving me from the pickles?" she asked with a breathy laugh.

"No, I'm going to kiss you," he said in her ear. "If you let me."

John felt her quick intake of breath and then she turned around in his arms, making his heart kick it up a notch. "I won't *let you*," she said, dashing his hopes, but when he would have turned away she put her palms on his cheeks. "I want you to. Big difference," she said in a voice that slid over his skin like silk.

John bent his head and captured her mouth in a kiss that could surely melt the ice outside. She felt so right pressed against him, and when her arms went around his neck he felt more than just desire. He liked her so much, and he realized the brightness he'd been missing all of his life. He could hear her laughter even when she wasn't around. He thought of something she'd said or her singing "Blue Christmas" a little off-key, and he immediately smiled right in the middle of fixing a sandwich or baking a cake. While he'd learned that happiness came from within, he knew that Betsy Brock would enhance his life in ways he'd never experienced.

And the woman could kiss . . .

John threaded his fingers through her hair and tilted her head back, wanting more, needing more. She was pliant and sweet and kissed with unpracticed passion that felt real . . . and oh so very good. This kiss was even better than the one in the deli kitchen, making him imagine how passionate she would be in bed. Reluctantly, he sat her on the counter and put his forehead to hers, his heart racing like he'd just run a 5K. "Damn, where have you been all my life?"

"Right here in Cricket Creek, Kentucky."

"Well, whatever you do, don't go anywhere."

She tossed back her head and laughed. "Not a chance."

24

Cabin Fever

DANNY WALKED INTO THE GREAT ROOM AND STOPPED in his tracks. He had to smile at the sight of Susan and Rusty sitting side by side looking out over the backyard. She cradled a giant coffee mug in her hands, taking a steamy sip here and there. She wore one of his T-shirts, which had been her wardrobe over the past two days—well, when she wore anything at all. Danny felt a hot shot of desire just thinking about their lusty lovemaking sessions, which had more than once lasted for hours. He didn't know everything about his life, but he knew one thing for sure: he could never get enough of Susan Quincy. And not just the sex. He loved her laughter, her quirky sense of humor, her gentle kindness, her earnest insistence that he enjoy the holidays . . . he could go on and on about her and never stop finding new reasons to love her. Danny knew she was everything he'd ever wanted in a woman . . . *everything*. If he really thought about it, and he had, the whole thing had started with prom night. One night . . . and he'd never gotten over her.

And now she was his.

He stood there, smiling, not knowing that love could feel this strong, this damned good. Being with her made him realize that he'd never truly been in love before because nothing came close to feeling like . . . *this*. Just looking at her put a goofy smile on his face.

Her riot of curls tumbled over her shoulders and down her back. Damn, he loved her hair. He loved the scent, the silky texture, and most of all he loved the curly locks trailing over his body while she kissed him everywhere. Danny was still amazed at how uninhibited she was with him, giving all of herself without holding back. But then again, he shouldn't be surprised because she was open, honest, and sensual in a natural, unpracticed way. Part of him regretted not pursuing her harder in high school but then again, they were both so different now. This was their time, now and . . . forever.

Forever.

Danny swallowed hard and his heart thumped. *So this is what it feels like.* Loving her made him feel stronger, sure of himself, and so damned ready to get on with his life.

He scrubbed a hand down his face. But just how was he going to do it? *Show her . . . damn it, just take Susan out to the workshop.* He thought of how satisfying woodworking felt to him and the pride of a finished piece. He knew working with wood was his calling, his talent, his passion . . . what he should be doing with his life.

But how could he tell his father he no longer wanted to run the marina? The answer was that he simply couldn't, could he? Perhaps he should at least approach the subject with him.

Danny closed his eyes and swallowed hard. A vision of his father lying in a hospital bed with tubes shoved in him while machines whirred and beeped went through his head. No . . . he simply couldn't do it.

Susan took a sip of her coffee and put the mug down

on the floor next to her so she could pet Rusty. He
rolled over, wanting a belly rub. Susan chuckled and
then obliged, while Rusty whimpered in ecstasy. When
she stopped he lazily pawed at her hand for more.

"Okay," Susan said. "You know I'm a sucker for
your sad eyes."

Danny shook his head, and fell a little bit more in
love with her right then and there. And he suddenly
knew he had to show her the part of himself he'd kept
hidden from her. He walked across the floor and sat
down next to them.

"Hey there," Susan said with a slow smile. "Mmm,
you smell good. Did you just shower?"

"Yeah, and it's not nearly as fun without you." He
noticed that Rusty stayed next to her instead of trot-
ting over to sit next to him. Apparently Rusty was in
love too.

"You should have come to get me."

"I heard you puttering around in the kitchen and
decided to let you make your coffee. You have to admit
that you need your coffee before you face the world."

"Yeah, but not before I face you."

Danny leaned over and gave her a tender kiss. "So
you love me more than coffee."

"I do. You should be totally flattered."

Danny laughed. "I am," he said and then inhaled a
breath.

"You look ready to say something important."

"I want to show you something," he said in a serious
tone that had her frowning. He reached for her hand
and brought it to his mouth for a kiss. "There's no need
to be alarmed," he said, thinking that she showed all
of her emotion on her lovely face.

"Okay," she said softly. "Can you give me a little
hint?"

Danny pressed his lips together but then shook his
head. "Nope, just get bundled up."

"The roads are still impassable, right?"

"We're walking." Mason had had the road through the marina plowed so she could get out today but he decided not to mention that little detail just yet. He wanted her captive in his cabin as long as he could before this vacation from reality had to end.

"All right. I'll get my jeans on and borrow one of your sweatshirts." She handed him the coffee. "It's my second, so you can have it if you like."

"Thanks, it smells good." He loved waking up to the aroma of coffee that she'd made in his kitchen. The three days they'd been snowbound made him wish they could hibernate here in his cabin all winter long. He didn't want reality to step in just yet.

Susan gave him a quick kiss and stood up. "I'll be back in a few minutes."

While Susan got dressed, Danny located coats and gloves. Rusty, knowing they were about to head outside, started running in excited circles. "I know, boy, I feel the same way right now," he said but wondered how Susan would react to what was in the workshop.

"I'm ready," Susan said, walking into the room. "And curious."

"Sweet, let's go." Danny helped her into her coat and they headed outside into the snow-covered backyard. He'd shoveled a path to the workshop, so the going was fairly easy. Still, he held Susan's hand, since she had a knack for falling down. "By the way, my mother has invited you to the Mayfield family Christmas."

"That works, because we open presents at my house on Christmas Eve."

"She invited your parents over too. Apparently our moms have been putting their heads together again. Don't be surprised if they get a little bit pushy. When my mother found out we were dating, she was already naming our children."

"Are you kidding? My mother made mention that she thought a wedding on Main Street at the gazebo would be lovely. She mentioned springtime and then a reception at the farm. I don't think the two of them ever got over us not dating after the prom. This is like a dream come true for them."

"It's a dream come true for me too." Danny smiled at her, loving the pink color in her cheeks from the cold breeze and the lively sparkle of her eyes. "I guess they knew something back then that we didn't," he said, but then tilted his head at her. "Although a certain someone felt the need to avoid me."

"Trust me, I will totally make it up to you."

Danny stopped and pulled her into his arms. "You already have," he said, and then bent his head and kissed her. "But don't stop trying," he added with a grin.

Rusty barked. He seemed to know that something special was going on and he wanted to be a part of it.

Susan laughed. "My dog aside, Rusty is the best dog ever."

"Mattie might not agree. Rusty used to steal her country ham from the restaurant on a regular basis. She would fuss and fume at him while she tried to chase him down."

Susan laughed. "I can picture her doing that. That makes me want some of her biscuits with a slice of country ham, her fluffy eggs, and cheesy grits."

"I'll have to take you to the bistro this week."

"If the snow ever melts."

Danny nodded and then started toward the workshop. When they reached the front door, his heart started beating a bit faster. He opened the door and then stood back for Susan to enter. He flicked on the lights and then looked to see her reaction.

Susan's jaw dropped and she looked at him with wide eyes. "Danny . . . oh my . . . wow." She started walking around, touching each piece with a sense of wonder. "This is all just . . . *gorgeous* is the only word that comes to mind. You are so very talented." She shook her head and then spotted a rocking chair. Sucking in a breath, she hurried over and then sat down. Tossing off her gloves she rubbed her hands over the smooth arms and then looked at him with tears in her eyes. "You built the rocking chair I have in my loft, didn't you?"

Danny nodded slowly.

"Why didn't you tell me?" She seemed perplexed and a little hurt.

Danny shrugged. "I'm not entirely sure. I wanted to a few times but I just . . . I don't know."

"This isn't a hobby. These pieces, especially the rocking chairs, are works of art. You need to share your talent, Danny." She stood. "I'm stunned." When she spotted the little rocking chair he'd made for Lily, she put a hand to her chest. "Why are you keeping this hidden? You could make a fortune selling your work."

"You know the answer, Susan."

"Oh . . ." she said slowly, and then swiped at a tear. "Does your family know all of this exists?"

"Mason does."

"And?"

"He pretty much feels the same way you do, but in a more casual way."

"Danny, you have to approach your family. This is your passion, your calling. This work is exquisite," she said but then stopped. "I get it now. You already know this and you didn't want to show me because you knew I would react this way."

"Yeah." Danny nodded, feeling both pride and pain. "Look, I've thought a lot about it, and I would like for you to sell some of the furniture in Rhyme and Reason. I know you don't have the space for all of this, but, you know, you could have a little bit at a time."

She suddenly seemed to bubble with excitement. "Listen, the store right next to mine is available. I was already thinking of leasing it, and hopefully buying the building sometime down the road. You can sell all of this there."

"But you'd need more inventory," he said, shoving his fingers through his hair.

Susan nodded and closed her eyes in understanding.

"This is years in the making," he said.

"In your spare time. If you did this full-time—"

"No." Danny pulled her into his arms and kissed the top of her head. "I love you so much for wanting this for me, but I've thought it over and I can part with what I've got here and slowly make more, especially during the winter. That way I can still help Mason and Mattie and run the marina for my dad. It's perfect. I can do it all," he said, even though his words sounded hollow even to his own ears.

"But Danny—"

"No, babe. I wanted to show you this because it's part of who I am and I wanted you to know everything about me. But this is the way it has to be. Please understand."

Susan nodded but he could feel her reluctance to give up. He understood completely, because if the shoe were on the other foot he would react the same way.

"Hey, it's a pretty good compromise. I get to do it all."

"Danny, you are such a good person. I've never met anyone with a bigger heart than you."

Danny heard a *but* in her compliment and waited for her to go on. He knew what she was going to say— that he needed to at least approach his father, but that wasn't even an option. He just couldn't risk his dad's health.

"Where am I in this picture?"

Her question took him by complete surprise. "You are the picture."

Susan shook her head. "Danny, I know that the marina is all but shut down right now but once season is in full swing and you work at the bistro and the brewery, when will there be time for me . . . for us?" She placed her palms on his chest and looked at him.

"Something has to give, don't you think?" She looked at him with such worry in her eyes, and damn if she didn't have a point. He barely had time for himself, so how could he be in a relationship and give her the time she deserved?

"I'll make time for you, Susan," he said, and as soon as the words came out of his mouth, he knew it was the worst thing to say.

She swallowed hard and gave him a small smile.

"Just trust me."

"I do," she said, and then made a visible show of brightening up. "Every relationship is based on trust and we have a strong foundation to build upon."

Danny nodded and should have felt relief but he didn't. Something of what he was feeling must have shown on his face because she put a reassuring hand on his arm.

"Let's just concentrate on Christmas for right now," Susan said, but her smile seemed just a little bit forced.

"You know what?"

"What?"

"I'm in the spirit! You did it! Let's finally go chop down a tree."

25

Something's Burning

$\mathcal{T}$HE TWO WEEKS LEADING UP TO CHRISTMAS EVE flew by in a flurry of continuous activity for Susan and Betsy. Even with the help of Aubrey, Rhyme and Reason was packed with so many customers that they had a difficult time keeping inventory on the shelf. Susan's mother made more Christmas cookie mix jars and brought in more hand-woven rugs. Aubrey and Macy made more sock snowmen and Betsy took several trips to Whisper's Edge for more handmade ornaments. Susan parted with many of the repurposed pieces in her loft, telling herself that she could replace all of them with new items as soon as the holiday season was over.

Danny's furniture sold as soon as she put each new item on the floor, and with the empty space, she was able to keep several pieces of his in the shop. His rocking chairs were the most sought after of all of the furniture he brought in, but Susan refused to part with hers.

She and Danny had spent nearly every night together, either at the cabin or up in her loft, and the passion between them remained smoking hot. But the unspoken issue of Danny juggling three jobs and trying to make more furniture hung in the air between them, even though they hadn't approached the subject since the day in his workshop and she'd seen very little of him other than late in the evenings. Even so, Susan fell more deeply in love with him with each passing day, but the uncertain future frightened her just a bit. She told herself that they could work things out . . . but how? She wanted so much to go to Danny's father and bring up the subject, but going behind Danny's back just didn't feel right. And what if the conversation led to his father taking over the marina but having heart issues? If the notion scared her, what must the thought feel like to Danny? In spite of her warm Jingle Bells sweater, Susan shivered. She understood.

Susan absently straightened a stack of vinyl records molded into bowls, glad that the day was nearly over. She still had gifts to wrap and tomorrow was Christmas Eve!

Susan spotted Betsy heading her way but struggled to put a smile on her face.

"Aw, sugar, what's wrong? I've never seen you this glum this close to Christmas. Want to go into the break room and talk? Aubrey can hold down the fort."

Susan nodded. "If you don't mind."

"Of course not."

Susan closed the door to the break room and sat down at the table with Betsy. "You know the furniture that Danny has been bringing in?"

"Yep. It sells nearly immediately."

"He's got an entire workshop full of furniture. All of it is exquisite."

"So with that kind of talent, why is he bartending and working at the bistro on top of running Mayfield Marina?"

Susan quietly explained the situation. "The thing is that his father doesn't know. And he's afraid to tell him, or any of his family for that matter. Although he did say that Mason knows."

"Have you thought of stepping in?" Betsy asked.

Susan nodded. "I just don't feel right doing it."

"I get that. But this seems so unfair to Danny. And if his family knew, they would surely find a solution. I just bet that now that they have the grandchildren the Mayfields won't want to stay in Florida. Seems like they're always up here nowadays."

"I know. Miranda Mayfield is always gushing about her grandkids to my mom. Surely she would rather live year-round in Cricket Creek. It just isn't my place to step in, but it breaks my heart that Danny can't do what he wants to do with his life."

Betsy reached over and patted Susan's hand. "Well, he's got you, and that's a good start."

Susan nodded but frowned. "I know the joy of getting out on my own and realizing my dream. I just don't think Danny can ever really be happy if he doesn't get the chance. He puts on a good front, but there's a certain sadness lurking in his eyes that I want to chase away . . . and I can't do it."

"And that makes you worry about your future?"

Susan nodded. "I mean, can you imagine if we leased the place next door for his furniture? If we joined forces and were in this together? You should see this little rocking chair he made for Lily," Susan said and her voice cracked. "But you know, I should go ahead and lease the space next door anyway. I'm so afraid that someone else is going to snatch it up, especially after the great Christmas season we've had on Main Street."

"So what are you going to do?"

Susan inhaled a shaky breath. "Hope for a Christmas miracle, I guess."

"'Tis the season."

"And I know that, even though we haven't talked about it again, this worries Danny too. He's been so preoccupied this past week that I'm afraid to bring the subject up."

"But it's the elephant in the room."

"Yeah, pretty much."

"Oh sweetie. Just get through the holidays and then you two can work it out."

"Thanks for letting me bend your ear," Susan said, still feeling a bit unsettled. "I'm going to head on upstairs, if you and Aubrey will be okay without me?" she asked.

"No problem, Susan." When they both stood up, Betsy gave her a hug. "Everything will fall into place, you just wait and see."

"Like it did for you and John?"

Betsy smiled. "I was so worried about how Aubrey would take it, since she wanted to set me up with Grady, but it turns out that she just wants me to be happy. She said free sandwiches for life!"

Susan laughed.

"And he won her over with his red velvet cake. Aubrey has already mentioned law school and they talked about it last night. He's a good influence on her."

"And John makes you just glow."

"Yes, he sure as shootin' does. All right now, sweetie, go on up and take a hot bath and relax. You sure deserve it."

"Thanks, Betsy."

"And I wanted to let you know that Aubrey and I work tomorrow. I know you're heading to your parents' tomorrow night so just take the day off. We've got this."

"I only planned on being open until noon for last-minute shoppers, so that would be amazing if you could do that for me."

"No problem."

Susan gave Betsy another quick hug and then headed up to her loft. She suddenly felt exhausted. A hot bath sounded amazing, so she headed straight to the bathroom and started filling the tub. She thought of Danny's claw-foot tub and how he'd washed her hair the other day. In all her life she'd never felt so pampered.

But her smile faded when she realized she hadn't heard from Danny all day, and even though she knew he was busy helping his family get ready for their family holiday celebration, it wasn't like him not to at least text her. Something was simmering beneath the surface; she could just feel it.

While she soaked in the tub, her mind wandered, and she had to wonder if she shouldn't have brought up the idea that Danny wouldn't have enough time for her. Had she sounded too needy, too clingy? Was he becoming distant because he didn't want the responsibility of being in a serious relationship?

"Love is hard," she said, and sank lower into the fragrant bubbles. Weary of second guessing herself, she put her energy into shaving her legs and tried to get back into the Christmas spirit. "Relax," she whispered, but when her phone pinged, she splish-splashed water all over the place in her effort to retrieve her phone from the floor beside the tub. When she read the text message from Danny her heart sank to her toes. *Something came up with Mason and I can't see you tonight.* "And that's all you're going to say?" she grumbled. She made a sound of exasperation as she sank back into the tub, sloshing water over the sides. "I think I need a glass of wine."

Her phone pinged again, this time her mother, who rarely sent text messages. *I need your help tonight.* "You need my help tonight? What is this, a conspiracy?" Susan texted she'd be over in a little while but felt a little bit put out. She'd just have to load her presents into the SUV and finish wrapping them at the farmhouse. She'd been so busy that she hadn't seen much of her parents, so this was actually a good thing that Danny begged off, she reasoned, not really believing herself. But she owed it to her mother and father to be in a good mood. She even wore another gaudy Christmas sweater, just for her mother.

26

We Are Family

"COME ON, DANNY, DID YOU HAVE TO GO AND THROW me under the bus?" Mason grumbled.

"I had to come up with some kind of excuse not to see Susan tonight."

"You could have blamed Dad," Mason said, nodding in their father's direction.

"I get blamed enough for things from your mother. Mason, quit your bellyaching and load that rocking chair into the truck. We have lots to do in very little time." He turned to Danny. "Son, I think you should have called Susan and not just sent her a text message."

"No way. Susan would know something was up from the sound of my voice. It's been hard enough keeping this from her for the past week."

"Okay, well, I just don't like her feelings getting hurt. She's such a sweet girl. I feel bad doing all of this behind her back."

"Dad, it's called a surprise," Danny said. "I wasn't even sure I could pull this off until a few days ago. It sure would have helped if you'd told me you wanted to take the marina over."

"I didn't want to hurt your feelings, Danny. Until Mason let me in on the secret stash of furniture you'd been making I had no clue that you wanted to make woodworking your main source of income. Your mama is over the moon to move back to Cricket Creek full-time. Let me tell you, being around the grandchildren is the very best thing for my ticker," he said thickly. "And thanks to my kids, the marina is thriving," he continued with a rare show of tears. "Ah damn . . ." he said and cleared his throat. "The sacrifices you made . . ."

"Dad," Danny interrupted. "We would do it all over again. And look where this has all led."

"We wouldn't have it any other way," Mason chimed in.

"All right, enough of this lollygagging around. There's work to be done," their father said gruffly.

Danny grinned at Mason. "Dad's right. I just got a text message from Mom that Susan has arrived at her parents' farm, so the coast is clear. Let's roll."

"I still don't know how we're going to pull this off by tomorrow," Danny said. "I think I bit off more than I can chew."

Mason grinned. "Uh, Dad and I called upon the help of a few more elves," he said. "In fact, they should be arriving soon," he added, and as if on cue, the door to the workshop opened. In walked Sophia and Avery, followed by Garret and Mattie.

"We've come to the rescue, baby brother!" Mattie hurried over and hugged Danny. "Mom's babysitting, so I get to pitch in and help. The bistro is closed tomorrow and Christmas Day, so I finally get to pay you back in a small way for all that you've done for me, Danny. I'm so excited for you!"

Danny hugged Mattie back, thinking he had the best family on the planet.

"Mum and Jimmy are on the way," Garret said. "So are my dad and Maggie."

Danny shook his head, reeling with emotion. "I don't know what to say other than . . . thank you." He had to get his emotion under control before he started blubbering. Clearing his throat, he said, "The funny thing is, I wish Susan could be here to see all of this happening."

Mattie gave him a jab with her elbow. "Uh, that would totally ruin the best Christmas surprise in the history of Cricket Creek, and this town has been around a while."

Danny laughed. "You've got a point," he said, still in disbelief as the whole crew arrived and started loading the furniture into various vans and trucks. "I hope Susan isn't mad at me for begging off tonight," he said to Mattie.

"Well if she is, she won't be for long," Mattie said. She spotted the tiny rocking chair. "Oh my gosh, please tell me that's for Lily," she said, and when he nodded her eyes filled with tears. In that moment, he fully understood what his furniture meant to people. "She is going to love it! We . . . well Santa is bringing her a baby doll. I can already picture her rocking her little baby," Mattie said, and went over to examine the little chair.

Danny knew his sturdy work would withstand time and would hopefully be handed down over the years. Babies would be rocked, soothed. His chairs would grace front porches and back patios. He smiled and then sprang into action. Tomorrow was Christmas Eve!

27

Coming Home

SUSAN AWOKE IN HER CHILDHOOD BEDROOM TO THE familiar aroma of bacon, cinnamon, and coffee. She breathed deeply of the comforting scent and snuggled beneath the covers. She blinked and for an odd moment felt as if she needed to get ready for school and felt a little pang of anxiety. But then she remembered she was an adult and was just here overnight for a visit.

Susan gazed around the room, which hadn't changed one bit since the day she'd left the farm for Main Street. This room had been her sanctuary, her place of peace, where she'd diligently done her homework and read endless books way past her bedtime. She'd written secrets in her diary, listened to boy bands, and dreamed of someday falling in love. She'd plowed through endless romance novels, becoming the feisty heroine instead of a shy, stuttering teenager who'd never been out on a date until Danny asked her to the prom. She knew that her dress still hung in her closet and she'd dried the wrist corsage, preserving it forever, never dreaming that she'd ever date Danny again.

Susan peeked beneath the covers and chuckled when she remembered that she was wearing an old ruffled flannel nightie, also from her teenage years. Everything meant to be long had been way too short for her legs, but for some reason she found comfort in wearing the soft nightie this morning.

Yawning and stretching, Susan realized she had a tiny bit of a headache and then stared up at the ceiling and chuckled. Her parents, who rarely imbibed any kind of alcohol, had felt the need to break into her father's treasured stash of Pappy Van Winkle aged Kentucky bourbon last night. The whiskey had felt like warm silk on her tongue and after sipping on a couple of drinks, there was no way she could drive back home, so she'd been forced to stay the night. Her mother had baked up a storm in the kitchen while her father watched *Elf* and laughed himself silly. Susan wrapped presents and really failed to understand why her mother claimed to need her help when it was clear that she didn't. Susan chalked it up to them simply wanting her company. And she'd enjoyed the evening, feeling the comfort and warmth of their love surrounding her like a soft blanket.

Stretching again, she reached over to her white wicker nightstand for her cell phone, hoping she'd missed a text message or call from Danny. She was disappointed to see that he hadn't reached out to her. She sucked in a breath and felt an odd pang in the pit of her stomach. Funny, but she'd had a sensation all night long that something was underfoot. But again, she'd always had a vivid imagination and so she was probably wrong and just absorbing the excitement of Christmas.

"Oh wow, look at the time!" she said, surprised that it was nearly ten o'clock. Good thing that Betsy and Aubrey were opening the shop!

A moment later there was a light knock at her door. "Come in," Susan said, and her mother rushed in, looking so happy to see her in her room. "Morning, Mom." Susan scooted to a sitting position and gave her mother a groggy smile.

"Somebody's a sleepyhead today." She handed Susan a big mug of coffee.

"Well, *somebody* fed me bourbon that apparently knocked me for a loop."

Her mother turned pink as if embarrassed. "Oh, just a little holiday cheer!" She looked ready to twirl around.

"Mom, have you had a little nip this morning?"

"Oh, heavens no!" She fussed around the room picking up this and that, almost as if she was a bit nervous . . . and her mother wasn't the nervous type.

Susan took a bracing sip of the strong coffee. "Mom, are you okay?"

"Yes, yes. It's just that it's Christmas Eve! Come on and get all prettied up. We've got quite a day ahead of us."

Susan tilted her head. "Like what?"

"Oh, you know, Christmassy things." Her mother waved her hands around like little birds in flight. "Let's get some breakfast in you, what do you say?"

"I say yes." Susan tossed off the covers and handed her mother her coffee mug. "I'll be down in a minute."

"Don't dawdle."

"Do I ever?"

"All the time. Getting you up for school was quite the chore, especially before you were old enough to drink coffee."

"True. When I woke up this morning, I felt as if I was in a time warp. I'm even dressed for the part." She pointed to her nightie.

"Oh, you sure did grow up way too fast for my liking." Her mother got all misty-eyed. "I miss you so much but I'm so proud of the young woman you've become."

"Mom, you gave me a wonderful childhood. I couldn't ask for better parents."

"Oh, sweetie, it's so good to have you here. But come on and get a move on!" She swiped at a tear and hurried out the door, nearly spilling the coffee.

Susan picked up a stuffed teddy bear and looked at the friendly face. "Well, that was a bit odd. What's the big hurry?"

After a hearty breakfast of bacon and eggs and her favorite cinnamon toast, Susan showered and tugged her jeans back on. Her mother had supplied her with another ugly Christmas sweater, making Susan think of Danny. Should she call him? She wanted to but he'd been acting so different this past week that she thought perhaps he needed some . . . what . . . space? The notion troubled her but she tried to shake it off. She didn't want to do anything to spoil her parents' Christmas Eve.

She hoped that Danny and his parents were still coming over. Shaking her head, she picked up her old hair dryer, which had seen better days. The sad little whir had her wishing she was in her own bathroom getting ready. She located a tube of mascara in her purse and put on some lip gloss. Rubbing her lips together, she looked at her reflection, unable to shake the feeling that something was going on with Danny.

Susan fluffed her nearly dry hair and headed down the narrow staircase, smiling at the familiar squeaks of the worn wooden steps. To her surprise, her mother and father looked ready to head out.

"Going somewhere?" Susan asked, noting her mother was wearing lipstick and her father had his hair slicked back, a sure sign that they were heading up into town.

"No," her mother said quickly. "Just getting geared up for tonight."

"Are Danny's parents still coming over?" Susan asked.

"Of course. They wouldn't miss it for the world."

"Oh good." Susan thought that was going a little bit overboard but nodded. "I haven't heard from Danny, but I guess he'll still be coming over," she said with a pang of uneasiness.

"Of course he will, dear," her mother said. She handed Susan her coat. "Well, you'd better get a move on."

Susan gave her mother and father a kiss. "Why do I get the feeling you two are trying to get rid of me?"

"Oh, don't be silly," her mother said, but urged her toward the door. "See you in a little bit."

"You mean tonight?" Susan asked and looked at her mother with a little bit of concern. Was she getting forgetful?

"Yes . . . yes, tonight," she said and nearly pushed Susan out the door. Susan stood on the front porch and shook her head. "Well, that was weird. Has the whole world gone plumb crazy?"

While she drove, her worry about not hearing from Danny grew stronger, and she decided that as soon as she was home she was going to give him a call. Trying to get into better spirits, she cranked up the Christmas music and did her best to sing along, but faltered. "Danny Mayfield, what in the world is wrong with you lately?" she grumbled as she pulled into the alley leading to her garage. Something odd caught her eye but she was too busy feeling grumpy to give it much thought.

"Bah humbug," she said as she all but stomped up the steps to her loft. She took off her coat, thinking the Christmas decorations even looked a little bit sad. And after such big holiday sales, her apartment appeared bare, and for some reason Susan felt a little bit like crying. "Stop it. It's Christmas Eve!" she told herself, and then heard a knock at her door. She hurried over, jingling all the way.

Susan opened the door expecting to see Betsy but it

was Danny standing there, sending her heart racing. "Danny . . ."

"Are you going to ask me in?" he asked with that bone-melting grin.

"Sorry, I was . . . I'm just surprised to see you."

"Well, it took you forever to get home."

Susan shook her head, perplexed. "Were you waiting for me?"

"Yes."

"Why didn't you call?"

"I was busy," he replied in a breezy tone, irking her a little bit.

"O-kay," she said, lifting her chin. To her surprise, he chuckled.

"Something funny?"

"Yes, you." Danny pulled her into his arms and kissed her until she forgot why she was angry with him.

"That's not fair."

"What?" he asked.

"All you have to do is smile at me . . . kiss me, and I can't stay mad at you."

Danny laughed. "I love your honesty. Why were you mad at me?"

Susan gave a little shrug. "You've just seemed so distant this past week."

"I'm sorry, Susan, but I've had a lot going on."

She put her hands on his chest. "But you know you can always talk to me about anything."

"Not about your Christmas gift. That would ruin the surprise. And I was afraid to talk to you or I'd give it away."

"Oh . . ."

Danny backed up and took her hand. "Will you come with me?"

"Where?"

"You'll see," he said, and for the first time she realized how worn-out he looked.

"Are you tired, Danny?"

"I was up nearly all night but I'm too excited to be tired." His phone pinged and he looked down and smiled at whatever was in the message, making Susan want to peek at the screen. He pocketed the phone and inhaled a deep breath.

"Tell me what's going on." She wanted to stamp her foot in protest when they got to the bottom of the stairs but she could feel the excitement buzzing through his body and the excitement suddenly transferred over to her as well. Too many things suddenly seemed planned . . . She tugged at Danny's hand, wanting him to give her a hint, but he kept walking until they rounded the corner of her building and stepped onto the sidewalk.

And then they stopped short.

"What do you think?" He pointed to the store next to Rhyme and Reason.

"Oh!" She looked at Danny and he positively beamed at her. "Rock Me Gently."

"Do you like the name?"

Susan gazed at the beautiful sign hanging above the door of the shop next to Rhyme and Reason. "I love it. Oh Danny. Your own shop!"

"Merry Christmas."

"Oh my goodness, now my gift pales in comparison."

Danny laughed. "All I want for Christmas is you," he sang, making her laugh with him.

"So this is why you've been so preoccupied. I was worried I'd done something wrong."

"Oh Susan, I'm so sorry to have worried you. I was so afraid that I'd somehow give it away, even in a text message. Baby, you never have to worry about how much I love you." He picked her up and spun her around. "Want to see the inside?"

"More than anything in the world."

Laughing, he grabbed her hand and they hurried up to the door and went inside.

Susan's heart seemed to swell in her chest as they

walked around the showroom. The overhead lighting cast a glow onto the polished furniture, making the wood gleam. One area was set up like a front porch, with two large rocking chairs begging to be sat in.

"So cute!" she exclaimed. Although rocking chairs were the focus, there were benches and stools and coffee tables. Soft music came from hidden speakers and the store smelled like polished wood and lemon. "Just walking through here makes me feel relaxed. Danny, how could you possibly have done all of this in such a short period of time?"

"I had a little help." He tilted his head. "Actually, I had a lot of help. My parents are moving back to Cricket Creek full-time and my dad wants to take over the reins of the marina."

"Oh, Danny! This is just the best Christmas ever."

"It will be."

"What do you mean?"

"Susan, I know we've moved at fast forward speed in our relationship."

She nodded, swallowing hard.

"But I love you with all my heart. I know this for certain."

"Danny, I love you too. More and more with each passing day."

He gave her a tender smile. "Our moms knew what they were doing when they wanted us to go to the prom together. And they also knew what they were doing wanting us to get married on Main Street at the gazebo. And naming our future children."

Susan's eyes widened when he got down on one knee. Her breath seemed trapped in her chest and she thought she might pass out and ruin the moment, so she steadied herself by putting one hand on the solid strength of his shoulder.

Danny reached into his pocket and pulled out a blue velvet ring box. He opened it, revealing a gorgeous engagement ring. "Susan Quincy, will you marry me?"

"Yes!" Her voice seemed to float out of her body and she watched with blurred vision while he slipped the lovely diamond ring onto her finger, a perfect fit. "Oh, it's beautiful."

Danny stood up, pulled her into his arms, and kissed her. "You've made me a very happy man."

"And I promise I will continue to do so. I love you so much."

A moment later the front door burst open. Friends and family rushed in.

"She said yes!" Danny shouted, and everyone cheered. He smiled at Susan. "Okay, now it's officially the best Christmas ever—with many more to come."

Don't miss another charming
Cricket Creek Novel
by LuAnn McLane,

WISH UPON A WEDDING

Available now from Signet

White Lace and Promises

"SOPHIA GORDON, NOW JUST WHAT IN THE WORLD ARE you doin' reading *Good Housekeeping*? For pity's sake, that's for my older clients, not for a young cutie pie like you."

Sophia looked over at Carrie Ann through her foil-covered bangs. "Well, there's a recipe for—" she began, but Carrie Ann tugged the magazine from her fingers so quickly that the salon chair swiveled sideways.

"This is what you should be reading, sweet pea." Carrie Ann placed the latest issue of *Cosmopolitan* in Sophia's hands.

Sophia gazed down at the scantily clad model on the cover and looked at the hair and makeup with a critical eye. "That eye shadow is way too shimmery."

"Oh, forget about that and turn to page thirty."

"Page thirty?" Sophia flipped through the magazine until she was staring at a hot male model lying in bed wearing nothing but boxer briefs and a wicked smile. "Twenty-five surefire ways to drive your man wild?" When Sophia shook her head and laughed, the foils made a light tinny sound next to her ear. "Well, unfortunately, I don't have a man to drive wild."

"I've seen you hanging out with handsome-as-sin Avery Dean a time or two. I'm pretty sure you could drive him wild all twenty-five ways and think of a few more to add to the list."

"We're just friends," Sophia insisted, but her pulse beat a little bit faster at the mere suggestion. She glanced at the article with renewed interest. Number two involved a feather trailing over certain body parts. "Oh my," Sophia said when the image of Avery popped into her head. She squeezed her eyes shut but the image remained.

"Share, please."

"These ideas are just silly."

"Really? I think this falls into the category of don't knock it until you've tried it." Carrie Ann looked at Sophia in the mirror. "My motto is to always be prepared." She arched an eyebrow. "Know what I'm sayin'?"

Sophia chuckled at the owner of A Cut Above. In her mid-fifties, Carrie Ann Spencer had the hair and curves of a vintage pinup girl and a sassy Southern attitude to match the look. She'd been styling Sophia's hair since last summer when Sophia arrived in Cricket Creek, Kentucky, to help out at her pregnant sister-in-law's Walking on Sunshine Bistro after Mattie had been put on bed rest. "You crack me up."

Carrie Ann fisted her hands on her hips and tilted her head. Her big auburn hair was so full of product that it barely moved. "I'm serious, girl. Hey, how about me and you head over to Sully's Tavern after your hair is all done up with those highlights? I'll be your wingwoman."

"Have you forgotten that I'm heading back to New York City soon?"

"No, but if you ask me, you don't seem in any big hurry." Carrie Ann took a seat in the chair beside her and swiveled it around. "But now that your mama, sister, and brother all live in Cricket Creek, I was hopin' that you might consider moving to this sweet little town too. I've grown fond of your smiling face here and when I have breakfast at the bistro." She leaned in closer. "Don't tell Mattie I said so, but I think you've mastered her melt-in-your-mouth biscuits," she said in a low voice. "I just add some strawberry jam and it's like there's a party in my mouth."

"Oh, thank you, Carrie Ann. And you know I'm fond of you too." Sophia shifted in her chair and inhaled deeply. Of course she'd thought about staying in Cricket Creek, especially recently. The peace and quiet of a small town drew her in more than she'd expected and she would sorely miss living in the same town as Garret, Grace, and her mother once she moved back to the city. "But Lily is nearly six months old and Mattie is back full-time at Walking on Sunshine. And while I love cooking and have enjoyed filling in as a chef, I'm a hair stylist and makeup artist. I've worked hard to develop my clientele, and it's time for me to head back to New York before I lose them. I really need to get ready for the June wedding season. I've already extended my stay way longer than I intended and my bosses are running out of patience with me. They will only hold my position open for so long before I'm permanently replaced at the salon."

Carrie Ann pressed her deep red lips together and gave her a level look. "And just why did you extend your visit?" she asked, but continued without waiting for an answer. "Um, maybe because you want to stay in Cricket Creek?" She raised her eyebrows. "Hmm? And you could have a chair here." She waved her arm in a wide arc. "I could certainly use someone with your reputation and skills. Girl, after you helped out with updos for the Snow Ball dance, requests for you started pouring in."

"You've mentioned that a time or two."

"Or ten." Carrie Ann gave her a slight grin.

While Sophia loved the little salon situated in the

heart of Main Street and honestly didn't miss the drama
of the bridezillas she had to deal with, her expertise was
in updos and makeup for elaborate events and weddings. But how could she tell Carrie Ann that working
at A Cut Above wouldn't be enough of a challenge without sounding uppity and rude?

"Hey . . ." Carrie Ann raised her palms upward and
inclined her head. "I know what you're thinkin'. You're
used to the hustle and bustle of that fancy salon in New
York City and this wouldn't be enough for someone
with your skills."

"Carrie Ann . . ."

"Hear me out, sweet pea."

"Okay." Sophia gripped the magazine and waited.

Carrie Ann nibbled on the inside of her cheek for a
few seconds as if gathering her thoughts. "We've been
slow today but A Cut Above still holds its own against
the chains popping up outside of town. I have lots of
loyal local clients and I could use a couple more stylists." She put her hands on her knees and leaned forward. "But I've been tinkerin' with the idea of opening
a salon up in Wedding Row. You know in that pretty
strip of wedding shops overlookin' the river?"

Sophia nodded her foiled head and felt a warm flash
of interest. "I've been up there with Grace. If I remember right, there's a florist, jewelry store, and lovely bridal
boutique, among other things."

"You're right. From This Moment is owned by Addison Monroe, daughter of Melinda Monroe, the famous
financial guru."

"I know." Sophia nodded slowly. "Um . . . Addison
was engaged to my half brother Garret before she married Reid Greenfield. It was a messy story in the tab-
loids until my mom's ex-husband came to Cricket Creek
to straighten out the crazy lies. Rick Ruleman was a
rock legend with a reputation to match, but he would
never have had an affair with Garret's fiancée." Sophia
shook her head in disgust.

Carrie Ann slapped her hand to her forehead and winced. "Well, hell's bells, how in the world could I have forgotten about that little detail?"

"Addison and Garret are on great terms now." Sophia lifted one shoulder. "My mom and Rick have mended their fences too. I never thought I'd see the day when he'd settle down in a small town." Sophia chuckled. "Life is so weird."

"Tell me about it. Did you ever think that your fashion model mama would marry a bass fisherman and run a fishin' camp for underprivileged kids?"

"Not in a million years. But she loves it."

"How about your Grace swooping in and helping Mason Mayfield save his craft brewery?" Carrie Ann picked up the mixing bowls and walked over to the sink.

"Now that I would have believed. Unlike me, Grace loves a challenge."

"That's a whole lotta movin' and shakin' going on. I'd say your family is pretty doggone awesome."

"Why, thank you. I totally agree," she said with a firm nod.

"And they're all here. This is why you need to consider staying in Cricket Creek." Carrie Ann walked over and checked one of the foils. "Not done processing yet." She folded it back into place.

"Carrie Ann, why are you so adamant about me staying?" she asked, but had an inkling of where this conversation could be heading.

"What would you say to opening up a wedding-themed salon as partners? I'm thinking I'd like to call it White Lace and Promises," she said in a dreamy tone.

Sophia's heart thudded with excitement but about a dozen questions popped into her head all at once. While her mom and sister were all about taking financial risks, Sophia was much more conservative. "Would there be enough weddings to keep the business brisk?"

"Good question. I spoke with Reid Greenfield's sister Sara who said that she's getting big barn weddings booked from Nashville, Tennessee, and Lexington, Kentucky. Sara's wedding reception venue with the gorgeous river setting is growing by leaps and bounds. She's also booking more intimate receptions at Wine and Diner right here on Main Street. We might be a small town but we're close to some big cities. And don't forget that there's a convention center down by the baseball stadium now. I'm sure there will be some black-tie events, which could mean even more business. Sophia, sugar, with your expertise and reputation I truly think the clientele would grow quickly." Her voice picked up speed and her hands did the talking as she became more and more excited. "The businesses up on Wedding Row support and feed off one another. There's a shop available for lease right next to Flower Power and it's located just two doors down from the bridal boutique! And it's already set up to be a salon. Can you believe it?" She paused to take a breath. "So what do you think? Not that you have to give me an answer right now. But thoughts . . . Give me some feedback."

"I think the idea has potential, for sure."

"So you're interested?"

"I'm . . . intrigued."

Carrie Ann smacked her knee. "Sweet! I've been thinkin' about this ever since Wedding Row opened up but I didn't have anybody like you who could take the reins for me. And I have to keep on top of things here at A Cut Above. My mother opened this shop and I want to keep the doors open in her honor." She raised her arms skyward. "This is so perfect! We definitely need to head to Sully's or down to the taproom at the brewery and celebrate."

"Carrie Ann . . . I said I'm intrigued." Sophia carefully added a note of caution to her tone. "I'm not making any promises, though."

"Okay then . . ." Carrie Ann flipped her palm over and put her index finger to her opposite pinkie. "Let's start a list of reasons why you should do this. You'd be your own boss. I would basically let you run the whole thing. You'd live in the same town as your family. The cost of living is nothing compared to New York City. You already told me that you love your condo overlooking the river." She leaned forward and put her hand next to her mouth and whispered, "And you already know that most of the hot Cricket Creek Cougars baseball players live there. Thought I'd toss in that tidbit."

"I hadn't noticed," Sophia said.

"Oh . . . well, maybe that's because someone else in this town has caught your eye. And that someone just might be Avery Dean."

"Pffft . . . no way." She pointed to her eyes. "Not caught. We're just friends."

"Right. And I'm a natural redhead."

Laughing, Sophia pointed to her own hair. "And I'm *about to become* a natural blonde."

Carrie Ann sat back in her chair. "You're gonna look that way because of my expertise. Actually, those highlights will be just the perfect little boost to your gorgeous caramel color. A very Jennifer Aniston look. You kinda remind me of her . . . So pretty but not in a flashy way."

"Coming from one of the flashiest women I know."

"At my age I have to pile on makeup and bling to camouflage my flaws."

"Oh, stop! You're gorgeous."

"Ah, bless your heart, Sophia. But, sweetheart, you're a natural beauty."

"The girl next door, right?" While Sophia didn't have the stunning long-legged beauty of her mother and sister, Grace, she was content with her looks, for the most part, anyway. Although it was irritating that Grace could eat whatever she damn well pleased and not gain an ounce. Having a slow metabolism really sucked. While she also didn't share the big personalities of her mother and sister, Sophia was happy to stay in the background. She'd much rather do hair and makeup than be in front of the camera. But being the quiet one also gave her the ability to get away with some pretty epic practical jokes. Garret and Grace were always blamed for things first, so there was a definite upside to flying under the radar. But she thought about Carrie Ann's offer and wondered if it was about time that she busted out of her comfort zone. But decisions didn't come easy to her. Here she was, a hair stylist, and it had taken her two weeks to decide to add a few highlights.

"Why so quiet? Did I say something wrong?"

"Oh no." Sophia shook her head. "Not at all. I'm just trying to process what you've thrown in my lap."

"You mean the twenty-five ways to drive your man wild?" Carrie Ann asked with a chuckle.

"No, I'm just a little blown away that you'd want to go into business together," Sophia replied, but glanced down at the article. Visions of Avery slid back into her brain.

Carrie Ann stood up and checked the foils again. "About another ten minutes." She patted Sophia's shoulder. "No rush on your answer. It's good enough for me right now that you're considering my offer," she said and hurried off to answer the ringing phone.

Because Sophia had come in rather late everyone else was gone for the day. She glanced at her reflection in the mirror and winced, thinking that she looked like an alien Medusa with the silver foils sticking out everywhere. The blond highlights were a bit of a whim but she was glad she'd finally made the decision to go for it. Of course, hair stylists should always be up for something different, but change, even something as simple as highlights, took Sophia longer than most people and it was so frustrating sometimes.

With a sigh, she started scanning through the article just for fun. The suggestions were mostly silly, in her opinion. The painting of each other with chocolate syrup and then licking it off seemed a little messy. She stopped short at the thought. Dear God, was she becoming a . . . *fuddy-duddy*? Yes, because she was pretty sure nobody her age even thought of expressions like *fuddy-duddy*.

Determined, she kept her eyes closed and tried to imagine the chocolate syrup scenario. Perhaps if you used thick chocolate fudge and warmed it up? Oh, now that might just be very nice. . . .

"Are you sleeping?" asked a whiskey-smooth male voice that slid over her just like the chocolate fudge she'd been daydreaming about. She smiled thinking that this body-painting thing might be the ticket after all. "Um, maybe I shouldn't interrupt," the voice continued, cutting through her chocolate-coated fantasy.

Oh shit.

Sophia opened her eyes and looked at the sexy country boy who had been invading her thoughts and dreams over the past few months. "Avery!" Foils sprung from her head and *oh dear God* the magazine in her lap was open to the twenty-five ways to drive your man wild. She gripped the armrest, wishing there was an eject button. "Hi." Her smile probably looked like a wince.

"Hey, Sophia. Haven't seen you in a while." He put his toolbox down and shrugged out of his jacket.

"I've been busy babysitting Lily a lot."

"Oh well, I miss seeing you at breakfast," he said, which created a vision of him sitting across a kitchen table in the morning all sleep-tousled and sexy.

She swallowed hard. "I miss you . . . I mean seeing you at the bistro, too." She glanced down at the nearly naked model. Her fingers itched to turn the page.

"Watcha readin'?" Panic set in when he angled his head at the glossy pages in her lap.

"I . . . um . . ." She felt heat creep into her cheeks. "I was just, you know, thumbing through a random magazine, while my hair is processing." She looked over at Carrie Ann, who was chatting away on the phone. "What, um, brings you here?"

Avery jammed his thumb over his shoulder causing Sophia to notice the bulge of his biceps that stretched the sleeve of his red T-shirt. "I'm here to fix the washing machine that's been giving Carrie Ann fits. I would've been here sooner but I was slammed with repairs all day. But it sure is a bonus to run into you."

"It's good to see you too, Avery."

"I'm sure glad you think so." He gave Sophia a grin that caused his cheek to dimple. His chestnut brown hair had grown out a bit since she'd last seen him, the dark tendrils curling around his ears and forehead. As though reading her thoughts, he shoved his fingers through his hair.

"I know. I need a haircut. Just been too busy to get it done."

"I like it longer," Sophia heard herself say, and lifted one shoulder in a shrug.

"Well then, maybe I should keep it that way." He shot her a grin.

"As a stylist I'm always thinking about hair," she responded quickly.

"Oh, I'd forgotten that was your career. If you ever decide to stay a cook you'll never be broke either." He flashed another grin that made her melt like the ice cube in "How to Drive Your Man Wild," number five. "I really do miss you at the bistro, Sophia."

"Oh, I was getting pretty good, but Mattie is still the best cook around."

"I was referring to your company," Avery said in a sincere but slightly flirty tone. "Your sweet smile was a great way to start my day."

"Why, thank you. I must look a fright right now, though." She pointed to her head and caught her bottom lip between her teeth. "Sorry."

"Aw, you still manage to look pretty," Avery said just as Carrie Ann hurried over.

"Hey there, Avery. You gonna take a look at my washing machine from hell?"

"Sure thing." Avery nodded. "Sorry I'm late. Been a busy day."

"Oh, that's okay. Still cold out there?" Carrie Ann peeked beneath one of the foils.

"Yeah, but I hear the snow is gonna miss us," Avery said.

"Humph, well, last time the weatherman said it was going to miss us, we got six inches. You're just about ready to get rinsed," she said to Sophia, but looked back at Avery. "We're thinkin' about heading up to Sully's Tavern later. Stop on in and I'll buy ya a beer."

"Well, now, that's an offer I can't refuse," Avery said, and angled his head toward the back of the shop. "I'd better get working." He picked up his toolbox, causing another delicious ripple of muscle. "See y'all tonight," he said, but his gaze lingered on Sophia. "Let's get you back to the bowl, sugar."

"Carrie Ann!" Sophia said in an urgent whisper. "Just what do you think you're doing?"

"Gettin' an early start on bein' your wingwoman," she whispered back. "Avery Dean's got the hots for you, Sophia. And judging by the blush in your cheeks I think you're sweet on him too. That whole we're-just-friends thing you keep saying is a bunch of hogwash. Why are you not taking advantage of the situation?"

"Because when we first met at the bistro he was just getting over a broken engagement. I don't want to be his rebound girl, and I didn't intend to stay here so I didn't want to hurt him all over again either."

"Well, now, I'd say enough time has passed since his breakup. And I'm hoping you'll take me up on my offer and move here."

Sophia stood up and had to grin. "I think you're playing matchmaker to give me another reason to stay."

Carrie Ann placed a hand over her ample chest. "Would I do something like that? Little ole me?"

"In a heartbeat."

Carrie Ann laughed. "Ah, child, you already know me too well. That's why we're gonna make great business partners. You just wait and see."

Sophia shook her head as she followed Carrie Ann back to the shampoo bowls to get rinsed. Through the open door to the laundry room she could see Avery bent over the washing machine. She couldn't help but admire his very fine denim-clad butt.

Carrie Ann turned and caught her staring. "What?" Sophia sputtered with a lift of her chin, desperately trying to appear innocent, which of course only made her appear guilty.

"Friends . . . ha." Carrie Ann laughed. "Thought so . . ." She clapped her hands softly. "I do love it when a plan comes together."

Sophia rolled her eyes, but when Carrie Ann turned around, Sophia angled her head to get another glimpse of Avery. Of course he picked that very moment to straighten up and look in her direction. She did one of those lightning-quick look-away moves but she caught the blur of his smile in the corner of her vision. A warm tingle of awareness washed over her as she leaned her neck against the cool porcelain bowl. She and Avery had been tap dancing around their attraction and for very good reasons. She firmly reminded herself that nothing should change if he showed up at Sully's.

No matter what matchmaking scheme Carrie Ann was cooking up, Sophia knew she needed to make her decisions with a clear head that wasn't clouded by the desire to know what it felt like to kiss Avery Dean.